The
TRACK
of
REAL
DESIRES

The
TRACK
of
REAL
DESIRES

A Novel by

BEVERLY
LOWRY

ALFRED A. KNOPF
NEW YORK 1994

Grateful acknowledgment is made to Warner/Chappell Music,
Inc., for permission to reprint from "Flip Flop and Fly" by
Charles Calhoun and Lou Willie Turner, copyright © 1955
by Unichappell Music, Inc. (Renewed). All rights reserved.
Used by permission.

Library of Congress Cataloging-in-Publication Data
Lowry, Beverly.
The track of real desires / by Beverly Lowry.—1st ed.
p.   cm.
ISBN 0-679-42939-5
1. Mothers and sons—Mississippi—Fiction.   2. Friendship—
Mississippi—Fiction.   3. Women—Mississippi—Fiction.
I. Title.
PS3562.092T73   1994
813'.54—dc20   93-34755
CIP

Manufactured in the United States of America
FIRST EDITION

For Colin, Andrea and Brandon

Special thanks to Brandon for the movies and the rat

The
TRACK
of
REAL
DESIRES

1

The black car came slowly down Strange Avenue toward Manilla Street, past the pharmacy, the doctors' offices.

"Go slow."

"I am." The boy shifted into first. He was tall, and the peaky ridges of his hair brushed the ceiling of the small, low car.

They had been on the road four days. Leland had wanted to come in her car, which was bigger and more comfortable, but he'd quickly argued her down. His sound system was better—they would need music on so long a trip—and he liked the idea, the two of them showing up in a 280-Z.

"Strange Avenue?"

"There was a rich man, somebody Strange, I don't know." Her face went back and forth as she scanned houses, one side of the street and then the other. "I should remember it. I think when I see it, I'll know it."

Her eyes were a smoky topaz color, the iris ringed in an arc of white. When she was frightened, her pupils narrowed and flashed, a wild look. "There's Manilla."

"Where?"

"One street up ahead. That's the house. Pull over a minute."

"Here?"

She flicked her hand. "Anywhere."

"Can you ease up a little?"

"Sorry."

The boy pulled into a space across the street from a pale pink two-story building with lacy grillwork around the windows, identified by a sign out front as the Eva Turner Home for Ladies.

Leland flipped down the sun visor, checked her makeup in the mirror, straightened one earring and licked a finger to smooth her eyebrows. "Okay," she said.

When he touched her hand, a muscle jumped. In the window of Eva Turner, a curtain was drawn back.

Pulling away from the curb, the boy reminded himself, as he drove the last half-block of their trip, why he had come: to take care of her, see her through, get her back home again in one piece, soon.

"See that blank?" she said, pointing at the sign. "It used to say 'White.'" There was a space between "Home for" and "Ladies."

"'Home for *White* Ladies'? Joke, yes?"

The curtain dropped.

"I wish."

The boy laughed. "This is going to be great. Just great."

"We're here." They crossed Manilla Street.

In front of the house on the corner, two identical green Toyota station wagons were parked at the curb. The cars were beat-up, trashed out and dirty. In the front yard was a huge dying sycamore tree, its yellowing leaves crisp and turning in on themselves.

Leland leaned forward. "Like fall." Large dead leaves carpeted the ground around the trunk of the sycamore in a wide circle.

"Fall? It's barely May." Toby backed the car into the space between the Toyotas.

"I know."

He cut the engine.

The house was hunkering and solid, dark brick with a porch that spanned the front facade and wrapped around one side. Pot plants—philodendron, frangipani, a ten-gallon cast-iron pot filled with herbs—took up most of the porch floor, and the grass in the front yard had been dug up and replaced with small flowering bushes. Cats patrolled the porch rails. The sidewalk was busted, the front steps leaned. Beyond the steps, double front doors—carved slabs of pale oak—were flanked by frosted panels of glass etched with swirls, loops, birds and flowers. Beyond the glass, something moved.

Leland looked frozen.

"Don't get out," the boy said, unfolding his long frame. "I'll open it for you."

He was lean and swoopy, she wiry and small with the coiled, springy look of a toy spaceship wound up for lift-off. Having attained his height early, he'd spent so much of his life bending to accommodate himself to her that he now had the patient, practiced stance of a servant paid to wait, an old man's stoop.

He thumbed the button of her door handle.

Studying a large bug smashed to pulpy smithereens on the windshield, Leland Standard wondered what she had been thinking about, coming back, bringing Toby, having made her escape all those years ago. She hugged her chest. Sometimes if she closed her eyes and concentrated, she imagined she could feel the process potentially, if not certainly, doing its slow work inside her, as pliant tissue yielded to chalky ossification, crusted and white like dried salt. Other times, she convinced herself it wasn't happening, she was fine.

The car door opened. Toby waited.

Leland took a deep breath and, hitching her purse over her shoulder, put her feet on Mississippi ground for the first time in fourteen years.

Three days, she reminded herself. Three days.

2

To cut the glare, Melanie Farrish cupped both hands over her eyes. "Oh, my God."

"What?"

"He's wearing a jacket."

"*What* he? Who?"

They had not thought she would bring the boy and hoped, once they remembered his existence, that she would not. Now there he was, lean, tall, on her case like a nursemaid. When Leland pulled herself from the car, her son gathered her up like warm sheets from the dryer.

"Draped."

"How do you mean, 'draped'?" Baker held up a limb of oak-leaf hydrangea. The Chinese umbrella stand he was using for a flowerpot was jammed, but he had the one last limb.

"Like . . ." Mell peered through the head of a cut-glass bird.

Baker did not wait for or particularly expect his wife to continue her thought; she was not exactly talking to him. Likewise, when he said, "Get in there, you goddamn son of a bitch," he was not precisely talking to a hydrangea limb. They had been married a donkey's age. They spoke to God, angels, whatever was up there, all the time, not just to each other.

Baker stuffed the limb in, and it snapped. Petals drifted to the floor. "Fuck you."

Mell came up with it. "Like bat wings."

"Bat wings?"

When people came Baker went nuts, tearing around the house with flowers and doodads, filling in dead spots. The oak-leaf hydrangea looked splendid but would not last, Baker having forgotten to add water. Also, the umbrella stand was in the way. Anybody who went upstairs would knock petals from the grapelike clusters, sending showers of white over the floor like rice at a wedding.

"What do you mean, 'bat wings'?"

Mell jumped. Behind her, Baker did his own version of draping, hands against the door frame, head turtled out over her shoulder. He smelled of greenery mixed with food, hope and damp inadequacy. His usual before a dinner party.

"My God," he said, "he's wearing a jacket."

Mell sighed deeply, impatiently. "I said that."

"She looks fabulous."

"I know."

The unexpected boy brushed something from his mother's blouse. Seen through the breath-misted glass, the two people on the sidewalk merged and blurred. As the glass panels flanking the front doors were frosted but the birds were not, if they positioned themselves just right, Mell and Baker could see out without being too much seen.

The boy's jacket was a black satin zip-up.

"There'll be a dragon."

He turned his back, and the dragon was orange. Red tongues of flame curled from its flaring nostrils.

"How did you know?"

"Mere brilliance. Isn't this fun, Doo? Isn't this just the best?"

Melanie sighed again. Leland Standard had first left home when she was sixteen, more than thirty-five years ago, her destination cities, the city, some place where acknowledgment, recognition and accomplishment came high, not cheap and easy like it was here.

"Law-zee me." For guests, Baker dumbed himself down, using Aunt Jemima phrases he hadn't uttered or heard spoken in years—his version of hospitality, a local ruse. "Look at them."

Mell gave up. "Baker, why in God's name do you think I'm standing here like a goddamn spy *except* to look at them."

"No, but the thing is—"

Mell swiveled to face him. "The thing is what, Baker? What what what?" Her dark hair was fly-about and wild, her gray eyes crazed and jumpy, her lovely face contorted into the telling snarl Baker hated.

Mell had lines at the corners of her eyes and around her mouth, a complex of road-map patterns as symmetrical as a spiderweb. She used makeup and eye cream with Retin-A, but nothing helped. Her left eye twitched. What was it this time—Xanax, Prozac or plain old Popov? She was supposed to be off everything, though with Mell you never knew.

"Mell . . ." Baker shifted his feet and the floorboards squeaked. He resisted a childlike urge to shift them again.

They lived in the old part of town, hard by downtown, in an area called Strange Park. The houses here were roomy, rambling and solidly built, with special touches like frosted glass panels on either side of double front doors, large front porches, huge kitchens, high ceilings, formal dining rooms with arched doorways, many halls, worn-out plumbing, no closet space. Strange Park had been named for the long-dead benefactress Wyola Strange. Never married, Wyola had founded the garden club, taught piano and played songs for Sunday school children at the Presbyterian church forever; when she died her money went to establish parks and playgrounds and to plant her favorite tree, the crepe myrtle, all over creation. Thanks to Wyola, in summer the streets, parks, schoolyards and, especially, the graveyards of Eunola, Mississippi, were awash in fluttery pink.

Time and federal programs changed everything. Strange Park had gone black. Longtime white residents swore they'd never sell but in the end, most did. Mell and Baker stayed on because they loved their old house, liked being thought of as eccentric and could not get away from the fact that the house was the last place Lucy had been alive.

Baker placed his finger on his wife's chin and lightly pressed. "They look so much alike, Mell. Look."

He knew she would not have noticed. Melanie was excellent at psychological detail—the dropped clue, the telling gesture—but a dud at anything strictly visual. Trees died, walls went; Melanie trudged on, oblivious. Baker let his hand drop.

"I swear, if you tell me to look one more time . . ."

Mell had been up for hours, scalding the cut-glass decanters, rewashing the cutlery and glasses, polishing the silver incidentals. Even so, she'd felt pushed for time and only in the past half hour had taken off the silk kimono she wore every morning and left on until after breakfast, when Roy went to school. As the kimono was the only revealing piece of clothing she wore anymore, Baker loved the clingy thing—the folds and drapes, the soft splashy colors up and down her back, those low, droopy armholes. Sometimes, when Mell reached her hand up, he caught sight of a breast slumbering beneath the ribbony straps of her sheer nightie. If he was on a roll, he even managed to hone in on a pinpoint nipple.

The two people on the sidewalk turned toward the house.

"So?" Mell wiped traces of her breath from the cut-glass bird.

"They have the same face."

Mell looked. It was true. "Oh, Baker . . ." She rippled her shoulders, inched her butt away from her husband, dug in her pocket for a Kleenex.

Light-years ago, through junior high and into high school, Leland Standard and Melanie Tree had been best girlfriends. Leland's mother rented, so she and Leland moved all the time. They once lived next door to Mell's family for eight months. From breakfast to late-night snacks, the girls went around together the way best friends do, wound around each other like vines on a tree. When Leland left Mississippi, their lives drifted in different directions, but their love had never paled. They didn't have to see each other or talk, even now, and both of them over fifty.

"Think, Mell," Baker said softly. "If you didn't know. If you'd never seen them."

Melanie blotted sweat drops. She was dressed as usual, in a plaid skirt, long-sleeved cotton sweater, stockings and low-heeled pumps. The clothes came from catalogs, the shoes from a store in the mall. Too heavy, too hot, but Mell would not change.

With thumb and forefinger, she pulled her sweater away from her chest and, pumping her hand at the wrist, fanned her breasts.

Watching his wife's hand, Baker Farrish had but one desire: to pull up her pink sweater, shove his cock into the cup of her hand, thump the head of it against her chest, come all over her veined and creamy breasts.

Mell let her sweater go.

Beyond stolen glances, Baker never saw his wife from collar-bone to thigh. She dressed and undressed in the bathroom, kept her kimono and lace nightie on a hook on the door. When they had sex it happened in the dark and fast, to quiet a jit-tering Baker felt inside his chest, pretty much all the time. He wasn't certain that its origin was sexual, but sex did the trick. Afterward they both fell quickly into sleep. Next morning Mell changed the sheets and that was that.

"If you didn't know," Baker whispered, "I swear, you wouldn't be able to say who they were to each other—brother, sister or what."

The couple on the curb had been told this many times be-fore. They had the same face, people said, the same gestures and expressions. Both walked in a wide stride—from the hips, gathering up chunks of ground as if they were on a treadmill and had to push hard to keep ahead of the machine—and held their heads like dancers in a love duet or underwater divers in Jacques Cousteau.

The woman leaned toward the boy, saying something. The boy looked up at the trees, around the yard.

Those two. Mell's breath went jumpy. Why were they here?

A smallish yellow kitten padded down the sidewalk toward them. Another—gray with white patches like milk stains on her nose and paws—sat like a statue on a concrete urn beside the front steps.

Baker's lips grazed the tip of his wife's ear. It wasn't so much screwing Mell he missed as the sight of her naked. Her milk-white flanks and soft stretch-marked belly, her lank behind and dishpan hips, sloping slim shoulders and thin pale arms. Not for him the taut muscularity of the modern woman dashing about a tiled locker room like a jock, easy in her nakedness. Baker liked modesty, soft sinking otherness, wide hips, night-gowns with ribbons and pleats. When Mell went to one of her meetings, he often spent the afternoon watching dirty movies from the video store. What moved him most powerfully was the first give of sex when the man pressed into the woman's silky—to him, almost holy—femaleness. After that, the rest was downhill, even the wild bump of climax.

He pressed on. "He looks older than, what, eighteen or nine-teen? She looks younger. They could be brother and sister, maybe cousins. Lovers or married. Like those people who live together so long they start to look alike."

Melanie shivered. She could feel the hinge of her husband's glasses at her temple.

"You'd never guess mother and son, I don't think. Ever."

"Like Miz Flake and Junior."

Eula Flake was a retired home-ec teacher, Junior her ancient pug. It was a standing joke in town how Miz Flake and Junior even walked alike, that puffed-up strut.

"Junior's a *dog*."

"I know that."

As if on cue, Lady Macbeth ambled up, did the down-dog stretch, yawned and sniffed idly at Melanie's backside.

"Hi, Boo," Baker said to the dog. "Speaking," he said to Melanie without moving his lips, "of d-o-jeeze."

Lady M. licked Melanie's instep, leaving drool on her shoe. Melanie sighed again. She didn't know how life got so far off the track of real desires. She had never wanted a big, slobbering boxer with an overbite; she wanted something small and soft she could hold on her lap and cuddle. It was true they needed a guard dog, but still . . .

Mell pushed out her shoulders and pulled in her chest, as if to withdraw her upper body from her sweater. "I can't believe it's just May."

She had been outside only once today, to take out a dripping plastic sack of garbage. In the backyard by the ground artichokes Baker planted to hide the garbage can, she came to a dead stop. For some length of time, she couldn't say how long, she felt outside of self, off and gone. She had come back in the house in a state she hadn't been able to shake, flushed, jangled and sopping.

"We say that every year."

"Say what, Baker?"

"'I can't believe it's so hot this early.' 'I can't believe it's just May.'" He threw up his arms flamboyantly. "Next year we'll say it again."

She twisted her head halfway around. "I am," she declared, "a puddle."

"Don't melt yet." Baker rubbed his hand down her long hair. "We have a long ways to go."

Mell sighed her sigh. "I know."

Her sadness broke his heart. He could not console his wife, not ever, really, but still made gestures in that direction. What else was there to do?

He lifted her hair and she bent her neck. There were two things Baker and Melanie Farrish never talked about. One was

Lucy. They could not imagine what good it would do to talk about Lucy. Lucy was dead and they would be sledgehammered with guilt for the rest of their lives; they didn't even go to the cemetery anymore. The other was money. They had none, lived on the float. The bank owned them, so what was there to say? Humming, Baker softly blew. The pale down along the columns of Mell's neck flattened, then rose back up again. She had dyed the front part to cover the gray. In secret places it shined with silver.

"Thanks," Mell whispered.

He let her hair down.

"I wish I could think of his name."

"Whose?"

"Whose do you think?" She nodded toward the sidewalk, frowning. "I keep thinking British. Or a dog's name."

"Derek?"

"Derek?"

"Lionel?"

"*Lionel?* Baker, I hate you. You never take me seriously."

"Bitch. I always do."

"Lionel, for God's sake. He'll have to," she reminded him, "sleep in Roy's room."

"It's clean."

"Don't you think you'd better do something—"

"Oh, my God." Baker slapped his forehead.

"—about the rat?"

Baker took off. At the stairs, his arm clipped the hydrangea and white petals rained to the floor.

"He certainly can't," Mell said to no one in particular, "sleep with *her.*"

Baker paused at the top step, one hand at his chest.

With her sweater sleeve, Mell wiped the glass. I will never make it through tonight, she thought, not ever. If only I hadn't gone outside, if I'd done one more slice of . . . She dribbled her fingers along the tip of Lady Macbeth's clipped, velvety ear.

For years there had been rumors: Melanie Farrish took lith-
ium, smoked grass, snorted cocaine, ate pep pills. While most
of the rumors were untrue, some were not. Soon after Lucy's
death, a doctor prescribed an antidepressant. As the pills gave
Melanie a new sense of self-worth, she became attached. For
balance and sleep she turned to Valium. In Zurich she discovered marijuana. Three years ago in Memphis, at a dream and
Reiki seminar, she found out about Xanax, and last year, at a
yoga workshop in New Orleans, Prozac. She managed to keep
a little bit of all of it stashed around the house.

In the downstairs bathroom, Melanie riffled the stalks of a
large potted dracaena. When she found the small envelope,
she poured the contents into her palm and dropped the last
white crescent down her throat. More, she said to herself. I
have to remember to get more.

In the front hall, Lady Macbeth hauled herself to her feet
and licked up the hydrangea petals Baker had knocked to the
floor. The flowers had no taste, but they went down with ease
once Lady M. soaked them in saliva.

The dog sniffed, drooled, wagged her tail.

On the sidewalk, the boy bent his head toward his mother
to catch a whispered remark.

Leland Standard lifted her chin.

3

Back when Melanie Farrish was Melanie Tree and her world
was different in every way, nobody took it seriously when she
went to Smith to study psychology. In 1958, Smith was the
going place for girls whose parents could afford better than
Millsaps or MSCW, and Mell Tree was brainy enough to go

east to college, not to mention oddball enough for the psych major.

It was after Melanie got her bachelor's degree and came back home to go to Millsaps to study more psychology that people, especially Mell's banker daddy, Marion, got nervous. Soon afterward, he suffered a mild heart attack, followed by the onset of sugar diabetes, then a thing with his prostate. Since quick early death was common in male Trees, after one semester at Millsaps his worried daughter moved back home, worked a couple of months at a nursery school, then quit her job to marry Baker Farrish, in a double-ring ceremony complete with rehearsal dinner, stag party and a reception that went on for an entire boiling-hot afternoon.

Baker was a lunatic all right, but he was local, Episcopalian, loved Mell, wasn't likely to move her away from Eunola. Marion Tree gave the newlyweds a two-week trip to Bermuda, and Baker had not crossed the Mississippi state line since.

In her thirties, Mell shocked her friends and family by going to Zurich to study Jung. Marion Tree was dead by then, not due to genetic inclination but from having driven, drunk, into an oncoming freight train carrying cars from St. Louis to New Orleans. When Melanie got the idea of going to Switzerland, the first thought to fly across her mind was "Daddy's dead. I can do what I want."

A trickle of sweat inched down the inside of Mell's pantyhose, past her knee. Maybe it was hormones, her first hot flash. She still bled—a paler, spottier flow than before, but regular as clockwork. Though she hadn't experienced anything she would call a flash exactly, sometimes she just felt so warm. Jack Threlkill said she would know when the final phase had begun when the time between periods stretched. "One month," he said as cheerfully as if he were predicting the sudden arrival of money to burn instead of the gynecological beginning of the end, "you will notice it has been six weeks instead of a month.

Then two months. Then . . . pow! You're finished with all that."

Jack Threlkill's middle finger was deep inside her when he said that, and he was pressing down on her belly with his other hand. Through her thin, pellucid skin, his fingers touched. Dr. Happy. Melanie hated messages of doom veiled as good news, more than maybe anything.

She stared at the shredded tissue in her fist, then looked around for somewhere to put it. Lady M. whined. Mell fed her the Kleenex, which the boxer minced with her tiny teeth and swallowed. Threads of white dotted the dog's great tongue.

Daddy wasn't the only dead one. Mell went to Zurich a little over a year after her and Baker's only daughter, fifteen-year-old Lucy, committed suicide by lying in a tub of warm water and slashing her wrists and ankles with a double-edged razor blade. Baker went along with the Switzerland idea, down to borrowing money to help her go, not from any feeling about Jung, Zurich or her career, only to pry Melanie from the watered silk couch where after Lucy's funeral she lay all day long, reading and hiding behind lank strings of unwashed hair. "When you refused to wash your hair," Baker told her later, "I knew I had to do something."

Leland was pointing into the backseat. The boy set a gray canvas bag down on the sidewalk, opened the car door and reached in. The car was so small he practically had to bend double to get into it.

Mell ran down the list of British actors' names. Jeremy? No. Laurence or Alec? No, no. Compact and athletic as ever, Leland wore tight black jeans, a soft silk shirt—taupe, to bring out the flecks of gold in her eyes—and earrings that dangled to her shoulders. Her shoes were flat black pointy things—maybe satin like his jacket?

Uncurling from the car, the boy struggled with a bundle of blooming ginger, its stiff straight stalks thick and long and woody, its hooded blooms a brilliant red. Leland took the flowers and laid them across her arm.

More flowers. The house already looked like a funeral home.

After Lucy's death, Mell spent a year inside the house making lists: groceries for Baker to get, errands to run, books to buy. Paperback mysteries got her through—short, choppy American ones, the bloodier the better. Then poetry. Rilke, especially the animal poems. And every book on suicide and the death of children she could lay her hands on. Mark Twain's dead son, Art Linkletter's daughter, Isadora Duncan's crushed babies, murdered children all over the map of time. The need for company was a grim and depressing fact about which she could do exactly nothing.

Mell didn't have a certificate from the Jung Institute. She had spent the entire time in Zurich smoking dope in her hotel room, sitting in small dark cafes dipping biscotti in espresso or red wine, going for long walks. She had a brief, thrilling affair with a pretty Jung groupie from Ojai. For a few months she escaped Lucy's death and the yappity-yap terrier of guilt. In Zurich she was happy.

She had not become a therapist—who wanted advice from loony Mell Farrish? It was like getting opinions on Alzheimer's from somebody who had it. But she did hold meetings. Once a month five women and a man came to discuss dreams and the collective unconscious, and to analyze works of literature according to the Jungian model. In the past few years, reading standards had dropped dramatically. Last year when somebody suggested doing *Gone With the Wind* in preparation for *Scarlett*, Mell gave up. Sometimes she and her group went to workshops and conferences. Piled up like teenagers, they'd drive to Memphis, Jackson, New Orleans, once even to Dallas, but that was too far. By Texarkana everybody was in a bad mood.

Again the boy put his hand at the small of his mother's back. Why was he treating her like an invalid when she was only fifty-two, young these days, and a known sports-minded person at that?

Mell scored grass all over the place, West Memphis, Hernando, across the bridge in Hamburg, Arkansas. For pills, she relied on a nurse at the Eva Turner Home for Ladies. Eva Turner used to be where white ladies from good families went to spend their twilight years. Now that good families were stone broke and everybody and his brother was on welfare—although nobody liked to call it that—and the federal government had ordered Eva Turner to make changes or lose the tax break, every kind of person on the face of the earth lived there, except men. And somebody said the family of a bilateral amputee from Lula Springs was getting ready to challenge that.

As a direct result of her study of dreams and the deep rivers of the unconscious, in the past few years Mell had begun to write—poems at first, because they were short. When brevity started to drive her crazy, Mell switched to prose. Her poems had been lyrical and personal, but the short stories were long, fantastical and erotic. She liked using a lot of paper, had a Mac, a laser, printed out daily.

Last year her son convinced her to try her hand at a film script. Mell provided the imagination, plot and character, while Roy gave technical advice and curbed Melanie's tragic nature. At twelve, Roy was an expert. He could recite passages from *Nightmare on Elm Street* and *Halloween* from memory, had seen all seven Freddy Kruegers and both *Nosferatus*, knew George Romero's scripts inside and out. Currently Mell was doing a sequel, and she was also trying her hand at romantic pornography in a Civil War setting.

There was no end to what people were up to these days. When they married, Baker had made a good living doing renovations and interiors. Now he stayed home cooking: banquets, conventions, weddings, debutante parties. Six days a week he got up at five to make cheesecake for Moe's, a local steak and tamale house that did extremely well because of write-ups in national magazines. Scholars and fans who came to the state to visit the shrine of Mississippi's dead genius writer often drove down to Eunola to eat at Moe's, and sometimes people ordered whole cheesecakes. Baker also grew things. He and Jane Scott Laws were trying out a new heat-hardy strain of ersatz raspberries in cleverly packaged jams and jellies.

Mississippi had a film commission. Farmers were growing funny lettuce. The yellow pages had to put in a new classification for consultancies. People made it up as they went, working in their homes at their PCs and printers and answering and recording and fax machines, dreaming up new ways to seize the time, exploit their expertise and make—they hoped—a living.

A friend of a friend had taken Mell and Roy's script to the state film commission. Mell had her doubts about their yuppie governor going for a splatter movie featuring the flower of southern maidenhood as the angel of death. But stranger things had happened.

Mell counted up. They had invited six people to dinner, so with the three of them and Leland that made ten. Eleven, now that she had brought the boy.

Eleven. Odd one out. Nobody with any sense had an odd-numbered dinner party, but it was too late to invite anybody now.

If only she could think of that boy's name.

Ian?

4

Time can drag if minutes do not, minutes being mathematically defined units—exact, precise, dependable—whereas time is neither mathematical nor dependable. In retrospect and memory, time can come to a stone-dead standstill.

Memory counts. So much was happening: Mell Farrish at the front door waiting for the dope to take effect, Baker heading down the upstairs hall to see about his son's pet rat, Leland Standard slicking her hair behind her ears with her free hand in an effort to appear calm and unperturbed to her son, Tobias relifting the canvas bag, adjusting the strap, wondering what he is doing in godforsaken Mississippi and why his mother insisted they take this trip without any real reason.

Lady Macbeth pants, waits. The rat sleeps. On the front porch, to give her nipples a rest, the mother cat pushes her babies away with her feet. The yellow kitten on the sidewalk rubs Toby's ankles, the gray one with the milk patches of white keeps watch from her post on the concrete urn.

At school, Roy Farrish, in his new black homburg, his black shirt and Sherlock Holmes plaid cape, his kung fu pants and Doc Marten sixteen-holes, sits alone in the schoolyard at lunchtime, nibbling his vegetarian sandwich—sprouts, hummus, tofu—and wishing he were home in his room with his masks and magazines, his new airbrush kit and his pet rat, Freddy Krueger. There, he is happy.

He is a strange boy. He makes the declaration himself, not as opinion but fact. Lucy had been strange, people told him, and he is too. Teachers point at his wool cape and ask, "Aren't you burning up in that thing, Roy?" instead of suggesting that he dress normally. He says no. No *ma'am*. His parents had brought his case before the school board, making the point that the child of tax-paying citizens had a right to dress however he wanted, making veiled threats of civil rights suits they probably wouldn't have seen through and everybody knew it, but the threat had weight enough. And since Roy Farrish was one of the few white children in Eunola who attended public school in whatever kind of clothes, the school board—about half white and half black—decided to take the risk and leave his costumes alone.

In addition to which there was Lucy. The suicide preyed on people's minds.

Baker and Melanie Farrish did not feel like heroes, keeping their son in public school when he got to the crucial age of twelve, when children left baby grammar school for the blackboard jungle of junior high, because they weren't. If it were up to them, Baker and Melanie would have dug up the money to send their son to Eunola Christian with the other white children. But Roy refused to go to a school where uniforms were a requirement, as he did to the plan of going to college in preparation for becoming an upstanding citizen. He didn't want to be an upstanding citizen. Not even close.

Roy knows things. His parents tell him things. How they live, what they long for. He can handle knowing things.

He loves his wool cape. He is not hot. He's fine. The black students—ninety-six percent of the student population, except for Roy the other four being the children of poor white rednecks who cannot afford Eunola Christian—think he's cool. The black students give him slack, room, some respect. Roy has one friend, a Chinese boy—Chinese in Eunola schools having long been counted as white. Huey is also strange. The only child in the Lum family who does not excel in school or attend a private one, Huey is fixed on spiritual matters, past lives, voodoo, and calls himself a pagan. Huey is absent. Huey misses a lot of school. Roy eats alone.

In other parts of town, those invited to the dinner party being given for Leland Standard—old friends, best friends, the oldtime high-school girl gang and their husbands—consider their options regarding wardrobe, hairstyle, general attitude and position toward the past, and wonder if she has yet arrived. At the Eva Turner Home for Ladies, Estelle Etheridge, a life-long Presbyterian and chief day-shift receptionist for some thirty-seven years, stands at the front window to see what's what in the Farrish front yard. Soon Estelle will be busy at her phone, punching numbers, speaking briefly, punching more numbers. Estelle wants to be the first in town to tell people that not only has Leland Standard arrived in a hot black 280-Z, but the boy is with her as well.

Time slows, speeds, folds back on itself. Grinds on, if unwillingly.

"Careful." Tobias Standard takes his mother's elbow, guiding her past the roots of a silver-barked cottonwood tree.

Leland shakes off the boy's hand. "I won't break, Toby. Christ. You make me feel ancient."

The boy releases her. He has no idea what he is supposed to do or how far to go; all he knows is he has to make sure she is safe and well and does not throw herself off another cliff or get caught up in situations where people can take advantage of her or, like Simon, win her easy heart, then dump her.

"This is going to be great. Just fan-fucking-tastic."

When Leland frowns, her eyebrows make an *M*-shaped crease at the bridge of her nose. She says nothing.

"You don't like that."

"What?"

"Me saying 'fuck.'"

"I didn't—"

"You don't have to."

"I never censor you."

"Not in so many words. But—"

"You're saying I do."

"Mom—"

"I don't know, Toby, sometimes I just don't know."

The boy takes a breath, pulls himself together. "Those

flowers . . ." He nods toward the blooming ginger. "They're outrageous."

She sashays her boyish hips. "Do I look like Miss America?"

"No question about it."

She smiles. He wonders what he would not do for her. For a while he was afraid he was going to murder Simon. And now there is this other, life-and-death matter, which she sees as one more challenge to her tenacious will, not only to control but to win.

They have the same haircut, zipped short around the ears, gelled in a long crew cut on top. The high crew cut gives them both a wonderfully startled look, as if they'd just heard good, if surprising, news. Feature by feature Baker is right: they have one face, the same prominent bones and large features, lush lips, clown nose, big eyes. Leland's hair is a reddish color, expertly, expensively dyed to conceal the gray, Toby's a darker shade of deep brown-black. But their gold-flecked eyes are widely placed in the same manner, set so deep in the sockets of their skulls that they seem to be peering from the far side of other worlds. Their noses are straight and strong, and they have the same juicy fullness about the mouth. Toby has a stronger chin and jawline, but then he is by now a mature young man—an altogether urbanized version of nineteen, wise in provincial city ways, ignorant as a sycamore ball in any other.

"Hold on." At the car, he opens the passenger door, to punch the automatic door lock.

"You don't have to—"

"We get back to L.A. and forget, you know what will happen."

"But . . ." She clams up, but not for long. Lines between them are fuzzed. Having lived together too long—in every way but one a couple—they are too close. "Toby, we're coming right back out for the rest of the stuff."

"I know." He closes the car door, testing the handle to make sure it's locked, turns, finds her gaze.

Her smile is dazzling. His head lifts. He comes to her.

"Aren't you hot in that jacket?"

"No." He pulls the jacket tighter. "I'm not hot." The jacket had been Jonathan's. Jonathan was Toby's chum; then he got sick.

"I'm sorry."

"It's okay."

"I'm just so—"

"Nervous."

"Yes. But I shouldn't—"

"It's okay." He places his hand at her waist. "It's fine."

The jacket had come from Hong Kong. Jonathan's mother wanted Toby to have it. "All right."

He urges her forward.

5

Baker clutched his chest. He did not do sports. Exercise, he had read somewhere, was not good for smokers. He had tried giving up cigarettes many times, but in the end he couldn't see the point.

Like Mell, he wore the same outfit all the time: dirty white Keds (not deck shoes or running shoes or any of the other currently fashionable sports shoes, but regulation low-cut Keds of the kind they used to call tennis shoes), loose khaki pants, no belt, a series of different-colored cotton knit polo shirts with a signature animal over the heart. Today's shirt was rosy pink, the traditional alligator a cerulean blue.

Retail, the shirt would have set him back fifty bucks or so. At Jack-Mart, he paid $8.89.

At Roy's door, Baker tiptoed in, holding his breath as if to minimize the intrusion. The room was tiny, no window, more like a closet than a room. The other bedroom was bigger and nicer and had windows, but Roy said small dark places made him feel like his own real self.

Baker stood on a round rug and, by the light from the hall, examined his son's tiny cubicle. Roy was no fool. Who could sleep in Lucy's room?

To see with a stranger's eyes, Baker squinted. Mell was right: it was clean. Roy never had to be prompted to pick up after himself. Nonetheless, there was a smell: wood shavings and a funky furry odor Baker had come to think of as essence of rat. One wall was plastered in a rotating display of movie posters. *The Texas Chainsaw Massacre* was currently up, along with *Night of the Living Dead* and *Near Dark*. Baker had built shelves to cover the far wall, and these were filled with horror-movie magazines, comic books, books and plastic skulls Roy had painted and filled with candles. A hand-lettered sign warned, Do Not Reshelve! The third wall was devoted to Roy's collection of rubber horror masks: Frankenstein, Dracula, Jason Voorhees's cover-up mask, Nosferatu in both the Max Schreck and Klaus Kinski versions.

The rat slept in a ball, feet tucked, tail at its ears, in a venti-lated rectangular Plexiglas box on Roy's desk. Baker placed a hand flat at either end of the box and lifted. Freddy Krueger did not stir. Holding the box well away from his midsection, Baker gingerly exited his son's room.

Three thousand centuries ago, when Baker Farrish was hope-ful and alive and doing interiors, he was known for his forward-looking walls of glass, openness, airiness, bleached-wood floors, skylights and track lighting, the geometric configurations. Back then, walls were the enemy. When Baker got a job, the first thing he did was find out which nonbearing ones could go. Then times got bad, Lucy went, and space and light became the enemy. Like Freddy Krueger, Baker now liked dark damp places. When people asked him what he thought they should do about their house, he just stood there.

From downstairs he heard Lady Macbeth rouse and stand, her nails clattering against the floor. He had to hurry, get the goddamn rat good and goddamn settled so he could go back down before Mell cratered completely. He passed Lucy's room. Mell was the fool; she worked in there. There was no place to put the rat except in their bedroom; if they left him in Roy's room, Leland's son wouldn't sleep a wink. In the night, like his namesake, the rat came alive, dinging the bell on his Ferris wheel contraption without pause.

At the bedroom door, Baker took stock. The problem with having guests was not so much that *they* saw through your disguised normality into the heart of your miserable weirdness, but that you did. Even vacuumed, perfumed and tidy, their bedroom gave them away. Mell's earphone radio and second-hand paperbacks, her Kleenex and Rolaids and breath mints, the Venetian dream notebook, her crystals in an ashtray. The two VCRs, three remotes, one set of earphones, videotapes, the TV guides and Baker's notebooks. Stacks of unread magazines around the bed, the Camels, ashtrays. Chaos, in spades. The general, unresolvable jitters.

Baker stepped over the doorsill. At the foot of the bed there was a throw rug, a kilim Baker had found tucked under some tacky reproductions at an estate sale. The rug had been at the foot of the bed forever, but this time it caught his toe. Baker fell forward, then caught himself.

On his feet, Freddy Krueger narrowed his beady eyes and, whiskers throbbing, squealed like radar.

Baker lifted the box until it was even with his eyes. "Don't you threaten me," he hissed, "you goddamn son-of-a-bitch rodent. I'll throw you to the goddamn toms." He shook the box.

Freddy Krueger fell to his knees.

Rats, Roy claimed, got a very bum rap. Rats were meticulous, as long as they were kept in a clean environment. "It's my money," he announced at the age of nine, "and I'm buying a rat. *Rattus norvegicus*, if you really want to know."

The rat was agile. In a flash he was back on his tiny feet.

Elbowing a stack of videotapes to the floor, Baker set the Plexiglas box on a table between the VCRs and stepped back, dusting his hands. "Eat shit and die, cocksucker," he said in parting.

Freddy Krueger jumped on his Ferris wheel. The harder he climbed, the faster the wheel turned and the louder the bell attached to the Ferris wheel dinged.

Tobias. That was the boy's name. Tobias, Toby. Mell was right—British *and* a dog's name.

It wasn't fair to have tried to raise a son; wrecked people didn't have enough of themselves available to give a child the attention and thought he deserved. Sometimes Baker wished he had gone back on his promise never to interfere with how Roy spent his own money. Sometimes he wished he'd taken up the position of a real father and said no to the rat, the way a real father—a real man—was supposed to.

But then, was there ever a time when he considered himself a real father or man? Here he was, fifty-two, a failure in many of the ways by which the world took measure, but nonetheless a living, breathing person—and a rat and a dog determined how his life went. Shirttail flapping, Baker flew down the stairs, muttering "Crazy goddamn bastard" to himself and then "Down, goddamnit, I said down" when he saw the dog standing on her hind legs pawing at the door.

Lady Macbeth obeyed. Baker rubbed the whining dog's ears and connected her leash to her collar.

Mell looked different. She'd taken something. Weird, Baker Farrish said to himself. We are all three just very goddamn weird.

"What are we waiting for, dollface?" he gently said to Melanie. "Let's go out and greet our guests."

Plaintive as Juliet, Melanie said, "Ah, me . . ."

"What, Doo?"

She rubbed her hands on her skirt. "Nothing."

Standing at the foot of the front steps, Leland stroked the head of the gray and white kitten. "I like you," she said. "You I like." The kitten momentarily yielded, then reared back and shook off Leland's touch.

"Why so many animals?" Toby said. "And what happened to the yard?"

"Yard?"

"There's no grass. It's all bushes."

Both front doors opened at once, and with such force that the doorknobs slammed against the wall and the gray kitten leapt from the urn. Melanie Farrish flew out, arms wide, with Baker and the bounding dog at her heels. Mell's hair had begun to slide from her barrette, and loose strands clung to her pale damp face.

"*Lela!*" Now that the moment was upon her and there was nothing to do but play it out, Mell was surprised to find herself feeling quite happy to see her old friend. Crookedly, ungracefully, a woman unused to moving fast, she ran to Leland, her heart feeling on the verge of disintegrating from all the love and need and unexamined grief.

Leland stood there, holding on to her red ginger, unable to move. She is still beautiful, thought Leland, thin and loony and quite unself-consciously gorgeous. I'm the tough city urchin, and she's the fragile china ballerina, dancing atop a powder box. We have changed and not changed.

The two women came together in a tight embrace, each hugging with equal force. All the years, losses, secrets, all that had been said or not said—now here they were, so many years later, as if they were still thirteen. The ginger stalks pressed into Mell's soft breasts. Leland rested her forehead on Mell's neck.

Bypassing the reunion, Baker and Lady Macbeth went straight to Toby. Lady Macbeth lunged, pulling her leash taut, all but choking herself.

Toby took a step backwards.

"Sit!" Baker ordered. Lady Macbeth obeyed the command but, because Baker neglected to give her the next order, did not stay. Pulling herself along with her strong front legs, she inched her bottom through the herbs and the berry bushes as drool poured from her black lips.

"It's okay," Baker assured the boy. "Drool means love. The bitch likes you, pardon my French."

Toby came forward to shake his host's hand. "Tobias Standard," he said. "Thank you for having us."

The dog kept coming.

"Yes, I know," Baker said, impressed with Toby's good manners. "And you are very welcome. Meet Lady Macbeth. Who seems to be in love."

Feeling witless as a tree stump, Toby shrugged. "Dogs seem to like me," he limply offered.

It was true. Toby's friend Joel had a dog, a Lhasa apso. Henry adored Toby, humped his leg, lay soft and silky in his lap, pliant as warmed honey.

While the men pumped each other's hands, the two women came apart. Leland handed Mell the red ginger, which she deemed *gorg*eous.

"Sorry about the goddamn dog," she yelled to Toby over Leland's shoulder. "She's a goddamn nuisance. I keep telling her to chill out, but she won't. If you think she's bad, wait till you meet the *rat*."

Toby looked down as Lady Macbeth threw up and stood looking at her vomit, a puddle of clear stuff dotted with white.

"The what?" he asked.

6

Estelle Etheridge closed the curtains and took off running. Waxed slick and shiny for wheelchairs, the tile floor was slippery, and even though Estelle was wearing her Reeboks, she missed a step rounding the corner of her desk and skidded to her left, whacking her funny bone on the corner of her laser printer.

"Damn," Estelle muttered, rubbing her elbow, but she did not slow down.

Flopping into her desk chair, she set her hand on the telephone receiver. The funny bone felt like a nonstop fireworks sparkler, winking and pulsing. "Hurts," she said, shoving the elbow into the meat of her middle beneath the rib cage.

If she positioned her chair just right, Estelle could see out the glass doors of Eva Turner to Strange Avenue. To get a good view of the Mell and Baker corner, she'd had to get up and go to the window. Estelle knew Leland Standard was coming home. When she saw the unfamiliar black car poking down Strange, she figured it had to be her. Estelle also knew about tonight's dinner party. She was in on Jane Scott Laws's dilemma and Sissy Westerfield's failed attempt to lose weight for the occasion. The only important details she was missing were wardrobe and side dishes. The legs of lamb she'd heard about from Dub Jr.

Estelle consulted Insta-dial. Her eyesight was clear, her hearing acute. At seventy-two, she wore neither glasses nor hearing aid. Thirty-eight years ago, when her husband keeled over and left her with nothing but debts and a tow truck the bank repossessed before the preacher finished "dust to dust," Estelle had to learn self-reliance at a late age. Before Dub Sr. went, she didn't know a mortgage from a pie pan. As it turned out, he'd done his wife a favor by leaving her in hock and alone. Grief and loss had forced Estelle out into the world, to find a job and learn things about life, happiness and technology for the first time in her life.

Estelle punched out Insta-dial #7. She had an entire computerized switchboard system at her disposal. The first in town to install touch-tone dialing, she had call waiting, call forwarding, a speaker phone, Insta-dial and a memory, not to mention three telephone lines, E-mail, a modem and a fax. She had learned WordPerfect on her grandson's Mac. She did spread sheets for Dub Jr., who was an excellent butcher but didn't know diddly-squat about the computer age.

Every time the jingling sound of numbers being punched on their own reached her ears, it gave Estelle a sense of power and control and made her feel connected to the whole modern world. Since the Eva Turner governing board didn't always approve of her purchases, Estelle applied to the government, got grants, found ways. At her left, the fabulous fax. Nobody much used the fax except Estelle, who sent messages to Dub III, her grandson in Rosesharon, and down to Jackson to her sister Juanita. Juanita didn't have her own fax machine, but there was a Kinko's just up the street she could walk to.

Cotton Plant, Mississippi, wasn't long distance, but the ring sounded different, a soft burr instead of the local Eunola blat. On the sixth ring, Sissy Westerfield picked up with her soft girlish "Hello."

"It's Estelle. She's in a black, jazzy sports car. And get this—she's brought *him* with her."

"Who?"

"The boy. You know."

"The *boy*. Oh, Lord, I forgot about the boy. Who does he—"

"Look like?"

"Yes."

"Well, Sissy, I can't hardly make out facial features from here."

"Oh. Then who drove?"

"Him."

"Did you say she did?"

"Him. I said *he* drove." Talking to Sissy could be a pain.

"What kind of car did you say?"

"Lord, Sissy, just never mind. I got to go."

"Listen, Estelle," Sissy said, dragging it out.

Estelle drummed her fingers. "Now like I say, Sissy, I got to—" To clear the line she punched Clear.

Because of her sensory gifts, Estelle felt it was her God-given duty to not hide her light under a bushel. In time people had come to depend on her for information and the kind of news you couldn't find in that poor excuse for a newspaper, the *Eunola Enterprise*. Connections were what people longed for, a distilled sense of what was going on. Hers was a talent for compression, isolation and choice. Chuck out the chaff, fix on the wheat; forget the general picture and eyeball details. She punched up Insta-dial #9.

The drug dealer nurse on the second floor—a Methodist of good works and solid reputation—operated along the same lines. After all, she said to herself, if my business brings "light to them that sit in darkness and in the shadow of death," it can't be all bad. Anyway, she didn't sell to kids, and her business brought many to Eva Turner who would not otherwise have seen fit to darken that institution's doors. Once they got there, to cover their tracks and do right by their unspoken agreement, people made visitations to the ill and infirm, the distracted, the shut-ins.

After speaking briefly to Jane Scott Laws, Estelle Etheridge set down the receiver, got up and went back over to the windows. Leland Standard and Melanie Farrish were hugging; Baker Farrish was shaking the boy's hand; their dog was puking. Most people hated Lady Macbeth, but when she minded her manners that dog was sweet as pie.

Estelle bustled back to her station, where she felt like a true hub. Everybody came to Eva Turner sooner or later, to visit or live. The infirm old-guard ladies had always been there; the only difference was, now their maids had rooms next door, as big and as nicely furnished as their own. Nobody came just to dry out. It was different. You could sit at the front desk of Eva Turner and chronicle the history of the town.

Estelle had a house, but her life was here. She ate in the cafeteria, washed her clothes in the basement, had her hair done at the in-house beauty shop. That way she could save up enough money for her and Juanita to go to the track, once a year to the fairgrounds in New Orleans, and once to Oaklawn in Hot Springs. At Oaklawn last year, Estelle hit the double three times, one exacta and several long-shot show bets. Juanita hit a trifecta and came close to the Pick Six until her horse pulled up lame in the last race and had to be carted off in a horse ambulance. They went to the Vapors to hear Tom Jones, ate fried shrimp and cherries jubilee, had a ball.

Estelle slapped her desk and picked up the receiver. "I know who."

Marlenetta L'Heureux had taught Leland Standard tap, acrobatics and ballet before Dolly Standard got ideas and started driving her daughter to Memphis to take ballet from that Cuban person. Marlenetta had given up dancing. She was getting ready to retire, but still taught business administration at Delta State. She had an 800 number.

Estelle rocked back in her chair. The double doors leading to the halls of Eva Turner proper were firmly closed, shutting out the moans and groans of Alzheimer's and Parkinson's, the clatter-chatter of the senile and sad. Every morning, ladies showed up at the nurses' station, bags already packed. "Call my daughter," they'd say. "Tell her to come get me—I can't afford this hotel."

Having been built in the old days when walls were thicker, Eva Turner kept its secrets. In the reception room, all gilt and dark velvet, furnished with settees and love seats and rocking chairs with antimacassars, you couldn't hear anything except soft, piped-in songs without words and Estelle Etheridge making her calls.

Rubbing her elbow, she listened to the delicious sound of long distance. They were sort of the same, the telephone and a funny bone. Not that her elbow hurt anymore. Only the memory of feeling, a lightning flash of the funny bone nerve doing its job, sending messages, jumping synapses.

Marlenetta's answering machine clicked on.

"Shoot, Marlenetta," Estelle said to the machine. "I had something to tell you."

She hung up.

7

In Cotton Plant, to steady herself Sissy Westerfield grabbed the bedpost and brought her other arm straight up over her head. A soft pretty skirt dangled from that fist, limp and blameless, like wet noodles. Looking at the skirt, Sissy hesitated. She wasn't stupid, she knew it was dumb to punish clothes instead of herself; on the other hand, so what? Like a lion tamer showing the cats who's boss, she shot the arm down, whapping the skirt full-force on her girlish white bed.

"Shit!" The flared skirt was washable silk in a rainbow pattern of muted colors, with a waistband she could not come close to buttoning.

Sissy's hair was newly colored and curled, her face done down to lined eyes, thickened lashes, base makeup and Very Peach cheek blush. Who could tell how clothes looked if your eyes weren't done?

She whapped the skirt again. Whimpering, Miss Lillian buried her curly head under a throw pillow.

"Can it, Lillian," Sissy ordered.

The Bichon Frise did as she was told.

When Mildred Sissy Pruett was thirteen, she had sworn on her mother's Bible never again to lay her head on a pillow in a house with a rural route address longer than three nights running. Not every vow came true. The PO had her at Route 2, Box 6, not even in Cotton frigging Plant but out from it, one mile past the junkyard and one beyond the rendering plant, at the end of a road that twisted past two equipment sheds, three shacky houses, two hundred acres of farmland and six catfish ponds.

She let the skirt go. It lay in a heap on her crocheted Heritage bedspread from Sears. Curling her toes around another clump of silk on the floor, Sissy lifted her foot. Once the foot was high enough, she grabbed a pair of pants. "Piss," she said, flinging them. "Piss and shit. *Balls.*"

Sissy didn't particularly want to be competitive with Leland Standard; she couldn't help it. There was only so much room in the boat.

The silk pants fell to the bed next to the skirt. Lillian poked her black nose out from under the pillow.

In high school, Sissy, Mell, Leland and the other girls in their gang used to have contests. They all voted: Prettiest, Most Talented, Best Legs, Cutest Mother. Because Sissy's talent developed late and nobody knew for years how good her voice was, Leland Standard, who could tie her legs in knots behind her head, usually won Most Talented. It wasn't until after Sissy graduated from high school that she started doing musical comedy and operetta. She even played Pitti-Sing at the Memphis Gilbert and Sullivan Festival one summer, a triumph.

Prettiest, however, belonged to Sissy Pruett, not only in the girls' private contests but in the high school yearbook as well, when the movie star John Derek looked at five girls' pictures and declared her the most beautiful. Sissy had a Marilyn Monroe look: soft white skin, full lips, melting eyes, cascading blond hair, a lushness about her body and walk. Sissy lost her little-girliness at about thirteen. At fourteen she was dating seniors, and by the time she graduated she was going out with flyboys from the Air Force base and Ole Miss frat rats home for the weekend.

Elastic waists were the answer; she should have known better than to buy pants and a skirt that buttoned. Leaning on the bedpost, Sissy rested, panting like a worn-out mule.

People thought because she dated older boys she was loose, but she wasn't. When she was young and dating flyboys, Sissy's life was simple, her goals clear-cut: she wanted out of the house, out of her family. It was the same desire that pushed Sissy into marrying Hank Westerfield. Hank was sweet, bless his heart, but he was boring, which made Sissy feel like she had been married forever when in truth it had been only thirty years in January. In her family, thirty years was not that long for a woman of fifty-two.

Hank Westerfield popped the question the Christmas Sissy's daddy went bankrupt for the second time in fifteen years, as often as a man could legally file in Mississippi. That was also the year the furniture store took back the living room couch, the radio-TV console and two beds. Since the family couldn't afford to send Sissy back to Ole Miss without the partial music scholarship she'd forfeited by having a low grade-point average, she was looking at living at home and getting a job selling cosmetics at the drugstore when Hank gave her an out.

At Ole Miss Sissy had been happy. Because of her talent and her looks she'd gotten a bid to go Chi O, had a date to every Rebel football game, went to the county line in Sardis every weekend, and sometimes during the week, to drink beer with her friends. She was a homecoming maid her sophomore year and everything. Giving up Ole Miss broke her heart.

The choices were not always great. At least, she told herself back then, married to Hank she would be secure. A big ha! on her.

At her free-standing full-length mahogany mirror, Sissy gave herself the objective once-over. She had on her prettiest underthings: an ivory-colored satin chemise from Victoria's Secret and a boned, lacy French bra with underwires. The bra pushed up her creamy breasts and nicely pinched in her rib cage. Men went for Sissy in a big way. She was not bone thin, but then men didn't always like leanness in a woman. When she went with a group of friends to Memphis to see a show or shop and they were all sitting in the Peabody lobby having drinks, it was Sissy men came over to, to offer a drink or a date, and not her fit, flat-tummied chums—who all but fainted with envy and disbelief when it happened.

Hank had just put in the catfish ponds, but he wouldn't take delivery of the fish until he had hired an experienced manager. The last one he found had been ripped out from under him by a grainfed operation in Rolling Fork. For now, the ponds just sat there. Catfish were a bitch. The water temperature had to be just so, and if you didn't keep the oxygen level adjusted you could go to sleep thinking profits and a new car and wake up with your assets belly-up on the surface of your ponds. Catfish decline was the current scare, the AIDS of catfish.

From beneath the hem of the chemise, Sissy's pearled thighs blossomed like moon skin. When she adjusted the angle of the mirror, her soft behind rippled and rolled. Tilting her chin, she moved to a three-quarters angle, her best. Her nose was good; she knew that. Turned up, it gave her a saucy look.

Catfish were the new hope of the state. Soybeans had been, then rice, towboats, crawfish, those stupid little pigs from Vietnam. Used to be, people considered catfish a trash fish which only southerners would eat; suddenly they were the media sensation, red-hot like mesquite and goat cheese. A woman from Indianola was Fed-Exing catfish pâté and smoked whole catfish all over the United States, maybe even Europe. Sissy had even seen a catfish feature on "20/20."

"Fat," Sissy said to her reflection, tugging at a roll of flesh beneath her rib cage. "You are *F*-period-*A*-period-*T*." When she went at herself for being fat, it was sometimes hard to tell which was stronger, her disgust or her purely perverse and counterproductive delight.

Anxiety was giving her a head rush. To settle her nerves she took six deep breaths—from the belly, the way the stress-reduction specialist told Hank to. In the past few years there had been two suicides in Cotton Plant, not to mention a number of unsuccessful attempts. After missing his heart with his .38 special, one friend of Hank's had saved himself financially and otherwise by writing a funny book on the subject, *How to Lose Your Farm and Hold on to Your Life*. The book had been a big hit. He was currently writing another, about his Weimaraner.

Breathe from the belly, the stress consultant advised. Sissy didn't know what that meant, since air was in the lungs and not down there. She didn't question the expert's advice. The trick was to *think* belly, and concentrating on air instead of trouble did seem to help.

The planters had done it with guns. In the mouth. Blam. A mess. Sissy had a great passion for true-crime books, which she bought in paperback, read in a flash, then gave to the dialysis center. From books she knew what guns did to a person. Not that pills worked the way people thought, laying themselves out in a pink peignoir like Sleeping Beauty. Horrible things happened with pills. Vomit, a blue face, the tongue.

Hands on her hips, Sissy whirled so that her chemise lifted to show the tops of her thighs and pale pubic hair. Her knees were cupped in cushions of dimpled fat. Now that the flesh there was beginning to droop like wet paper, it looked awful. She'd gone on a diet the minute she heard Leland Standard was coming to town. She had even paid M.L. Brown to be her diet coach. People made fun of M.L., but she knew her business. Otherwise, how could she have made a name for herself throughout Mississippi and around the Mid-South as the expert on getting ready for beauty pageants? Turning in profile, Sissy sucked in. She was thinner from the side. Her breasts were nice—still high and pretty much rounded, especially in the underwired bra.

Hank had ordered the federal government pamphlets on exotic vegetables. Except for arugula, they mostly turned out to be Chinese. Arugula was plain old rocket, which southern ladies and their maids used to grow for flavoring in salads. Hank said he wasn't desperate enough to grow Chinese, since he didn't even eat it. And then he paused. An unspoken "yet" finished out his thought. When Sissy said maybe he'd prefer doing European salad mix, Hank said, "European *what?*"

Turning from the mirror, Sissy made for the walk-in closet with the built-in shelves and the PVC-pipe clothes rack Hank had designed and built for her. Hank was a good man, decent. He couldn't help being dull, and Sissy felt terrible when she went at him for being what he essentially was, but time was running out. She ran coat hangers down the pipe, one by one.

M.L. Brown taught girls poise, posture, weight and cellulite control, how to do a full-circle turn on a runway so their skirt swirled enough to show their legs but not their underwear, how to Vaseline their teeth and the insides of their mouths so they could smile the whole time they were on stage without their lips sticking to their teeth.

Six weeks ago, Sissy started paying M.L. forty dollars a week for a diet and exercise plan. M.L. had gone all out, even loaning Sissy her own stationary Tunturi with the rowing device on the handlebars. To work on her inner thighs and quadriceps, she had Sissy walk back and forth in her swimming pool in skintight blue jeans and high-heeled shoes while swirling her arms in the water as a triceps toner, a trick M.L. swore by.

The diet she recommended was protein sparing. Sissy couldn't understand where the sparing came in, since all she ate was fish and chicken. Anyway, M.L. said protein sparing made your body burn off fat and not muscle and as a result helped speed up metabolism, the latest thing: readjust your metabolism, be thin for life. To Sissy's mind, a big ha! But it worked. Eating mostly poached chicken breasts, water-packed tuna and the occasional raw vegetable, Sissy dropped eight pounds the first week. She couldn't believe it; the last time she lost weight that fast, she had the Hong Kong flu. But, my God, how many chicken breasts could she choke down? To help out, Hank went on the diet with her, though Sissy had seen wrappers from hot-chile pork skins and boiled peanuts on the dashboard of his truck. Nonetheless, he kept getting skinnier, while after the initial eight-pound loss Sissy plateaued.

By the end of the second week of the diet, Sissy started to feel weak and nauseous. That Saturday, she had a wedding in Shaw. Weddings were a bitch, and she could not manage one with a sick headache. People were always changing their minds. The groom wanted the "Wedding Song"; the bride liked "We've Only Just Begun"; one mother doted on "Because"; the other one said a wedding wasn't a wedding without "Oh, Promise Me." There was always some fool who wanted "When You Wish Upon a Star," the Jiminy Cricket song from *Pinocchio*.

The one in Shaw was a fiasco of the first water. The groom wore running shoes with his tie and tails; the bride was pregnant. At the rehearsal dinner both mothers blew up and stormed off. At five a.m. on his wedding day, the groom went out for a jog; he lowered his personal best by thirteen seconds, but stepped in a rabbit hole at the end of his run and got shin splints. The bride was having morning sickness and second

. thoughts. Nobody could agree on music, so at four that afternoon, an hour before the service, Sissy and the organist worked it out to do the "Wedding Song," "All I Ask of You" from *Phantom of the Opera* and "Because." In the end, nobody approved except the stepfather of the bride, who everybody was going around pretending didn't exist, even though he was footing the bill.

Sissy ate plenty of wedding cake in Shaw. Back in Cotton Plant, she drove straight to Food King and came home with all the things she loved—fresh fruits and vegetables, cheese, mayonnaise, potato chips and her favorite food in the whole world, crackers. Saltines, Wheat Thins, Club crackers, Triscuits . . . Sissy loved every cracker ever made.

The next day, she called M.L. "Protein sparing," she announced, "is history."

M.L. said Sissy could go back on the diet without doing that much damage.

Sissy said no, she could not: "If you're not on the diet bus, you're off it."

Hank took back M.L.'s Tunturi that night and paid her the forty dollars she was owed. Sissy's eight pounds came back in four days. Since then she'd probably added a few more, though she hadn't weighed. Her new afternoon passion was Sesame Wheat Thins with mayonnaise, capers and Gorgonzola, which she sometimes topped with a sliver of Black Forest ham. Yesterday, while reading *Baser Instincts*, she and Lillian had shared an entire bag of garlic bagel chips.

She raised her arm and slipped a silk caftan over her head. Silk was Sissy's trademark, and she wore it all the time, even though it clung to your skin and held in odors. The caftan came to her ankles. The peacock blue and jade green of the swirly print set off her pale skin and green eyes and freshly tipped hair, which curled about her face like a feathered cap. Hands at her waist, Sissy swiveled her hips.

Sometimes she thought about John Derek and wondered if he remembered her. She wasn't far from the Bo Derek type. At Ole Miss she won the Marilyn Monroe look-alike contest both years. Plus, no matter how fat she got, Sissy could outdance the world. In high school, she was queen of the dirty bop, bumping and grinding her soft hips in a sly and subtle way to "Hearts of Stone" and "Sixty-Minute Man." From movie clips she'd figured out the steps Elvis did at his peak, and she had James Brown's swoop down pat; she could do Tina Turner's strut and Michael Jackson's moon walk and had memorized every jog and dip in the dirty-dancing movie and the one about the shag. To get into the new dances she watched "In Living Color" and MTV. Hip-hop was tough. Whenever whites thought they had a move nailed, blacks went the other way and swagged when they used to sway, zigged when zagged felt right.

In dreams, Sissy was a diva. She did recitals at Carnegie Hall. Singing Puccini, she brought the house down, hitting the high notes like Leontyne Price. Secretly she thought she should have been the one to go to New York, not Leland Standard. She was still beautiful, her cheekbones like small knobs, her chin creased and arrogant. Her eyes had that floating-in-jelly look that made men think she was up for anything they asked. Even now, her lips were like cushions, and she hadn't even entertained the notion of a facelift.

"Not bad for a fat lady," she said, looking at herself in the caftan. "If I do say so myself."

Lillian came out from under the pillow, and Sissy got out her green leather sling pumps with the four-inch heels. She had slim ankles and tiny feet and could walk in spike heels better than other women did in running shoes. From her jewelry box she selected a pair of jade earrings that dangled to her creamy-white shoulders. Hank had bought the earrings for her in Chinatown the year they had their way paid to the Rotary convention in San Francisco. She put a long strand of beads around her neck. "Eat your heart out, Leland Standard," she said, plumping her curls. "Eat out your fit, skinny L.A. heart."

Hank farmed in partnership with his mother, but didn't own the land. Whenever his mother died, three other Westerfield brothers would be waiting in the wings, each one hotter than the next to sell the land to developers. Meanwhile, Hank had had four disastrous years in a row. His cotton was ginned and sold for this year, his beans picked. It hadn't been as bad a year as last, but that wasn't saying much, and, in truth, they would never catch up, not ever.

Sissy sat on her bed and stared out the window, running her hand down Lillian's curly coat. The land was so flat you could see to the edge of the sky. The sky pressed down like a huge hand. To the north of the house a dust cloud rose up, then disappeared. The combines were out, turning the defoliated stalks under, getting ready for fall and the next repetition of the same old thing. It never ended. There was always a next season, and they would never retire or move or have time to take off and see the world. To the east of the cotton rows, the catfish ponds looked like rectangular invitations to small children to tumble into and drown.

One thing was clear. Sissy Pruett Westerfield had to sing if she wanted new clothes and expensive makeup, and she was by God going to have new clothes and expensive makeup. And since all-out weddings were still big in the Delta, no matter how far down the tubes the economy had gone, and because there would always be a funeral in the works, she could depend on getting work. She'd also done some jingle singing in Memphis and Jackson—local commercials for Jax beer and the Tote 'n Carry convenience-store chain—and still had the voice to sing the ingenue lead in musical comedies, though she was far too old for the parts. Her voice was neither big nor truly great, but it had sweetness and purity and truth at its heart.

The flat land looked like a sad future she could see to the end of. Sissy flopped back onto her bed. Hank would be home for lunch. She checked the clock. She had time. Twisting around until her feet faced the full-length mirror, she kicked off her green pumps and drew the chemise and caftan up around her waist.

When Jack Threlkill tried to talk to her about menopause, Sissy had clapped her hands over her ears. She didn't want to hear about menopause and didn't want to read the stupid book, either. All menopause meant was, you dry up and then you die. Why would she want to hear that? Anyway, didn't she have to have her uterus and one ovary out when she was thirty-eight, and wasn't she taking hormone pills already—didn't that mean she didn't have to worry about the change? Not necessarily, Jack Threlkill said.

Sissy had her ways of checking herself out. Fluffing a pillow beneath her head so she could see herself in the mirror, she opened her rippling thighs.

All this talk about HIV and the new monogamy. Sissy had never been unfaithful to Hank Westerfield in her life; adultery just wasn't in her. Dressing for men did not necessarily mean making yourself available to them. Not that Hank was enough. Hank was all business: put it in, get there, take it out. And while of course Sissy would never tell Hank, would not know how to get the words into her mouth, like most women Sissy liked play—liked to dawdle, as if there were no such thing as orgasm or any point to get to, as if the point itself was the doodling and dawdling. She had never told that to a soul, never talked to other women about her private self, but kept it inside.

Looking at herself in the mirror, she rubbed her soft belly, pressing the soft wads of fat toward one hipbone and then the other. Lillian crept closer, her nose at Sissy's breast. Sissy ran her hand down to her navel and then to the top of her pubic bone, hips lifting slightly in anticipation. She checked the mirror. Pink as a shell, pink and oyster gray. Lips and folds. Pale crinkly golden hair. What the silk and satin kept secret. And wasn't that a drop of moisture? Sissy reached down, brought the finger to her lips, ran it up and down her curled tongue. The taste was salty. She stroked herself and there was more. It made her feel triumphant to know she was still juicy. With the other hand she pulled Miss Lillian closer, and after a time began to hum and then to sing, a Brahms lied and then "O mio babbino caro" from *Gianni Schicchi*.

Love, life. To sing was to love; singing was life. Her hips came up higher. She put three fingers inside herself.

Fat wasn't the worst thing in the world. Fat did not come close to poor. Fat was negotiable but poor was not. She would never be poor again. She would go to her grave in her silks, singing her songs. That was the one good thing about not having children, even though she'd always wanted at least one: she would not have to worry about failing them, and could concentrate on herself.

Sissy pressed her pretty dimpled knees together, clamping her hand in its soft trap. "Ahhhh . . ." she said in her real voice, and "Ahhhh . . ." again.

Her arm went limp. She let go of Lillian, and the dog shook herself, leapt down off the bed and stood on the fluffy rug beside the bedpost, looking back up at her.

In seconds, Sissy sat up and straightened her clothes. "Show's over," she told Lillian. She took off her caftan and jewelry and, humming a new tune, put on a soft pink cotton shirt with matching elastic-waist pants.

For an appetizer before lunch, Sissy had four Triscuits with mayonnaise, goat cheese and black olives, washed down with a sixteen-ounce Diet Coke. As she chopped celery for tuna fish, she hummed k.d. lang's new song "Wash Me Clean." She shared her last Triscuit with Lillian.

Chopping, she began rehearsing a conversation with Hank, in which she informed him that he was not going into Eunola with her to Mell and Baker's dinner party tonight in a way that made it seem like his idea and not hers. It wouldn't be far from the truth. Hank hated dinner parties in general and said that Mell and Baker Farrish gave him the sick headache.

Sissy stuck a tablespoon into a Hellmann's mayonnaise jar and dug out a glob.

8

Fanning her face with her hand, Mell all but fell into an overstuffed rocker. "So . . ."

To Toby, the living room looked like a padded cell for an idiot king. Satin plush and velvet everywhere, in muted colors, nothing disturbing to set the king to raving. The walls were covered in a quilty, gunmetal-gray fabric with a soft sheen; the rugs were plush off-white with pale rose and green accents; the oak floors, bleached and rubbed to a warm, pale yellow. In front of the small fireplace was something that looked like a Viking shield; in front of that, stiff greenery in a brass spittoon. Displayed on every surface of all the little tables around the room were small everyday items turned into adornments: an ivory baby brush, a dented silver cup, a set of ancient barber tools, a collection of sewing machine bobbins on a crocheted doily.

Baker finished Mell's thought. "We're having a supper party in your honor tonight."

"Dinner," Mell corrected him.

From a small china pencil cup, Baker selected a cigarette.

Mell turned to Leland. "When *people* come," she said, "Baker goes extremely Deep South."

Leland shook her head. "Okay by me," she said. "I still say it sometimes."

Toby checked out the dog, who was curled at his feet, her chin on the floor. To be polite, he asked, "What?"

"'Supper,'" Mell explained. "Instead of 'dinner.'"

Toby nodded, which seemed the thing to do.

Baker turned to Leland. "We'll be . . ." he said, then paused for a moment. "Eleven," he concluded.

"Eleven?" Leland glanced through the archway into the dining room. The table was set with crystal water and wine glasses, linen tablecloth and napkins, polished silverware, family china; for a centerpiece, lilies, rosemary and achillea in a pale green pasta jar. Baker had put Leland's blooming ginger in a battered copper umbrella stand beside the table in the hall that served as the bar. Like the hydrangea, the ginger looked splendid but was exactly in the way.

Baker fiddled with his unlit cigarette. "Yes," he said. "Eleven."

When he looked her way, Leland held his gaze. Baker had been balding since he was in his late twenties. By now he was shiny on top, clean and hard. A fringe of reddish brown around his ears and the back of his head made for a softening effect, like ruffles on a plain dress. With a finger he pushed his glasses back up on the bridge of his nose.

He was lying, Leland was certain. Melanie and Baker would never invite an odd number of people for dinner. He looked away, and Leland's heart sank. They hadn't been expecting Toby. Why should they? She hadn't told them he was coming. She kept planning to, then hadn't, thinking . . . She didn't know what she was thinking. Of course no one would complain or say anything; they would all go on. That was how they did things. "Eleven," she said. "Sounds good."

"Doesn't it?" Baker offered.

Leland dipped her head. "Table looks fabulous. I can't believe I brought more flowers."

In high school Baker was a drip: horn-rimmed glasses, too thin, and he didn't play sports. It took him some time to grow into his looks. In his twenties, having discovered that, in truth, women didn't that much go for hunky he-men, Baker had become the town ladies' man. A couple of times, when she came home to see about her mother and then to bury her, Leland had experienced Baker's newfound expertise. He was just so alive and charming. The first time he wasn't married, and then he was.

"Don't be silly," Mell said. "Ginger's the best. Bert did the table arrangement—you remember Bert."

"Bert? Of course." Leland smoothed her hair. She had no idea who they were talking about.

Mell turned to Toby. "Roberta Frazier," she explained. "Used to be towboat money. Now she does flowers."

"They're really nice." Toby felt like a plastic dog in the car rear window, head swiveling this way and that.

Baker offered cigarettes around, and when no one accepted—Leland would have, but she'd promised Toby—he shook a kitchen match from a toothpick holder. "I'm sure you know, the only people around here with any money are the banks, and—" Mid-thought, he lit his cigarette while the others waited. He looked up. "Sorry. And Doyle Granger."

Leland shook her head. "I don't know who that is."

"From Detroit. A right-wing nut case and meat magnate. Supplies frozen hamburger patties to franchise food operations."

"Jack in the Box," Mell said in an aside to Toby. "And like that."

Toby smiled.

"My friend Jacky Nelms does okay." Baker took back the floor. "Jacky's a plumber. This swamp burg of ours swells and contracts. Houses shift, pipes burst—he keeps busy, then a lot of times, people don't pay. But if we're talking real money, forget it. You remember Johnny Callouiette—played French horn in the band, spat when he talked? He owns Jack-Mart. John does well."

"Sweetie."

Baker turned to his wife, whose pale eyes drifted like paper in a wind.

"She doesn't know what Jack-Mart is."

"You don't know about Jack-Mart?"

Leland shook her head again. "It's okay."

"Oh, you have to go. It's an institution. John buys last-chance sales merchandise from Saks, Bloomingdale's, I. Magnin, you name it. When Jack-Mart has its Saks sales—"

"Twice a year," Mell told Toby.

"Twice a year, in late summer and winter, they have to—"

"Put bars over the windows." Having got her foot in the door, Mell wasn't about to pull it out. "People come from all over Mississippi and, oh, Arkansas and—"

"Tennessee. Louisiana. All over. They bring giant plastic garbage bags, tear around the store, dump clothes in the bags—"

"We're talking designer—"

"Armani? Gianni Versace? Unloaded at the cash register like macaroni from a sack."

Mell clucked. "No credit, no checks, cash only. No dressing rooms. I wouldn't be caught *dead* in Jack-Mart." She poked her thumb toward Baker. "He goes."

"This shirt?" He plucked at his chest. "Fifty dollars anywhere. I got it for eight eighty-nine."

"Wow." It was the only thing Leland could think of to say.

"You'll see. Everybody's in Calvin Klein and Donna Karan, carrying Vuitton and Gucci. Names don't mean beans here."

"So . . ." Mell turned to Toby. "Where were we?"

"I don't believe I . . ." Without understanding exactly why, he liked her enormously.

"Oh." Baker slapped his chair arm. "Money. Anyway, Johnny Callouiette does okay. And of course Carroll."

Toby looked up.

"Carroll Cunningham," Mell added.

"He got out of real estate just in time."

Lady Macbeth had drifted into sleep. On her back, she pawed the empty air.

Mell touched Toby's forearm. He jumped, then Mell did.

"Sorry," she said.

"That's okay."

"I was just going to say, we'll get finished with all this past history before long. You must be bored to tears."

"Not at all. Please, I'm fine. It's just . . ."

"What?"

"Nothing." When was lunch? He was starving.

"So . . ." Leland resumed the conversation. "Now, who's coming?"

Baker set his cigarette down and placed his right index finger in his left palm. "Well," he said, "there's the four of us." He glanced at Toby, then raised the middle finger of his counting hand. "Sissy and Hank."

"How is Sissy?"

"Mean as a trapped possum and fat as a Swift's Butterball."

"Mell!" Baker scolded.

"It's true."

"True's not the point."

"*God*, Baker."

"What?"

"Give me a fucking break."

Toby looked up. So much for not saying "fuck."

Leland stepped in, realizing that this wasn't fighting but just the way they exchanged information. "And Hank?"

"Boring as a dishrag." Mell looked at Baker. "But fine—a nice man." Her voice went icy. "Don't you just love nice men? If we're lucky, Sissy will convince him he doesn't want to come."

"Why?" Leland asked, without caring one way or the other.

"Catfish decline, for one thing."

"Catfish what?"

"Hank's lone topic of conversation."

Baker looked puzzled. "Why would Hank Westerfield want to talk about catfish decline?"

Mell rolled her big eyes. "You haven't heard? Hank's got ponds."

"Hank?"

Mell stared.

"Has *ponds*?"

"That's what I said, Baker. Ponds."

"Sorry, gang." Baker stabbed out his half-smoked cigarette.

"Don't you guys talk?" Leland pretended it was a joke.

"Not if we can help it." Mell's tone was flat and humorless.

"Moving right along," Baker said. "Paul and Pat were coming, but he's in Houston having a grandchild. So they can't."

"Pat?"

To be the one to tell, Mell spoke quickly. "Pat Greener. You might not remember her. We didn't grow up with Pat; she's from Eustace." She turned to Toby, who wasn't listening. "Eustace," she said, and suddenly something inside shifted, a tiny crank of a lever into another gear, and she thought she heard an odd dripping kind of sound from the kitchen—or was the slim white chip in the potted dracaena kicking in? She couldn't quite get her rhythms right, and there was a steady whirring, a furriness in her head, that distracted her. "Eustace is ten miles out Highway 1 on the lake."

Toby did not respond.

"Pat makes pots," Mell said to nobody in particular.

"Ah." Toby nodded, studying Mell. She was an odd but provocative combination, both bony and cushioned, with thin arms and legs, high bony shoulders set off by large breasts, wide hips and thighs, a nice round belly. When she talked, her hands made wavy gestures, soothing and gentle.

"Her daddy," Mell said to Leland, "you remember, was Stick Greener?"

Leland shook her head.

"Sure you do," Baker said. "Stick Greener had the shoe store."

"The one with the x-ray?"

"Greener Shoes, exactly." Mell poked Toby's arm. "We used to x-ray our feet on a daily basis."

Leland frowned. "Not daily, Mell."

"Well, I know, but we stuck our feet in this machine—has your mama told you this?" She pressed her hands against her knees. When Toby didn't answer, she went on. "Then we'd look through this dark *window* kind of thing, like a what do you call it—stereopticon?—and Lord, just stand there. We could see through our skin like Superman. It was *magic*."

Baker remembered Mell saying "bat wings" earlier on. What had she meant, "bat wings"?

"I didn't," Toby said, "know that."

"*Anyway* . . ." Mell used the word "anyway" the same way Baker did a cigarette, to keep the floor. She returned her attention to Leland. "Pat was in New Orleans studying with some, I don't know, master *potter* when Paul went down there after his brother was killed in the Bronx buying cocaine in that shooting gallery?"

Leland couldn't believe her ears. "Paul's *brother*?"

Mell nodded. "His brother. Shot dead."

Toby jumped in. "What was he doing in the Bronx?"

Leland nixed that line of pursuit. "So Paul went to the French Quarter to recuperate."

"He was at some bar, and he was a Kappa Sig at Ole Miss when Pat was a Tri Delt, and so, like they say, the rest is . . ." Mell shrugged.

Leland turned to Baker, who'd been quiet for too long. "Pots? Like what kind of pots?"

"Urns. Geegaws."

"Art." Mell's tone said it all: art was a joke.

"*Objets.*"

"Exactly. There's one." Baker pointed to a large brown ceramic urn with a wide base, a narrow mouth and concentric ridges around the center like lines made in dirt by a yard rake.

"It's beautiful."

"Like I say, she's good. Little bitch."

"History." Emboldened by hunger, Toby jumped in.

"What?" Mell brushed her dark silky hair behind her ears and peered through her bangs at the boy.

Toby shifted in the velvet love seat. "'The rest is,' you said."

"Yes, of course." Mell was nothing if not kind. "That's what I was about to say—'history.' Thank you—I can be vague. Sometimes I lose my place."

Baker cleared his throat. "So why are we talking about Pat and Paul when they can't come?"

"Because we're talking about them, Baker. We aren't on a schedule. Do you hear something?"

They all were quiet.

"No." Leland broke the silence. "Do you?"

Dreamily, Mell waved the thought away. "So that's two, four, six . . ."

"Jane Scott."

"I was hoping for Jane Scott."

"She's the one you were with when—"

"When I fell off the horse. I've told Toby the stories."

"Not too many, I hope."

They all laughed.

Baker pressed on. "Totty and the Dog."

"My god, the *Dog*." Except for a startling, erotic dream some years back, Leland had managed to forget Dog Boyette.

"Well, I know, but—"

"She's bringing her *dog*?" Toby said.

"No, sweetie." Mell smoothed her hair. "Her husband's name is Dog."

"Oh."

"Same old Totty, I guess?" Leland smiled.

"Arched eyebrows, shaved neck and spit curls."

"Our gang." Leland watched as Melanie studiously rubbed one knee. They had been young when the thing happened between them, thirteen or fourteen. Mell had been the aggressor, standing before the mirror pulling at her nipples until they stiffened, asking Leland to touch her there . . . there. It was a long time ago. They were babies. Still, it was odd having been first with Mell and then later her husband and neither of them knowing. Or so she assumed.

"And of course Carroll."

Leland lifted her chin to one side. "Of course. He's well?"

"Fine." Mell gave Toby a chance to say something, but he didn't. "So," she went on, counting up. "That's one, two, three . . . ten. Who have I left out?"

"Roy?" Baker gently suggested.

Mell laid her head in her hands. More hair slipped from her barrette. "I mean, would you believe I forgot my own son?"

Leland had not lost the knack of maneuvering through a southern conversation. The trick was to ignore subtext and focus on chatter as if chatter were the point, meantime keeping steady in mind the fact that subtext was everything. "How old," she asked like a doting aunt, "is Roy now?"

"Twelve," Baker answered quickly, in case Mell didn't know. "Thirteen in July."

"Twelve, imagine. A baby."

"Thank you for leaving out the rest." Baker lightly stroked his bald head.

"What?"

"At our age."

Leland placed her hand on his chair arm. "Not at all. Haven't you heard? Women in their forties are having babies all over the place these days. A woman in Orange County is having twins and she's menopausal and fifty-three."

"Oh, well," Toby cracked. "Orange County."

Mell and Baker waited.

"No," Leland said. "I was just thinking how lucky you were."
Baker reached for another cigarette.

"Why don't we take your bags up," Mell suggested. "After
y'all freshen up," she said, dragging out the "y'all" until it was
hard to tell whether she was being ironic or just lazy, "we'll
have a little—"

Baker kept a sharp lookout on his wife. Mell made a big show
of her goofball vagueness, all the while not missing a trick. She
had seen the quick exchange between Leland and him. Stored
it up. "Drinky-poo." Baker finished her sentence.

Toby checked his watch. He had tried to get his mother to
stop for lunch at a Burger King, but she said they had to wait,
Baker and Mell would have fixed something. It was past one
now, and they were sliding over lunch into drinks.

"Lunch." Mell ran her fingers distractedly up and down the
length of her face. "I could swear . . ." She looked off toward
the kitchen. She had caught Toby's drift. Hungry, he was
doubtless expecting peanut butter, Velveeta and Jell-O pie
from the Elvis Presley cookbook. Instead, lunch was a platter
of smoked salmon with capers, minced red onions, sour cream,
cream cheese and tiny French pickles. There was another platter of assorted condiments: raw vegetables, pickled okra, mari-
nated green beans, some of Jane Scott's watermelon pickles
and sweet gherkins. On the kitchen counter was a nice and
runny wedge of German blue Brie. The wine was only so-so;
nobody in town cared that much about wine except Carroll
Cunningham and Jacky Nelms, and Jacky didn't even drink,
for God's sake. But they had Heinekens on ice and Bombay
gin and Absolut Citron in the freezer.

Toby eased his toe out from under the head of the sleeping
boxer. When he got up, so did the dog. Toby pulled his satin
jacket tighter.

Baker led the way up the stairs. At the top, he closed the
bathroom door.

"*Baker!*" Mell screamed from the kitchen.

The bathroom door edged back open.

"Oh, God," Baker muttered. He pointed out where Toby and Leland would sleep, then excused himself and sped off down the hall toward the stairs.

Leland leaned against a wall. "Toby . . ."

"You didn't tell them I was coming."

She lowered her eyes.

"It's okay." He shrugged. "We're here. Forget it. She's stoned out of her tree, you know."

"You mean Mell."

He nodded. "But I think she did hear water. I heard it too. I think from the kitchen." He cast a glance behind him, toward the tiny room Baker had said was his. "Did she say something about a rat?"

9

Old money. Continuance. Regeneration. Manners. In Beall Park, the magnolia limbs dipped to the ground like long gowns from another era. The trees were old, most of them prewar— the one Eunola's older citizens referred to as "the Waw of the Nawthun Invasion." Having been allowed to branch out low, the trees needed no raking, as the great green leaves fell within the skirt of shapely limbs and composted themselves in cool dark solitude, adding iron and raising the pH.

In her Beall Park kitchen, Jane Scott Laws shifted an unlit True to the other corner of her mouth and, hefting a five-pound sack of sugar, tore open a spout and poured.

When I get lonesome I jump on the telephone. The volume on her boombox was up to six. *I call my baby, tell her I'm on my way back home.* Big Joe Turner.

Earlier this spring, the air had turned sticky sweet with the

lemony smell of magnolia blooms, white and irregular as pop-
corn. May now, the season was over. There were no more flowers. Only the stiff green leaves.

The sugar came out in an even spray. When the sack was
empty, she tossed it aside and opened another as Joe Turner
did the "flip flop and fly" line. Personally Jane Scott hated
magnolias. The smell, the drippy implications, nostalgia and
other lies. She was glad when the blooms turned brown,
dropped off and died.

The older houses in Beall Park were made of dark brick, in
the swoopy-roofed style known as English manor. Turrets, ga-
bles, amber frosted glass. Some of the homes had been reno-
vated, opened up, walls torn down, windows put in; most were
still dark, heavy and brooding, filled with Victorian furniture,
weighted down with imitations of another country's past. One
of the larger homes in Beall Park, with its four magnificent
magnolias, two in the front yard and two leading to the arbor
where the rose garden used to be, the House of Laws had once
reigned over its block, the cul-de-sac dowager queen.

Jane Scott set her cigarette in a metal ashtray inscribed with
"My heart's in San Francisco but my ass is not," and punched
the boom box up to eight. When she did jelly, she liked her
music loud. Estelle Etheridge had had to shout to be heard
over "Corrine Corrina." Maintaining a steady flow of sugar,
Jane Scott picked up a long wooden spoon and began to stir.
The white crystals pouring into the blue-speckled jelly pot reminded her of old times in San Francisco, where in the space
of a fair number of lost and wonderful years she ran wild and
almost killed herself. Whatever there was to try, Jane Scott
went for, and in a big way: ups and downs, but mostly she liked
the hallucinogens—mushrooms and acid, the mind openers
that took her to new worlds. In figures of speech, drugs were
prepositional. Out beyond, over under, around and through.
Friends used to call her All-out Jane.

She tapped her foot and boogied. *Here comes my baby*

flashin' a new gold tooth. Big Joe liked repetition. He said it again.

What difference did it make if Leland Standard had brought her mystery son home to Eunola? Estelle Etheridge was a pain. Small towns could always be divided neatly in two: who left and who didn't. It didn't matter how long you went away for, just that you went. Extra points for doing it as a grown-up. Once you saw how much more there was to the world than who came to which party and who wasn't asked to be a debutante, your perspective changed a little.

With her wooden spoon Jane Scott dipped up berries from the bottom, folding the sugar in, then checked the clock. In two minutes she would allow herself a real live cigarette.

Soap opera had its enchantments. Jane Scott had often wondered if Baker Farrish wasn't Leland's boy's father, or maybe Carroll Cunningham. More likely, it was somebody from New York. But there was a period back there when Leland was coming home regularly to see about her mother, and . . . The time frame fit, but who knew or cared anymore? Jane Scott understood absolutely, Leland's keeping her son secret. The real question was, Why bring him back now?

More sugar. Jane Scott had made enough jams and jellies not to need to measure anymore. The trick was to open up the sack and just pour, more sugar than you thought you could stand to think about, much less eat. She lowered the flame.

She was still in her robe, a soft rose-pink chenille thing she'd found, brand-new and in a shopping bag on a shelf in her mother's closet. One thin hint of rebellion, wearing her robe past noon. "Jane Scott!" her mother would snap if she saw her. "You weren't raised like that!" So? Samme wasn't there anymore, only the leftover hull of what she used to be, clinging to a tree trunk like a locust shell.

Eight years ago, when Jane Scott told her San Francisco friends she was moving back to Mississippi, they came down hard. They'd all done their Family of Origin work; they loved her. Going back was destructive, they said—regressive. It went on and on.

Her best friend out there was a writer who was doing serials for the *San Francisco Chronicle*, stories of city life that left his readers hanging at the end of each installment. Lucien Monet—his real name—was from Virginia. His father had been a state senator; his mother raised fox hounds. If anybody knew about southern families, Lucien did. Don't go, Jane, he'd said. You'll never leave if you go back now. They'll get you. Loosh was right, but what could she do?

The sugar was starting to turn translucent. Thirty seconds and she would light up. Meantime she folded, lapped and stirred.

In your forties you figured it out. The choices weren't always what you hoped for. A middle child, when all medical, financial and psychological hell broke loose in the Laws family, Jane Scott felt she had to come home to take care of things. One death, one Chapter 11, two and a half drug rehabs and a nervous breakdown later, here she still was, stirring jam to Big Joe Turner in her mama's kitchen. *I'm like a Mississippi bullfrog sittin' on a hollow stump.*

Even Lucien had to admit her decision wasn't easy. His boyfriend said, fuck 'em, live your life, but then Tony had an inborn sense of working-class rage. When he found out he was HIV-positive the same month he met Lucien, the coincidence validated his suspicious nature. Wouldn't you know, he said. Love and death in the same month. Bowl of cherries, piece of cake, no free lunch, choose your cliché.

I got so many women I don't know which way to jump. The sugar was beginning to melt, and the thirty seconds were up. Jane Scott lit a cigarette, drew deeply.

When she arrived home those eight years ago, lugging seven suitcases and a secondhand leather hatbox filled with antique jewelry and feather boas, nobody was at the airport to meet her. She had told Samme and her little brother, Gus, she was flying to Jackson, which flight, what time. Nobody was there, and nobody had left a message. She called home, but the line was busy for two hours. Finally she hailed a cab. Eunola? the driver said. It's a hundred twenty miles to Eunola. Jane Scott gave him a hundred-dollar bill and a pair of antique filigree earrings she'd bought at a yard sale in the Russian District. Besides a couple of ones and some loose change, the hundred dollars was all the money she had in the world.

In Beall Park, the front door was wide open. The cab driver helped her haul in her suitcases. In the living room, she found Gus blotto on the velvet settee, the phone off the hook on the Oriental rug beside his dangling foot.

Long-distance, every time Jane Scott had asked about her brother, Samme had said, oh, Gus was "fine, you know, just fine." When Jane Scott inquired what she meant, Samme feigned ignorance. You had to know Samme. Samme never talked like that without a reason.

When Jane Scott banged the telephone receiver in place, Gus lifted his head. "Sis," he said. "Hey." Then he laid his head back down on the needlepoint pillow and folded his hands over his chest, lifting one finger in greeting.

"I thought," she said, "I was the dope fiend in the family."

"I have no idea what you're talking about," Gus replied, his face as sweet and flat as a vanilla Moon Pie. "No idea." He sat up. "Want a drink?"

Gus. Their brain baby, the hope of the Laws. It turned out you didn't have to go to San Francisco or even Memphis to get drugs; as long as you stayed friendly with a certain employee of the Eva Turner Home for Ladies, you could get whatever your heart desired right here in Eunola.

Jane Scott took another drag from her cigarette, then put it in an ashtray. Dipping up jelly, she set her wooden spoon on a saucer. When the jelling pink stuff was cool, she gently stuck her finger in and sucked off the juices, smacked her lips, winced, set the spoon down on the stove, picked up the sugar sack, poured more in. Baker wasn't kidding when he said Southern Razzmatazz berries were sour.

The death of Jake Laws—"If Daddy hadn't gone and died on us . . ."—was the family excuse for bad behavior. The Family of Origin people were right: you couldn't become a grown-up until you stopped blaming your parents. But sometimes parents asked a lot. Life in the House of Laws had never been smooth, but until Jake's death it did make its way.

Like many good white citizens of the Mississippi Delta, Jake and Samme had lived life as if the good times would go on forever. When the lumberyard business cratered, Jake took to drinking straight Jim Beam from a coffee cup at all hours of the night and day. When it went under, he jumped into Samme's Valium. The policeman who picked him up for driving under the influence had never heard of Jake Laws; all he knew was a man had driven his Mark V straight through the front yard of a Presbyterian deacon, uprooting the ligustrum and flattening little Choo-Choo, the family spaniel. They booked Jake, put him in a cell. He refused to call anybody, but the police thought he'd change his mind once he slept off his drunk. Instead, Jake hanged himself with his belt. All Samme could say was, "How dare they put Jake Laws in jail!"

Jane Scott stirred the sugar in. She was in San Francisco when Jake died, living with Roseanna Dallas. Her one lesbian fling had been good, fine, sometimes extraordinary. Only in the end, Jane Scott found she went for difference, preferred men—which in many ways was too bad for her. Meanwhile, older brother Clyde was in Eunola. After flunking out of Ole Miss, he'd come home to run the lumberyard. Two months later, the bank plastered a sign on the front door of the business. At the moment Jake was unbuckling his belt in the jail cell, Clyde was sitting drunk on his usual stool at the Yacht Club. Gus was at Tulane maintaining a four-point average, preparing himself to lead the family into the age of technology and computers. After Jake's death, things went haywire. When Jane Scott came home, they got even worse.

The boombox went silent. "The Chill Is On" was next, Jane Scott's favorite. So here she was, making jelly and smoking Trues in her mama's kitchen. She'd held an estate sale and sold off anything she didn't specifically need. Except for her bedroom and Gus's, one bathroom, the sun porch and the kitchen, the house was mostly unfurnished. Jane Scott had moved the ten-foot pine table from the kitchen to the sun porch, where she did her sewing.

When Big Joe came to her favorite line—*I been your dog ever since I been your man*—Jane Scott sang along. She didn't often feel sorry for herself. Every now and then, in the face of it all, she indulged. What was it Dr. John used to say—"the right place at the wrong time," or was it the other way around? Life was about timing. She had learned to pace herself. Five cigarettes a day, one Big Joe cassette's worth of self-pity.

She stared out the kitchen window. There used to be a swimming pool in the backyard, where Jake had taught them all to swim. There had been such parties. Jake had to have a special liner built to keep the cement walls of the pool from cracking as the wet, black Delta ground groaned and shifted. The concrete cracked anyway. Everybody thought they were just about the best family in town. Horses, a cabin cruiser, the house on the lake. Jane Scott had the pool filled in, then planted the space with thornless blackberries. Gus wailed like a baby when he came home and saw it. Not that there had been water in the pool for at least seven years; but like most addicts Gus was a romantic, especially when it came to things he couldn't have and didn't matter. The blackberries had had their season. Soon Jane Scott would hack the canes to the ground, for the new growth next year.

She had promised herself: no more married men. But then this time, maybe married wasn't the bottom line. Maybe lawyer was. Maybe redneck. She was his dog. The dog of Dog Boyette.

With a gentle, practiced motion of her wrist she spooned up berries from the bottom of her pot. Jane Scott had had more boyfriends than she cared to remember, but only one husband—for about five minutes nine years ago, an experience that left her with no desire for another. By now her pattern was clear. She chose men badly. Better to go for temporary if she was going to do it at all.

Dog Boyette was a new low. Friends called him Dr. Dog. Former all-American halfback, former county commissioner until the handsome new governor came and broke up their tea party, Rayford D. "Dog" Boyette was your typical aging southern man, full of stories about possum hunts, pussy chasing, coon conking and how great life used to be. Though he was also the most recent in a long line of territorial, irreverent and slightly mean peasants—her type—Jane Scott nonetheless could not believe she could be in love with Dog Boyette. Maybe it wasn't love; but she did long for him, moon around the house over him and feel happy when she was with him. Dog had his sweet side. Sometimes she thought she lived her entire life to provide country songwriters with material.

Dog would be at the party tonight, and so would his beloved Totty. Wilhemina LaGrande Boyette had never been called anything but Totty in her life, with good reason. Who wanted to be called Wilhemina? Totty had been in Mell, Jane Scott and Leland's girl gang. Totty always won Best Legs, and usually Sweetest Smile. As far as Jane Scott knew, neither Totty nor Mell had a clue about her affair with Dog. Baker was in on it from the beginning. Jane Scott told Baker everything.

By expert and cannily indirect manipulation of the great sympathy people—including creditors—still felt for her family, Jane Scott had managed to hold on to the House of Laws. But her fiscal triumph, by the time she achieved it, didn't mean a lot. It was late summer, moving into fall, no rain in three months. The lake was down, towboats scraping bottom, farmers red-eyed from sitting up watching for clouds. The drought broke on the night Clyde Laws staged a show-down with a nasty curve on Reed Road. The asphalt was just wet enough, and Clyde was going so fast that his Sting Ray climbed straight up a telephone pole. Word came in the middle of the night. Jane Scott was awake, drinking cheap champagne and scanning the new GQ. Clyde was killed instantly.

Samme blamed the rain. There was no mention of Yacht Club stingers, just as, when Jake died, she never once uttered the word "suicide." The coping skills of southern women were a marvel. Most people thought Samme made it through Clyde's funeral fine, but Jane Scott knew better. An occasional twitching of her right eyelid, the way she sat from time to time in a cold dead stupor, her shoulders slumped so far down they seemed on the verge of landing in her lap: those moments Samme looked *gone*. You only had so many choices. Coping skills and the human spirit could only take so much.

Alzheimer's, the doctors said. When Jane Scott suggested that maybe Samme just checked out, emotionally and other-wise, they would neither confirm nor deny this unscientific di-agnosis. She knew what they said behind her back, that she'd gone California or whatever. Whys didn't count for much when the end result was Samme Gamble Laws in the blotto ward at Eva Turner.

Once the new dose of sugar was fully incorporated into the berries, Jane Scott turned up the heat. She refused to be de-pressed. She had her health, her home, and would not fall back into dark times. Those were the choices. And trouble wasn't the only reason she stayed in Eunola. In fact she liked it here. She knew how to operate, found value in limiting her options, liked feeling free to talk with an accent again, making use of the stylish and metaphorical shorthand you either got the drift of or not. Talk southern in San Francisco and they thought you were Blanche DuBois or George Wallace.

Gus was in Pascagoula in a halfway house. After his last four-week stay in the drug rehab program down there, Jane Scott told her brother to stay where he was, away from Eunola and Eva Turner. She drove down every two weeks for the requisite family session. The interminable rehash. Endless coffee and cigarettes. Doughnuts. Leo Buscaglia, John Bradshaw, Marianne Williamson. The chemical dependents said how they wanted to love themselves again. The therapist talked about shared pain. Gus gave her winking looks from across the room. Still and all, it worked. By the end of a session, Gus had abandoned irony. His face was shiny, his cheeks warm and red from hope and determination. Sometimes Jane Scott had to remind herself that Gus was a forty-one-year-old man and not a boy.

The tape switched off. "Fuck it," she muttered, and fired up another True. Today was going to be hard. By the end of the dinner party she might have used up tomorrow's allotment.

Besides jellies, jams, fudge, cucumber pickles and pickled watermelon rind—sold in tearooms and gift shops from Memphis to New Orleans—Jane Scott also made hot pads and hand puppets in the shape of prehistoric and imaginary animals. The puppets had a wide-eyed expression kids went for. Jane Scott had hired a woman to help out, and the two could barely keep up with demand. They did especially well in Natchez and Vicksburg, where tourists came in the spring for pilgrimage.

To get a patient into Eva Turner, you had to sign an agreement allowing the nursing home to draft monthly payments from a bank account. If Jane Scott put everything in her own name and signed a form declaring her mother a pauper, she could apply for Medicaid. But then Samme would have to have a roommate, and Jane Scott could not imagine any such thing. Medicaid patients were treated differently. Staff lied when they said they weren't. Medicaids didn't get an afternoon toddy like the other ladies, and nobody bothered to call them to the cig sessions in the common room. If she got Medicaid, Samme would have to give up physical therapy, which Jane Scott didn't want; the aides said her mother slept better on days she had PT. The rock and roll of massage and being forced to walk when she didn't want to had its effect. Right down to it, Jane Scott stayed in Eunola because she could not—would not—abandon Samme.

The jelly was coming to a rolling boil, bubbles popping on the surface. She and Baker had agreed to a seventy-thirty split, Jane Scott providing the jars, the cooking and the gas burned while driving to gift shops and tearooms. Baker grew the berries and worked up the recipe. Jane Scott thought $2.95 was about right for a half-pint jar. Baker found that a ridiculously high price for such a tiny amount of jam, but he didn't understand the tourist mind.

She had pinned her dyed hay-colored hair in a pile on top of her head. Tonight she would do the top part in two French braids, gel and mousse the rest in a wild frizz. She was going to wear a loose brown see-through chiffon and bugle-bead blouse she'd found at an antique store in the Mission District, and underneath it a black camisole, sheer stretch leggings, medium-heeled Lucite sandals. Then, maybe her barracuda earrings, or possibly the snakes. Dog liked the way the barracuda mouths grazed her shoulders. On her arms she would stack as many jangly bracelets as she could fit between her elbows and her wrists.

A few minutes past one. She would have to shower and get dressed before long, in time to get to Eva Turner by four. Then back home, dress for dinner, hope to have time to masque her face and do the collagen thing on her eyes. She had saved up for an eye tuck a couple of years ago, but it was wearing out fast. Her skin was getting crepey again.

She hated seeing Dog with Totty. Totty looked younger than everybody else, because Totty had never changed: same dark spit curls, same shaved neck; same life, same church, same giggle. Totty was real local. She still bragged that the only time she had left Mississippi was in the fifth grade when she went to Amarillo to church camp. That wasn't quite true: Totty had been to Memphis. But nobody counted Memphis as being out of Mississippi.

A fleck of cigarette ash dropped into the jam. With her spoon, Jane Scott carefully flicked it out, then set the spoon on the stove top.

Traditionally, the way to get by in the Delta was to drink hard and hold on to your eccentricities. Jane Scott was working at both. To a Laws, eccentricity came easy, as did heavy drinking, even though both in the long run took a lot out. Jane Scott kept a supply of champagne in the refrigerator, a cheap Spanish brand she had convinced Duke Shamoon to stock. Weekends she smoked dope. Dog didn't know about the grass, of course (though from time to time he enjoyed the blissed-out results of her little habit, without realizing), Dog being a card-carrying family-values Republican—maybe the true bottomest of lines.

Gus's counselors issued dire warnings. Addiction was in the blood. Jane Scott knew she'd gone too far in San Francisco, but that was the past. She didn't do hallucinogens or hard stuff anymore, even though she thought they were still back there, tiny sleeping mind worms. Brain waves, genes, whatever theories the chemical-dependent people came up with, she was not about to con herself or be conned into thinking she could live sober in Eunola.

She flipped the tape over and punched Play. The song came on about the curly-headed chicken in love with the chicken hawk, and Jane Scott sang along. Driving past the House of Laws at that moment, Jocelyn Bible, in her brown UPS truck, had to smile. When hot music was on Jane Scott's boombox, she was doing jams and jellies. When she worked on puppets and hot pads, she went for sweeter stuff, like Chet Baker and Al Green.

Jane Scott was one of those southern rich girls. They were wild. But they knew who they were.

10

"Call Jacky."

Mell lifted her foot. Drops of water fell from the sole of her shoe.

"Mell, my God . . ."

The sink was full, and water was spilling onto the floor in a gentle sheet. To flush some down, Mell had turned on the garbage disposal, which ground on behind her in a high horrible whine.

"What happened?"

"What difference does it make what happened?" Mell shouted. "It was the goddamn"—her face went scarlet—"*artichokes.*"

"*Artichokes?* You didn't—"

"No. I took them out, but some got . . ." She was on the verge of screaming, so she stopped. "Do we have to have a goddamn discussion about this? Why can't you just call—"

"Jacky."

Mell lifted her hands palms-up. "Yes, Jacky." Hairy strands of artichoke and glittering shards of shrimp peel floated on the surface of the water like twirling paper boats.

As Baker's hand touched the phone, it rang.

Mell reached for the disposal switch. "This isn't doing any good." The high whine abruptly stopped.

"Thank God," Baker said into the telephone.

"Thank God what?"

"Sissy, hey. I adore you but I can't talk."

"Is anything—?"

"Plumbing."

"Like you said, thank God. Listen, Hank says—"

"He can't come."

"Is it a problem?"

"We'll miss him, of course, but—"

"Seven-thirty. Bells on. Bring anything?"

"Just your gorgeous self." Baker had his finger on the button when he heard Sissy ask, "Our guests arrive?"

Guests? Baker said yes and hung up, then dialed Jacky Nelms's number as he muttered Estelle Etheridge's name under his breath. Jacky said to use the plumber's friend until he got there. The problem was the pipe under the house he'd jerry-rigged the last time; he'd have to get under there again to fix it, and Baker was lucky he caught him at home eating lunch, he was just getting ready to leave again.

"You know we—"

"House guest, I know. I'm there."

Baker hung up and the phone rang again immediately.

"If you get the water down?"

"Yes?"

"Don't use the faucet."

"No."

"Or the disposal."

"No." Baker hung up and turned to his wife. "Jacky said . . ."

Mell was way ahead of him. At the drain she had hold of the wooden handle of the plumber's friend and was plunging it down. When she pulled it up, the thick rubber cup made a sucking sound. Mell paused to get her breath, then shoved the stick back down again.

Baker edged to her side. "Here, Doo."

Mell shook him off. "I'm getting it." She went up again and then down, hands in monkeylike fists on the wooden shaft of the plumber's friend. In the center of the water, a small but widening whirlpool churned the choke hairs and shrimp peel in circles.

"You are indeed, Mell-doo. You are."

"Get some towels."

Dutifully Baker made for the laundry room, where there was a basketful of rags to be used for just such cleanups. Their entire plumbing system needed replacing. As they couldn't afford to do it all at once, Jacky Nelms did it piecework, joint by joint and pipe by pipe. Baker and Mell kept him busy, doing things like leaving shrimp peels and artichoke hairs in the sink to float down into the disposal and clot it up.

At the kitchen door, to catch one last glimpse of his wife at work, Baker turned. Mell sent the plumber's friend down hard, her shoulders folded in with effort. When she poked her butt out, her long skirt lifted in the back, and Baker could almost see the backs of her knees, tightly girdled in pantyhose. He ran his hand over the top of his head. Mell the sexpot. He liked fucking her from behind. She used to lie on her belly with her shoulders against the mattress, seat in the air, wide open, more vulnerable than he could even imagine being, much less wanting to be, her head to one side and her long lashes fluttering. He would go in and out of her for a long slow time. The true Mell. In the damp, dark laundry room, Baker held his cock.

This was not a crisis, not even close. By the time Leland and Toby came downstairs they would have cleaned everything up. Lunch would be served. Jacky would be under the house patching pipes on the cheap. As it was Friday, Jacky would have brought last Sunday's New York and London papers. No one would know a thing.

Baker gathered up the towels and held them to his chest. He had to stop thinking about fucking Mell all the time. But then again maybe he didn't.

11

"Do they know?"

"What?"

"You and me. I'm queer, you're sick." Lying on his side, he struck a silly pose.

On her back, head against a wall of pillows, Leland laughed.

"You know," he said, flipping his hand through the air.

She raised a finger in a teacherish gesture. "I'm not *sick*."

Toby pulled his jacket closer. "I hate this cold air."

They were on Lucy's bed. Pushed against a wall beneath two windows, the bed was queen-sized and covered with a pretty floral spread. In a window behind them, an air conditioner blasted icy tunnels of air through the room.

"You wouldn't if you knew how hot it can get here. Anyway—"

"I hate it when you tell me what I would or wouldn't feel."

She made a sound in her throat. "All right."

"Anyway what?"

"You're right in front of the thing. Here." She shifted her position, patted the bed.

The fogged panes of glass dripped with condensation. The room was immaculate and very much arranged—books, magazines, tiny vases of flowers, dentist's tools, darning needles, crochet hoops, a collection of ceramic thimbles.

"So do they?"

"No." Leland sank back again into the pillows. "Nobody knows. Any of it." Her eyes went soft and she drifted off to that safe place she went to when she felt trapped.

"Are you okay?"

"Tired, but . . ." She looked up. "I'm fine."

"You didn't tell them I was coming."

"Toby. They should have known."

"Why?"

"You're my son."

"I'm nineteen, Mom—I don't have to go anywhere. Oh, forget it. You never tell anybody anything." From as far back as he could remember he was her secret. He knew it, was a willing participant. It was exciting, as if they lived on the other side of walls where no one else could go. From her he learned, and in time he kept his own secrets. His stomach growled, and he flopped across the bed. "I wish we'd gone to Burger King."

Leland sat up.

"What?"

"I thought I heard—I don't know, *something*."

The bedroom door inched open.

Toby sighed. "Who else?"

Lady Macbeth sat on her stubby tail and wagged it at the same time.

"Talk about murdering sleep."

"There was a rat in my room."

"Baker said he moved it."

"I can smell it."

"It's your imagination."

"I hate it when you say that. It's patronizing." He thought, And condescending.

"I'm sorry. This is hard."

He sighed. "You've got this huge bed. I've got like a *cot*."

Leland smoothed the flowered bedspread. "Lucy's bed."

"Is that the bathroom where she did it?" he said, nodding toward the door.

Leland nodded. "I came home for the funeral. It was horrible. Baker and Mell looked like they'd been hit by a train. They had Lucy laid out downstairs."

"What, dead?"

"They kept the casket closed, but she was in it, in the living room. Her first-grade teacher came up to me. Hilda Bunch—everybody had her. Miss Bunch said, 'Where's Lucy?' I told her, 'Over there.' 'Where?' she said. I said, 'In the box.' Hilda Bunch could not believe it. Lucy in the box, dead in the living room."

Toby stared at the overhead light, which was shaped vaguely like a breast.

"And then she said something I never forgot. 'Some children,' she said, 'walk in your classroom and you know. You wonder what you can do to help. Sometimes you figure it out, but mostly you don't.' I started to ask what you figured out, but then she pointed at Lucy's casket. 'It doesn't have to end up this way. It doesn't have to go this wrong. But you look at them and you see it in their eyes. No hope. Nobody home. I don't know *what* Baker and Melanie could've done to help.'"

Leland shuddered. "I don't know if I even believe it. But I never forgot that 'Nobody home.'"

Toby raised both hands. "I wish we'd gone to the Ramada."

"You can't come to Eunola and stay at the Ramada."

"*You* can't."

When he pouted, he looked about four. Frowning was part of his face. In the picture the hospital took of him when he was only hours old, he had bunched one hand up in a fist beside his ear and screwed his face up in a worried little prune. Holding him, rocking him, Leland used to put her index finger at the bridge of his nose and, as she sang, press upwards against the insistent curled ridges of his forehead.

"Three days," she reminded him, studying him. "Three days."

"It feels like the rest of my life."

She looked away. They had grown up together, brother and sister, mother and son, roommate and companion, all in one. That he loved her more than life was not the problem. The problem was what to do with that love.

Now he resorted to a childish whine. "I wish we hadn't come. I wish we weren't here."

She never had told him who his father was. Astonishingly,

he never had asked. Leland convinced herself that if and when he wanted to know, he'd say so. A couple of times she'd prodded him, and when he didn't respond or even seem curious, she let it go.

"Can we just take it as it comes, Toby?"

He lowered his head. "Jesus, Leland, you say you don't have a Deep South bone in your body, but sometimes . . ." He took a long breath. "Now who is Roy?"

"The son."

"I got that. I mean—"

"Adopted. Another story."

"I'll bet."

Who told people how to be a parent? From the time she was nine, hellbent on being a dancer, Leland was fixed on purposefulness and singularity. Dance class became her life, ballet positions a kind of manual of structures to tell her what to do. Instead of memorizing multiplication tables, she moved through the required shapes, feeling in her imagination the dream of heels coming together in first position, butt tucked, shoulders down, head high. Then second: legs apart in a pretty squat, Chopin in the background. Perfection was possible if you worked hard enough. Perfection, control.

"Okay." Toby slapped the bed and sat up. "I'm going to wash up and see what's for lunch."

"Are you sure you aren't hot in that jacket?"

In the bathroom doorway, he gave her a scalding look. "No," he said very simply. "Like I said before." Then he closed the door.

Leland put her face into a pillow. She would not have chosen, if she had had the right to say, for her son to be gay. Once, realizing what was up, she consulted a friend, the heir to a candy-making fortune and a self-described aging queen. "Of course," he'd said. "Naturally, you would as soon the facts were otherwise. Life would be easier for Toby if he were straight, but frankly, I don't think there's anything for you to do."

She turned over and drew up the covers. Her friend was of a different generation, a man who'd spent the best part of his life hiding from the truth about himself. The world had changed, but only so much. Most of the world still hated the fact of what her son was. The next step was obvious and inevitable—they hated *him*—and it was impossible not to take that personally. Dangerous not to.

Easy to say, "Some of my best friends are . . ." When it came to your son, it was hard, facing up to preconceived notions you didn't know you had. She'd been to counseling sessions with him, on her own and in a group, and a lot of wrinkles had been ironed out. So many people dead. He was alive, that first. Mostly now she worried for him, about him. She wanted him safe, well, alive.

She sat up. Toby was right. The room was like a meat locker.

When she found out she was pregnant—she was thirty-two, living in Manhattan—it felt like a gift: for the first time in her life she wasn't alone. She began reading books as soon as she knew—natural childbirth, diet, vitamins. She attended prenatal class, did careful exercise, went around with her hand on her belly to protect her new friend, companion, life mate. Fatherhood seemed incidental then, alien to her purposes and her understanding.

She had planned on having the baby at home. Everything was ready, the midwife in attendance. She'd been in labor eleven punishing hours when the midwife called an ambulance. Between contractions, enraged by failure, Leland lashed out. The midwife stood her ground. She didn't know what was coming out first down there, but it wasn't the baby's head. At New York Hospital they put Leland under and performed an emergency C-section. There wasn't room. Leland's hips were narrow, and Toby had a big head. They found him upside down, tangled in cord, set to come out knee-first. The nurses said it was a wonder he was normal.

Two days later, Leland went home. Nurses argued against it,

the surgeon said she'd had major surgery, and the other mothers in the maternity ward told her to relax, why rush? But she didn't want other people taking care of her baby, couldn't stand the thought of him lying in a hospital basket, crying. The nurses said they wouldn't let that happen, but how could she be sure?

She could hear Toby through the bathroom door, splashing water. She'd breast-fed him for a year. Welfare kept her going for a while; then she went back to work—temp work mostly. As soon as she got home, they'd play. She read him books. They had fun.

"Can I?" She knocked at the door. Until Toby was twelve they lived in a one-bedroom floor-through on the Upper East Side, all but under the Fifty-ninth Street Bridge. He slept in the bedroom. She was on a convertible couch in the living room, and had to go through his bedroom to get to the john. They'd made their rules.

He opened the door. She reached to touch his shoulder. "We'll be fine," she said.

He wiped his face. "How do you know?" He wadded the towel and shoved it behind the towel bar. Making his exit, he tried to slam the door, but it only swung shut a little, then came back open again.

In the hall, he zipped his jacket halfway closed. He felt like a baby, wishing all the time, but he couldn't help it. He wished he was back in L.A., where he belonged, or in New York, or in fucking Tehran, anywhere except godforsaken Eunola, Mississippi. He wished he was at the Ramada instead of this nuthouse. Wished his mother was well so he could say things. "Come on, ugly," he murmured to Lady Macbeth, who came down at his heels for two steps, then pushed past him.

"Ta-*da*." Mell had pinned her hair up. Her face was flushed and radiant. There was a wide wet spot on her skirt. She stood behind a long, sturdy oak table on which were arranged two gorgeous platters of food, a basket of bread, cloth napkins, small ceramic plates, silver knives and forks, a bowl of apples, a wedge of softened cheese.

"Hey." Toby's face brightened. He looked at Mell and smiled.

"I'm not sure what y'all *drink* out there, but we have a pitcher of mint tea. Do you like iced *tea*?"

"I love iced tea. Thank you."

Toby felt so grateful he thought he might cry.

12

Leland placed her toiletries bag on a shelf beside the sink. Reaching across her chest, she gingerly touched her left breast.

Nothing. It felt soft and familiar, her normal, small breast. But then, they'd told her, it was too soon to feel anything. And in fact, nothing might come of the process they referred to as a "thickening" of tissue. Nothing—or something.

The shelf had been cleared. The sink was a wide cracked bowl with two separate faucets for hot and cold. She turned on the cold, cupped her hands, splashed her face. The water came out a rusty brown.

She looked in the mirror, lifting her chin, patting the flesh along her jawbone with the back of her hand. She didn't look old most of the time, didn't feel it. She took the appropriate vitamins, calcium and E; but looks and feelings aside, she was getting there. Friends and magazine articles convinced her to have a checkup, get a mammogram—her first ever—and the reading came back questionable. Five years ago, her doctor told her, they would not have been able to detect the change. Even now they couldn't guarantee anything, one way or the other. The only way to know was to go in there. Of course, if she could live with not knowing . . .

She'd tried alternative methods: acupuncture; a mixture of vitamins, herbs and juices; meditation. Her doctor kept at her. So did Toby. She couldn't hold out. She was scheduled for a biopsy in ten days.

She slicked her hair behind her ears and straightened one of her earrings. Coming to Eunola was a last-minute, possibly panicky decision. "In case you die?" Toby had asked point-blank. She didn't know. Her age. So many people dead; the thought of Toby—in a worst-case scenario—alone. She wasn't used to being brought to her knees by anything. When she and Simon fell apart—when, face it, Simon dumped her—she felt old, vulnerable, open to attack. Then this . . . *thing.* She tucked her shirt into her jeans, then bloused it back out again.

Last week she had called Mell to ask if she could come for a short visit. Mell said of course, come right away, she couldn't wait to see her. She was gracious, but Leland heard questions in her voice; nervousness, like background music. Two days later she and Toby were blazing east on I-10.

Her jeans were black and short, her belt a bright beaded thing she'd bought secondhand at a flea market in the East Village. In her bedroom, she hung up her nightgown and the clothes she was wearing tonight. The black silk blouse was wrinkled. She shook it, took out her steamer and piled her exercise clothes, underwear and socks in an empty drawer. On top of the bureau, next to the thimble collection, she laid out twenty-four plastic packets of capsules and tablets so variously and brightly colored they looked cartoonish. Vitamins, each packet labeled: "To be taken all at once three times a day." Beside the vitamins, her Baggie of oat bran. Was it possible, she wondered, that Mell and Baker had a juicer? She had learned to keep tidy, to insist on a sense of order as rigorous as ballet positions.

Tonight, there was no telling. She hadn't seen Sissy, Jane

Scott, Totty or the Dog since Lucy's funeral, and then they hadn't really talked.

She opened a second drawer for the rest of her clothes, and it was filled with books and papers and articles clipped from magazines. A book about Jack the Ripper, another about Gilles de Rais, articles about serial killers and poisoners.

Leland closed the drawer and put the rest of her stuff in the other drawer. She noticed Mell's computer on a built-in desk across the room, covered with a plastic hood.

Carroll would be her anchor. Carroll used to come to New York regularly, to have his flings and see shows. This past Valentine's in Santa Monica, he and Leland went to dinner on the promenade, ate cotton candy on the pier, gave all their pocket money to ragged homeless beggars, then went back to the Shangri-La, where he and his companion were staying. Leland put her empty suitcase in a closet.

Melanie was yelling up the stairs. Lunch was ready, so what would she like to drink—iced tea, wine, a Bombay cooler or what?

Iced tea, Leland hollered, and said she'd be down in a minute. Then she took off her shoes and stood on a throw rug at the foot of the bed, doing fire breaths. Her father had been a career Air Force colonel. Born and raised in Colorado, John Standard met Dolly Vogel at an officers' club party in the Midwest. Small, pretty, her dream was to be either a model or a singer, even though she was short and had no singing voice, so when she met the colonel, Dolly moved fast. John Standard was tall and read newspapers. She thought he was smart, patient and orderly. She hoped he might get her out of Iowa.

John Standard was neither smart nor patient nor orderly, but he did get her out of Iowa. Dolly's husband didn't even particularly like women, and had no instinct for fatherhood. Above all else, he valued his privacy. When Leland was born, Colonel

Standard began volunteering for extra duty, more courses. He was shipped to Eunola, where there used to be an Air Force base. Dolly barely had the curtains up before John Standard keeled over. The sea-level altitude got to him, not to mention the humidity, fatherhood, marriage, the suffocating presence of a child.

Undaunted, Dolly pulled herself together, got a job at the elementary school as secretary to the principal. When Leland advanced to junior high, so did Dolly. She moved as Leland did, taking jobs that enabled her to be near her only child, bumping her ambition to be a model or a singer over one notch, from herself to her daughter.

When Marlenetta L'Heureux praised Leland's dancing ability, Dolly envisioned a grand future for them both. From the time Leland was nine Dolly drove her to and from Memphis every Saturday—some 160 miles each way—to study ballet with a Cuban famous for having known and danced with Alicia Alonso. The Cuban did not give easy compliments. It was clear he found Leland talented, plus she had the stubbornness and high pain threshold that dancing required. When her toes bled from point work, she blotted the blood, dabbed the rips with iodine, stuck wads of cotton between her toes and kept dancing, as Dolly hovered, pushed and drank.

When she was fourteen, Leland went to a horseback riding party Jake and Samme Laws gave for Jane Scott, out at the stables on Reed Road. Not wanting anybody to know she'd never ridden, she lied, and Jake assigned her a spirited gelding. Leland ended up with her whole left side bashed against a concrete silo, and that was it for dancing; young hips didn't usually crumble so easily. Six months later there was another accident, a silly slip on some sawdust doing a scarecrow routine for a high school play. Leland's wrist snapped. Her mother started drinking in the morning. Leland dislocated a shoulder. A year after that, her pelvis cracked when she came down too hard after doing the Russian splits.

Downstairs, a phone rang.

Expanding her rib cage, thrusting breath out in small explosions, she pressed her shoulders down, tucked her pelvis to stretch her lower back, inhaled. Back then, she took calcium, drank vitamin supplements, ate Tums. Remedies helped but did not cure. Muscular agility and perverse mental obsessiveness made Leland Standard all the more determined to succeed in the very area in which she was fragile, the physical. At sixteen, she left home.

Six years ago, when she announced they were moving to Los Angeles, Toby threw such a fit she almost didn't go. But four good friends had already moved out there, and one of them had shouldered her way into a rent-controlled apartment she was holding in Leland's name. The opportunity was too good to miss. Leland outwaited Toby's panic. L.A. had its downside, but life there was easier by a long shot than in New York.

"Lela?" Baker yelled up the stairs.

She went to the top of the stairs. "For me?"

Baker was on the landing. "It's the paper."

"The newspaper?"

"They want to do an article."

"About me?"

"Would you like me to plug a phone in up there so you can talk in private?"

Leland skimmed down the stairs like a young girl. She was past Baker before he knew it.

She was exciting, Leland, but far too up-front for him. Sometimes he wondered, however, could he be Toby's father?

In Mell and Baker's front hall, sitting in a velvet-cushioned church pew beside the Chinese umbrella stand, Leland put the phone to her ear. A woman identified herself as Roxie Sidwell from the *Eunola Enterprise*. Above Leland's head, a white hydrangea petal slipped from its perch, floated through the air, came to rest between points of her ferociously gelled hair.

Roxie Sidwell said she'd like to come over in about an hour. After Leland hung up, Baker stole quietly down the stairs so she wouldn't know he'd been listening.

13

Carroll Cunningham folded the *Journal* and put it on a shelf stacked with several weeks' worth of papers. The market would close in an hour and a half. Except for the U.K. currency flap, nothing had happened all week. Fridays could be dull, and anyway, Carroll had no great ideas. Taking a sharpened yellow pencil from a cup on his desk, he played with it, tapping it on its pointed end, running his thumb and forefinger down the shaft, tapping the eraser.

Across from his desk were sliding glass doors leading to his deck. His office was on the second floor, the deck cosseted by cleverly contained bamboo. Sitting outside, except for the traffic on Reed Road he could almost believe he was in a world of his own, not in any place in particular, just alone, closed off and very safe.

When he bounced the pencil on the eraser, it made a light and thudding sound. He had a terminal to watch the market play, a computer, a printer, but still used pencils, yellow legal pads, small index cards. He would never yield entirely to electronically trained habits, so that all he did was sit there watching a screen; he was not even remotely interested in that. The pencil was yellow, a number two Dixon Ticonderoga with the picture of a revolutionary soldier on it—his brand since high school.

As a boy Carroll had been as boringly pretty as a photo on a color postcard. The hooded lids half-covering his pale green eyes were his saving grace, adding a sense of dark potentiality to his otherwise outright unmitigated availability. In his early fifties now, he was still pretty. When people asked how he managed to look so young and stay so slim, he credited the genes on his mother's side. Lady Beall Cunningham had been a beauty, a drunk, a melancholic, a suicide. But her skin was good, her face unlined and her waistline trim, and so were Carroll's. On a good day he could pass for ten years younger. When he was in a mood, however, his fair skin turned sallow, jowls formed beneath his chin, his eyes went dull. A tan would help, Robin told him. But Carroll was allergic, and sunlight made him break out in hives. On the tennis court, he wore a visor, covered himself in SPF 15 and played in sweats whatever the temperature.

At fourteen, he'd been sent off to prep school. When he came back home, tall and blond, lean and sulky, girls flocked around him. He seemed so different from the local boys. To preserve that reputation, and maintain the strongest sense he had of himself, Carroll kept the walls up and didn't reveal himself to anyone, except the girl he married. When Emma was killed in a car crash, Carroll thought his spirit had been crushed for good. But what was there to do, go off the deep end?

After a number of years he married again, a vibrant blond divorcee with two daughters. Annie, such a spirit. Within a year, she slipped on a wet diving board and hit her head against the concrete edge of the swimming pool. She was unconscious for a week; and with nothing more to show for the accident than a small comma-shaped mark behind her right ear, his second wife also died. The girls were eleven and thirteen. Carroll tried to raise them, but when they hit puberty and started to go wild their grandmother came and took them away. Jessica called every now and then, usually from jail or some rehab program, asking for help. Her doctors told him not to send any more free money, so he didn't. He had paid for Kate's college and wedding.

After Annie died, Carroll sealed himself off. He did his work, fulfilled obligations, sent flowers when flowers were called for, attended weddings and funerals. His mother had given him rigorous training in manners, so he always knew what to do. But he in no way felt alive and did not think he ever would again. When his mother got to that point, she checked it in; jumped off a bridge. Carroll had too much of his father in him for that.

It wasn't that he woke up one morning feeling hopeful. Being depressed simply got old, and he realized he was bored with waiting life out, crossing off minutes like so many errands he'd run. He threw himself into work the way other people read spy novels. He began making money.

With the pencil he wrote "Flowers for M and B" on a scratch pad.

By then, sexual ambiguity had become Carroll's strongest feature. In his thirties he found himself attracted to and desired by both sexes. Both were drawn by his ambivalence as well as by the mystery of not knowing who he was or what he was after, more even than by his money.

He thought of the dinner party tonight and the deaths they'd all been through. Well, they were past fifty. It happened. By now people had seen lives bloom and wither in the most horrific and unexpected ways. And in the end, he thought, they'd all done pretty well, considering. Hanging on by fingernails thin as tissue, but still . . . He scratched out "flowers," substituting "champagne." Baker would have the house looking like a funeral home already.

Making money was a knack. Carroll had an instinct for anticipating the peak of a fad, for knowing when a hot idea was about to chill. He was not greedy. He made money on real estate while it was possible, and had gotten out—a little soon, perhaps, but not by much—when other people were still saying land would never go any way but up. He had enough money to get him through his life, but he still enjoyed the game of it, reading the *Journal,* trying to pry from all that information a story, a narrative that made sense, that he could act on, test, watch.

When his father died, Carroll sold the family house with thirty acres to Doyle Granger, the frozen-meat-patty magnate. The rest of the land around the house, some two-hundred-odd acres, had been carved up and sold. Willow Run Condos were his, out in one of the more recently built suburbs of Eunola. When the condos went up, part of the deal Carroll made with the builder was that he would have the biggest townhouse, with a private deck, closest to the swimming pool and the tennis courts. The mother condo—walled off, quiet.

He got up and went to the window. Leland was back. She had called from Tucson, left a message: "This may be right or wrong, but Toby's with me." Carroll just laughed. What else was there to do, with the two of them halfway home already?

He strolled out onto the deck, closing the sliding doors behind him to keep the cool air inside. Passing a planter, he deadheaded a rose.

Leland was too brash and nervy for her own good, but she was hopeful, lively and vulnerable, a combination of qualities that Carroll envied and found so endearing that it made his heart hurt.

In the Delta, a deck was a joke people played on themselves, pretending they had California weather with cool evenings, warm sunshine and no mosquitoes. The builders played along, and except for the few days of each year when they had a California kind of bug-free evening, the decks just sat there. People had the right idea a long time ago, before openness was everybody's idea, using window screens to wall indoors from out, with such small squares in the screen that not even the most minute mosquito could squeeze through.

A drop of sweat rolled down his eyebrow into his long lashes. He was wearing a soft cotton knit shirt and slim khaki trousers, leather loafers. Everything immaculate, clean. He smelled of

Camay soap, his favorite, and the Oil of Olay he applied to the skin beneath his eyes. Deadheading another rose, he left the soupy steam of the outdoors and returned to the merciful cool of his office.

At his desk Carroll Cunningham made a call. Robin worked nights and was sleeping when the phone rang. But yes, why not come for a visit, spend the rest of the afternoon? They might play tennis later on; nobody else would set foot on the courts until after seven, when the temperature began to drop.

Making money perked up his life and reminded him that he was, yes, still alive. So did being with Robin. He went to his small kitchen to get out two large glasses for iced tea.

14

Totty Boyette did not have to do Dog's shirts; she and Dog could easily afford to send his shirts out. But ironing was comforting and peaceful, and people let Totty alone when she did it. She could stand there with the soaps on watching the hot triangle go back and forth over the material as folds and creases vanished, and she could *think*, and it just made her feel very fine. She'd liked ironing—the smells!—since her mother taught her when she was little and wasn't tall enough and had to stand on a footstool. Back then she used a dampening cloth to steam out stubborn wrinkles, or a water-filled Coke bottle with a sprinkler cap. Now she had this fancy GE with steam.

Totty knew what they all said about her and the Dog. Fine with her was her attitude; Totty by God had what she had, knew what she knew, about Dog and whatever trash he was currently screwing, Jane Slut Laws and all the others before her. There was a line for Jane Scott to get to the back of, longer than the checkout line at Kmart on Friday night. The most

Totty could say about the Dog's women was, oh for God's sake—they knew Dog was married, did they think she was invisible, stupid or what?

Fine, she told Dog way before Jane Slut's time; fine. Do what you want, come in at whatever time, smelling however; just don't think about leaving me and the boys. I don't care what else, but don't even think about that. She didn't say anything else, just went on, and left the threat hanging. It was enough. Down deep, Dog Boyette was a coward. She didn't have to sit him down and make him a list; all she had to say was "Don't you dare" and he fell to.

Totty had what she wanted: a brick house in Cottonwood Acres with wall-to-wall carpeting soft enough to sleep on, custom-made drapes, a sunken tub and hanging plants, built-ins, a microwave and a breakfast nook, a circle drive out front. Totty knew what they said about her, that she was ignorant and silly and had never left Mississippi except that time she went to church camp in Texas, that she was still wearing her hair the same after all these years, spit curls and shaved up the neck, and wasn't that an ignorant thing when women were doing perms and highlights, and all of that was fine with her.

She ran the point of the iron up the sleeve. Steam billowed from the gathers at the cuff. Dumb Totty. Ignorant Wilhemina. They didn't know who she was underneath and what she had been through and how she had managed to come out on the other side—nobody knew, not even the Dog, which was fine. It was over, and she could go on, and what she had was what she wanted, right here: a home, a life, college-educated sons with good jobs . . . what more?

Totty balanced the iron on its heel. The shirt was blue; blue was good on Dog. She'd chosen it herself, since Dog didn't care and men were a piece of shit. Leaning on the board, Totty closed her eyes. If she went on like this, by tonight she'd be a nervous wreck. She was flibberty enough inside as it was; she had to slow down, down, down. Earlier in her life, when the boys were small and Dog was running amok taking any kind of financial advice from anybody who flattered him enough to convince him that there were special deals in honor of his great abilities on the football field, Totty had chewed the insides of her cheeks until the flesh there hung in bloody strings. Then she quit that and started gritting her teeth, until the doctor said if she didn't stop she was going to grind down her jawbone for life and wouldn't have a bite anymore, and did she realize what it meant when you didn't have a bite, that your jaw just hung there?

Staring at the weave of her husband's blue shirt as if hoping to melt into it, Totty held it up like an offering, then laid it carefully back down and lifted the iron.

Her sons were her life. Her sons adored her. In college they wrote long newsy letters and she sent cookies; Jody played football, Arthur was the brain. They were the kind of boys who, if you asked what they'd do if they won the lottery, first off would say, "Buy a Cadillac for my mama, build her a house, have her a rose garden planted"—whatever it was they thought their mama dreamed of, as their dream was whatever hers was. Not that she needed or wanted this, but it was satisfying to know they were that kind of boy, the old-fashioned kind. White boys didn't so much come that way anymore; they were ungrateful, spoiled and selfish. The black ones still gave the credit to their mamas. You could see them during football games on TV after making a catch or scoring a touchdown, mouthing "Hi, Mom" no matter if they were six-four, two-ninety and going on thirty. But not the white ones.

She didn't know why she named her baby Arthur. Art had been her father's name, and he'd ruined her life; but by the time the baby was born, Big Art had moved to Memphis, where he married a whore and was out of her life. Maybe that was what she was celebrating—the fact that he was gone. Now he was even more than gone: Big Art, thank the Lord, was dead. Maybe she thought it was what she was supposed to do, name a son for his grandfather; or maybe it was for cover—if she named her son for him, nobody would ever suspect what he'd done. Why would she name her darling son for a man who had done what he did?

Dog said he thought Art was a good idea, but Dog didn't know his ass from third base. Anyway, it was too late to think back now. Just so long as Big Art stayed good and dead. Totty went to the cemetery every now and then to make sure he hadn't risen up out of it. Even though he'd been buried for years, it didn't matter. Her father had such power about him, and with all the church talk about the Second Coming, wasn't it possible that after even a number of generations, if a man had power enough, he might rise up out of his grave, break through the earth, come back?

Sometimes, in some store, at the mall, somewhere where there were strangers all around and you never knew who might come flashing by, she would hear a thin, nasal voice—no need to raise it, since he knew his rights and just how far his domain extended. Hearing the voice, that tone, that cold rusty nail slipping beneath her skin to leak into her soul and infect her heart, she went dead cold. Stopped, froze, could not move. If Dog was with her, or the boys, they would jostle her. Totty? Mama? And she would come to and look around, and there would be some stooped old stranger back there whom she had never seen in her life, and he would have the same tyrannical spirit as Big Art, and Totty would know what he was up to. And she wanted to strangle the stranger with her bare hands then and there.

She draped Dog's shirt on a hanger, buttoned the top button, shook the cotton shirt so it hung straight. Totty insisted Dog not get slimy polyester, which he'd do in a hot minute if she didn't tell him not to. She always went to Jack-Mart for the Saks sales, was among the first ones there with her brown plastic garbage bag, in her running shoes, leaning against the barred windows with the rednecks and the niggers and the

Asians, waiting for John Callouiette to open his doors, and did she care what color the other ones were? She was after quality, and she had a good eye. She had her own kind of doggedness, not unlike the kind Dog showed on the football field, determined by God to get where he was going, however big the linemen who were trying to bring him down and keep him from his goal.

Totty had never liked Jane Scott Laws, even when they were girls. Jane Scott came from Beall Park, and Totty LaGrande lived in a shotgun house behind the tourist court her mama and daddy ran out on the highway, and so what was there about Jane Scott for Totty piss-poor LaGrande to like? When Jane Scott went out to San Francisco with the hippies, that took the cake. She was too old to be a flower child and looked plenty stupid in her drippy clothes and wild hair and earrings. Totty hated the whole thing. It was out of control, silly and scary. People ought to have more sense. People ought not to be out in the street. They ought to stay home.

Totty hung the shirt on the hook on Dog's closet door, so he would know what to put on. She did everything for him except that one thing. Which he got from Jane Slut Laws and let him. Totty was known to be sexy and flirtatiously seductive, and she was too. The one change she made in her hair was to dye it, so it framed her face and set off her dark eyes. Men liked that, and how she was known and thought of was fine with her as long as she could keep it to what she was known to be and not have to do anything. Curvy waist, bubble butt, tiny, her same cheerleader self, smiling like there was no tomorrow, until she thought her face would break. Smiling was what she did, how she got by, how she made believe it was not happening and he was not hitting her and doing what he did to her again and again, until it was over and he was dead and by then the smile was a part of her, permanent, glued on. Like one of those stupid yellow faces with no nose.

Totty spooned powdered Crystal Light into a glass, added

water and ice and stirred. In the den she sat in her recliner chair—right beside Dog's—put her feet up, hit the automatic push-back lever, fixed her cat-eye glasses on her nose and settled in to watch the one soap she didn't like to miss.

She'd already been through the change. It was a snap, and she was glad to be finished with all of that. No hot flashes, just the gradual slowing up and then nothing. Not that she didn't pretend to have symptoms, just to make Dog feel sorry for her and wait on her a little bit, but then he owed her that much. Two abortions after Jody and Art were too big for another sister or brother had sealed Totty's mind. No more, not any of it. She would have had herself sewn up down there if she could.

Tonight she was wearing a dress. Simple, white, sheer, a pinafore kind of thing with ruffles, underneath it this body stocking that covered everything up but gave big hints as to what was there. The women at the party would wonder who she thought she was—a child?—to be wearing such a girlish dress, and the men would be reminded of times when they were secretly drawn toward young girls in school uniforms and ruffled pinafores, and nobody would give her credit for knowing all of that, nobody would have the slightest clue. They would say, Oh, ignorant silly Totty in that child's silly outfit. But she took *Vogue* and *Elle* and knew the Alice-in-Wonderland look was big this year, especially since that movie came out about the sexy little girl.

With her zapper she turned up the volume on the TV. Organ music rolled, swelled. The TV screen covered the better part of one wall. Dog had bought it for football season, so the ball didn't look like a fuzzy dot he couldn't make out who was in control of until the announcer said. Dog hated sportscasters, especially those over-the-hill athletes they hired for color. Especially the black ones. Totty took a sip of her drink and kicked off her shoes.

Dog had troubles again. What with the economy gone to hell and the federal government horning in on every minute of their lives, he had lost his place in town and the state, lost the road inspector job he loved because it was a nothing job; he could go out on the road and jaw with people, talk about the glory days at State and get paid for it. There had been a scandal how Dog and others had gotten their jobs, the scandal having to do with blacks, who else, not that there hadn't been some bad things done to blacks. It was just that *everything* had to do with either them or queers these days, and for God's sake nobody's life was perfect. A black pencil-pusher for the county found out how Dog and others were letting contracts for road work—giving jobs to their friends, especially State alums— and reported it to the new congressman from the coast, also black, and that was the last wag of old Dog's tail as a road inspector. The story even made it to the news on that stupid left-wing public radio station people were so hot to get, then they finally did, and now look: Dog Boyette out of work, except for this new piece of shit he'd picked up, selling the idea of graduation rings and pins to high schools when the high schools were all black and nobody had a pot to piss in. A com- mission salesman. God, Dog, Totty had told him, next thing you know it'll be used cars. Dog looked struck dumb. He knew it was true.

Totty had told Dog he could be in all the financial fixes he wanted, but if he knew what was good for him he'd stay clear on one little matter, and that was not to dare lose her her house. A home was the one thing Totty truly needed and by God deserved, and he just better not lose it. She was doing her part, selling Amway and steak knives. Dog just looked at her when she said all of that. Totty could read his mind, so she knew what he wanted to come back at her with, which was a big fat "Or what?" He was too scared to bring himself to say it, too much under her thumb, too much of a pure unadulterated chickenshit coward. Dog had spent the best years of his life proving his manliness on a football field, and he was manly then, no question. Third down and twenty-three? Hand off to the Dog. Football was easy compared to real life. Totty dealt with real life.

On Totty Boyette's closet door hung her white pinafore, ironed, waiting, a ghostly girlish presence, like cast-off dreams from some other time. The main reason for the abortions was she was afraid the baby might be a girl.

She had written a note to Jody and Art. One day she was sitting at the kitchen table making a grocery list on her tablet when for some reason she flipped over to the next page and started writing it all down. When she was finished she folded the pages in a neat three-part letter fold and wrote, "FOR JODY AND ART ONLY!!!!! TO BE OPENED AFTER MY DEATH OR ELSE." And she'd drawn a perfect picture of a skull and crossbones, using a bottle of iodine for a guide. She'd put the note in the very back of her underwear drawer—Dog never even reached to the back of his own underwear drawer, since she was the one who kept his Jockey shorts clean and folded and put away, much less hers. It would take them a while but eventually somebody would discover it, probably one of those wives of theirs. And they would know. The big cover-up would be history.

"Darling. I've missed you."

"Oh, Roger . . ."

Totty turned the volume up. Dog had wired the TV sound to go through their stereo speakers so when you sat in the recliners, the sound wrapped all around you and filled up your mind, and your ears.

She didn't know why she wrote the note, really. It wasn't like she was trying to prevent anything or help anybody. She just wanted to set the record straight in that one area. Nobody would ever know about the abortions, of course, because Totty was a firm right-to-lifer. Mostly she wanted to get back at Art LaGrande—even if it was after she was dead and gone and nothing was left of him but what the worms wouldn't have.

The phone rang, but she either didn't hear it or decided not to. Totty Boyette had an extremely useful talent for closing herself off from things she wished weren't happening.

Letting her head sink into the cushioned Naugahyde, before long Totty was lost in the comforting pea-soup fog of daytime romance.

The phone rang an unusual eleven times, then quit.

15

Leland looked out the kitchen window. The side yard was a jungle of unpruned fruit trees, oak-leaf hydrangeas, weeds, tall stalks of ground artichokes and perennial herbs running wild. Anyone who didn't know Baker would assume that here was a piece of useless ground, left to go wildly to seed. Leland could imagine Baker shoving a careful hand down among the Johnson grass, coming up with a peerless stalk of rosemary or bunch of mint, the hydrangea for the umbrella stand, a peach, a plum, some particular kind of greenery for the table, perfect for a fill-in.

She reached for the faucet, then drew her hand quickly back, remembering Baker's parting instructions to not, for God's sake, turn the water on. Mell was upstairs resting. Baker and Toby had gone to pick up Roy from school. Leland was alone, waiting to have her interview. Baker and Mell wouldn't say too much about this Roxie Sidwell, but when Mell said "Wait till you meet *Roxie*," in the same unfathomable way she'd spoken about the rat, Leland had to wonder.

The kitchen was a wreck, stacks of plates and bowls on every surface, waiting for the sink to get fixed. Leland checked the clock on the microwave. Half an hour.

Hearing a light tapping sound, she brought her attention

back to the window. She looked for a bird, but the sound wasn't at the window, exactly. She leaned over the sink to look out and heard a voice faintly calling, as if *from* the drain itself. And then the birdlike tapping sound came again. Leland leaned her head down, ear first, toward the drain. Mell's hard work had done its job, and except for scraps of shrimp peel and bits of debris the sink was empty.

The voice came again, faint and ghostly, like a far-off cry for help. Leland straightened, looked around. There was nobody, nothing. Retrieving a small white espresso cup she thought had been hers at lunch, she refilled it with coffee from the French plunger pot. The coffee was inky with chicory and, because it had been sitting since lunch, barely warm.

She listened for the voice again, but all she heard was the squeak of a floorboard somewhere.

These Strange Park houses, full of ghostly creaks and whispers. Leland used to walk through this neighborhood on her way to class at Marlenetta's studio in the old Elks Lodge on the edge of downtown. The hulking brick houses looked to her like bank vaults, symbols of the safe life—the father with a steady job, the mother making cookies, the life of homeowners and good citizens. When her mother died, Leland discovered they hadn't had to live like gypsies all those years, moving in the middle of the night to yet another rented house. John Standard had insurance; the Air Force took care of its widows. Dolly might have bought a house, made their life better. Leland had no idea why she hadn't. Fear, perhaps, that the money might run out, and then she'd have to go back to Iowa. When Leland dreamed about Eunola, she was often standing on a street in the dark, looking into the window of a Strange Park home.

She took a sip of the thick black sludge Baker called coffee.

"Help." It came again, from the walls.

Leland gripped the cup. She did not know how Melanie and Baker managed to get up the morning after Lucy died, take the next breath, much less find a way to make a life for themselves. Once again Leland looked out the kitchen window. Lost in thought, she was turned in profile to the door leading to the laundry room and the back door when the man came in.

For a moment he stood there, not knowing how to keep from frightening her. Gazing out the window as if transfixed, she lifted the cup halfway to her mouth and then—clearly sensing his presence—hesitated.

He extended a hand in her direction, as if to calm her, and spoke in a low voice. "Don't let me startle you."

As she gasped, her hand came up and the cup hit a tooth, then dropped to the floor, spraying dark, heavy droplets across the linoleum.

"Ahh, that's exactly what I did *not* want to do." He came over, picked up the cup and lightly placed his hand on her arm. "Are you okay?"

"Yes. I don't know why I—"

"I'm sorry." He took his hand away. "I was trying to prepare you . . ."

She fingered her tooth. "No harm done," she said. "Really." She took a step back. "No harm." She ran her tongue across her teeth.

"I was down there"—with a small crescent wrench he pointed toward the floor—"tapping the pipe." He set down the wrench, the cup. "I thought you were Mell."

"You're the plumber."

He held out his hand, looked at it, withdrew it. "I'm also filthy," he explained. "Jacky Nelms. And you're Leland."

"Yes."

"Not Mell at all."

"No."

He was wearing a faded blue work shirt with pearl buttons, blue jeans, no belt, worn leather lace-up boots, the shirt open one button too many to be an accident. He had a faintly Mediterranean look, his naturally tan skin stretched taut and smooth across his skull, so that the high cheekbones and broad forehead beneath seemed on the verge of breaking through. His eyes were an intense dark brown, his convict-cropped hair altogether gray. He was slim but not skinny, and there was a sense of athleticism about him, of wired, insistent focus. He looked sculpted, a madman, fabulous.

Realizing she was staring, Leland came to, enough to realize he was staring back. "I'm sorry I didn't answer," she said. "I heard. You were under the house?"

"Flat on my back."

"I thought you were . . ."

"A ghost?"

"I started to say."

"I thought so."

"You were calling Mell."

"Yes."

"'Mell' sounded like . . ."

"'Help'?"

"How did you know?"

He shrugged. "Figures." He turned his back, went to the sink, opened the tap, watched the water disappear.

"This ought to hold," he said. "At least through tonight and dinner."

A frozen moment. Leland studied his back.

He turned around, hooked his thumbs through the loops of his jeans and frowned. For a second Leland felt him back off into the safe reality of the situation—his friends' kitchen, a clogged drain, a job—and pull away from her. For a second, in self-protection she did the same thing. It was crazy. He was as obsessive, as single-minded and as rapt as she. She didn't know who he was or how far this would take her, but she knew what he was up for. She wanted to leave the room, the house, just go. She wasn't even, for God's sake, over Simon yet.

Jacky Nelms made a slight adjustment within himself and came back, eyes hard on her. "Well?" It was a challenge.

"Yes. All right." She met him halfway, holding her ground, doing her bluff tough-guy dancer pose.

He smiled and gave a little laugh. Briefly, her brusque matter-of-factness, so unsouthern, had thrown him, the way she stood there, shoulders squared, head thrown back.

When she spoke her voice was low. "Listen . . . umm . . ."

He waited. He had learned. If you waited, women declared themselves much more straightforwardly than men. But you had to shut up first. Let them talk.

"Do you have plans?"

He cocked his head. "Plans?"

"We have an extra place at the table tonight. A last-minute cancellation."

The front door opened, the dog's nails clicked and Baker came into the kitchen. Standing in the door, he heard Leland, saw the whole thing. "Ahem." He said the word. "Yes, Jacky . . . ah . . . would you like to come for supper tonight?"

Before Jacky could answer, Baker tacked on a requirement. "Only if you've fixed the pipe. Otherwise . . ."

Jacky reached behind himself, turned the water on full force.

"Jesus," Baker said. "God. Oh well, fine."

Leland felt a flutter of panic. She was moving too fast—again—hurling herself forward without thinking. "Baker . . ." She looked to him for help.

He waved her doubts away. "Don't be silly," he said. "Anybody's better than Hank." He pointed at Jacky and grinned. "Even you. But, oh God, you do know who's—oh . . ." He threw up his hands. "I don't want to think about it."

Arms flailing, Baker left the room. Light quick steps pattered down the stairs, and the front door slammed.

Leland tilted her head. "I have something to tell you."

"Oh my God, serious. Are you sure I want to know?"

She laughed lightly. "I'm positive you don't."

"Then don't. We haven't even shaken hands."

"No." She held out her hand.

"Let it wait."

Toby had told her over and over again, wait, go slow, she was always jumping the gun, declaring herself too soon and without much warning, or need. "All right." She let it go. "But—"

"Let it wait. Now . . ." He picked up his wrench. "I have another job, then I'll freshen up for dinner. What time?"

"Seven-thirty, I think Mell said."

"You think?"

She narrowed her eyes. "Seven-thirty. Tough guy."

"Look who's talking. I'll be back."

"My son is with me."

"And?"

She shrugged. "Nothing. I . . . Why don't I know you?"

"I moved here in the tenth grade—you were gone by then."

"So you're younger."

"Than?"

She circled her arm. "Me. Us."

"Not significantly. A year or so. I remember stories about you. It was a huge deal, you know. 'Leland Standard quit school. She went to Memphis to be a dancer.'"

"I didn't go to be a dancer."

"Whatever."

"But I did go to Memphis."

He was quiet.

Her face was a little crooked, a joke kind of face. When she dropped her macho stance, the soft side of her emerged. She was arrogant and at the same time vulnerable, innocent and clever, knew what she wanted but not always how to ask for it.

"At any rate, I remember."

"Your parents did what?"

"Ran a store, over by Moe's. A Greek, a Jew. She was the Greek. We ran an Italian grocery store and deli." He shrugged. "You tell me."

She laughed. "About what?"

"You know. Their only child—I was supposed to be a rocket scientist, educated from money made by their long labors and hard work, but—"

"You liked plumbing?"

"Hardly. Took a long time to figure out. The words dancing on the page when I tried to read was no letter ballet. They danced because my mind was making them." He touched his broad forehead. "Wires crossed."

"Dyslexia?"

"By the time we knew, I was fed up with failure and school—and besides, I was good with my hands. Also, I have this strange, continuing belief in a full life as the point of living, not a job, maybe because I gave up rocket science early on and lost the feeling of being called to a profession and found other ways to occupy myself. I do my job very well, but it's the smallest part of what I am."

"An aristocratic notion."

"Go on."

"Work as a sideline, the life well lived as the goal, the point, the satisfaction. I'd call that leisure-class thinking."

"From a plumber."

"Don't be coy."

"It's what I do."

"Be coy?"

"Plumb, woman. Plumb." He lowered his voice half an octave. A trick, but she liked it.

"Aren't you the one who brings Baker the New York and London papers?"

"I didn't say illiterate. But I am a plumber. I stick my hand down toilets and grease-clogged disposals, live my life in people's dark and dirty nether worlds."

"You are a phony, Jacky Nelms."

He came to her, placed his hand on the tips of her spiky hair to feel the points, slid it to her neck, cupping her jawbone. He

was not tall; she only had to stand a little on tiptoes to reach
him. She pressed her mouth to his. Her tongue darted between
his lips.

"I knew that," he said.

There was a noise from the other room, Baker screaming
something about soup.

Leland pulled back. "Yes." She touched his cheek with her
fingers. "You're warm."

"Genes." He brushed away a bit of dirt he had left on her
blouse. "Until later, Leland Standard," he said. And he drew
his top lip inside his mouth as if to taste her tongue once
again. His lips were thin. A deep scar cut the bottom one in
two and ran toward his chin. Leland wondered what kind of
trouble he'd been in. He turned and was gone.

"Well." Baker waltzed in, having poured himself a gin and
tonic. He shook the glass, rattling the ice. "You like a drink,
Lela?"

"No thank you. Jesus, why did I do that?"

"It's fine. Jacky's my best friend."

"Can we make another pot of coffee?"

"Sweetie, of course. There's only one thing."

"Oh God, what?"

"Jacky and Dog Boyette."

"What?"

"Like oil and water."

"Oh God, well." She shrugged. "Is Toby back?" She looked
around as if he might be there in the room.

"He and Roy are walking the goddamn dog and Freddy
Krueger."

"Freddy who?"

"The rat."

"They took the rat for a walk?"

And then somebody was knocking at the door and Baker
was gone and Leland was running upstairs to get a packet of
vitamins, wondering as she went what in the world had pos-

sessed Toby to take a walk with a dog in love, a twelve-year-old boy and a rat.

16

After arranging her pad, pen, tape recorder and cigarettes on the coffee table, Roxie Sidwell rocked back and settled herself on the sofa cushion. Then she reached forward to turn the cassette recorder on its side. "I don't know how I got into this business." She poked the head of the microphone wire into one hole and then another. "Bad as I am with machines. There." She looked up. "I thought being a reporter meant a steno pad and pencil, like Roz Russell in the old days."

Leland smiled. The important thing to remember about an interview was, it wasn't a conversation. If Roxie Sidwell thought Leland was fooled by the aw-shucks routine, she could think again.

The *Enterprise* had once been considered quite special, the editor taking brave rare stands against racial inequality in the late fifties before the civil rights movement, when nobody thought they had anything to worry about when it came to race. When the editor died, his family sold the paper for millions to a corporation out of Knoxville and that was it for brave stands.

As Roxie Sidwell murmured "Testing . . . testing," Leland sipped her coffee.

"You like that stuff?" Roxie gestured toward the cup. "The way he makes it? Rot out your floorboards." She punched Play, and her voice came on. She propped the mike in a holder and aimed it in Leland's direction.

"I do, in fact," Leland said.

"Be awake all night."

From the kitchen came sounds of violence and Mozart, as Baker cleaned up lunch dishes to Kathleen Battle. When Lucy died, Mell lost herself in books while Baker turned to music. Musical comedy and Mozart saw him through, and still did.

"But . . ." Roxie gestured toward the dining table. "I see y'all are planning a do, so you'll probably need some stimulation, time they get supper on. Probably won't be till ten or so."

Mell called Roxie "obnoxious," Baker said "pushy." Nobody said anything about fat. Or black. Roxie Sidwell was a rock-solid mountain of a woman, her skin a deep mahogany, her hair cut in a close-cropped helmet. She wore a one-piece jumpsuit, a sparkly stud in one nostril and many earrings. The jumpsuit was white, unbuttoned to reveal serious cleavage.

"You know, I think we don't have much time." Leland made a big show of checking her watch.

With two businesslike fingers, Roxie pushed the red Record button. "Now," she said, "I know in the vaguest kind of way what you've done up east and out west, but as a fool can plainly see I'm no Jane Fonda." She chuckled, patting her middle. "So how about explaining it to me. How'd you get started—as a dancer, I mean?"

Leland cleared her throat and in a practiced voice began to tell Roxie Sidwell, the *Eunola Enterprise* and the town she had grown up in and felt so little a part of what she wanted them to know. "It wasn't so much the dancing as the injuries. You never know. I was never going to be a great classical dancer." She held up her feet. "Bad feet," she explained. "Being injured forced me to reconsider my options, learn to work within the givens, to think a little."

In New York, to get by, she'd worn feathers doing the chicken in a cage at a disco, and pigtails and a milkmaid costume giving away cheese in Gristedes. She had passed out rye bread at Zabar's, spritzed perfume in people's faces at the front doors of Bloomingdale's, worked the Schenley display in Grand Central Station, conducted interviews about lunch-meat preferences for a market research company, sold light bulbs over the telephone for a company she swore hired only the handicapped.

"All that time," she told Roxie Sidwell, "I kept up my work-outs. I went with the times. Dance class, exercise class, yoga, Feldenkrais, weights, Pilates . . ."

Roxie looked blank.

"The Alexander Technique. And, as you say, Jane Fonda."

She had had her polarities balanced, had been on the hurt-ing side of deep tissue massage and the Rolfers, had fasted, done solo on Outward Bound, had her high colonics and her auras read. Because of her injuries, some forms of exercise were out: jogging, certain twists, too much pounding.

"I had a teacher in the third grade, Mrs. Grace?"

"I'm not from here—and let's face it, if I was . . ."

Leland blushed. "You wouldn't have gone to—no. I'm sorry."

"It's okay. You were saying."

"When the class misbehaved, Mrs. Grace made us stay in after school and do numbers. We started with a hundred, sub-tracted three, added two, all the way down until we got to zero. Took a while. My career went like that. Three steps forward, two back. Three up, two back. I'd go too far, push too hard, hurt myself, do a reassessment."

Her yoga teacher, a former anatomy professor at Columbia who'd gone hippie during those years, helped Leland stretch her spine and align her injured internal organs. From him she had learned about physiology and breath. For a while, she'd read *Gray's Anatomy* nightly, as if it were a long, thrilling novel.

"I taught all over the city. At YMCAs, the YMHA, in com-munity centers in New Jersey. Little by little I started to de-velop a . . ."

"Following?"

She hesitated. "A group. People who came to me. Then I moved to L.A."

With the help of some friends, a bank and some leftover inheritance money from her father's insurance, three years ago Leland had gone into business for herself. She and Toby moved from the rent-controlled apartment—in spangly West Hollywood, on noisy Fountain—into the lower half of a rent-controlled duplex north of Pico. The duplex had a large back bedroom she used for a studio; even so, it wasn't long before her morning class—starting at seven, before people went to work—outgrew the studio. A friend helped her do a video, and she'd been on a couple of cable talk shows.

"And now you're famous."

"Not even close." Not by L.A. standards, and not in the way she and Dolly dreamed of all those years ago when they were driving to Memphis to study with the Cuban. "But I've done pretty well. It took a long time to get away from the need to perform."

Leland listened to her voice roll on; meantime her mind went in other directions. She sometimes did that while teaching—gave instructions and at the same time daydreamed, then came to. The real story was not in her words or what she had accomplished, but in why she was here, what brought her, how it had been to raise a son through all that, what they'd been through together. And what happened next.

Roxie shifted her bulk, tapped a foot, fooled with her machinery. She knew that Leland Standard was not attached to the words she was speaking; but then, subtext, motivations, real reasons were not Roxie's business.

"Roxie. Hey." Mell had floated down the stairs, eyes glazed from sleep, her dark hair down about her shoulders. "Don't let me interrupt you, I need to . . ." She lifted a flyaway strand of hair and tucked it behind her ear.

Roxie paused the recorder.

"Don't worry about it, Mell. Come on in. Me and Mell," she explained to Leland, "do yoga together with my girlfriend. Don't we, Mell?"

Mell nodded.

"You ought to see my inversions." With her palm Roxie cupped her belly. "It's a riot."

Mell smiled distantly and went down the hall toward the kitchen. Roxie turned the tape recorder back on. "Okay now, you were to the point of getting your studio."

"I had a lot of help, as they say, from my friends. . . ." Leland checked her watch, and Roxie consulted her notepad.

"Let me ask you this."

"Yes?"

"What do you see as up next for you? Help us out down here in Podunksville. Some new kind of whatever workout thing on the horizon?"

"I'm doing some volunteer work at an AIDS hospice, and . . ." Her voice drifted off, and when she looked up, Roxie Sidwell was waiting. "I have some ideas I'm working on, but I'd as soon not talk about them."

Roxie smiled. "Reasons?"

Leland shifted her gaze. "No reasons. Just superstitious. If I talk about it too soon, it could . . ." She waved her hand through the air.

Roxie Sidwell didn't believe a word of it. But this wasn't the first time Leland Standard had worked an interview. Cutting her losses, the newspaperwoman fired her last shot. "What made you come back down here to Eunola to see us?"

Leland fiddled with an earring. "To see my friends." She crossed her legs. "And anyway . . ."

"Yes?"

"Nobody wants to stay gone forever." Big smile.

Roxie punched the Off button, reached into a large black fake-leather case on the couch beside her and pulled out a small camera.

"I'm no photographer, but we're short-handed. Do you mind?"

Posing at the front door, looking toward the street, Leland saw Toby, Lady M. and a boy in a homburg heading toward the nursing home.

"Smile, dear."

Leland lifted her head. The boy seemed to be wearing a cape—and was that a skirt? And was there a small, furry *animal* wrapped around his neck?

The surprise and uncertainty in her gold-flecked eyes as she faced the lowering sun gave Leland the look Roxie was hoping for. She pressed the button of the camera. "Let's hope I had film in this thing," she said with a chuckle.

Leland smiled; then Roxie yelled "Bye, y'all" into the house and left her standing on the front porch watching the odd foursome make their way toward the rest home.

17

The front door of Eva Turner crashed open and Estelle looked up, shading her eyes against the glare. "May I help you?" she said in her best receptionist's voice. You never knew who was going to come through those doors these days, state inspectors, the welfare police or what.

"It's me," Roy Farrish said brightly. A loved child, he did not feel the need to give his name.

When Estelle stood up, her remote phone fell to the floor. "Roy." Her face went warm as a flattered girl's. "Hey!"

A tail dangled down one side of Roy's chest. "I brought somebody," he said.

Roy wore round, horn-rimmed glasses. His face was babyish and soft, his mouth a perfect bow. Small for his age, he looked vaguely Middle European, a little Slav child. The homburg turned him into a tiny old man, just off the boat. There was a sweetness about him which people instantly responded to, even when he went punk and wore Sid Vicious shirts and a dagger in one ear. All he had to do was smile.

A tall boy followed Roy in. On the other side of the glass doors, Lady Macbeth waited on the front stoop. Estelle retrieved her remote.

Roy brought the other boy over. "This, Estelle," he said, "is Tobias Standard."

Estelle came around her desk, out of the blinding light. Shaking the boy's hand, she saw Leland Standard all over again, the same face. "I'm glad to meet you," she said. "I heard you were coming."

"You did?"

"Your mother was coming, I meant. Say, I love your Zee."

"You saw it?"

Roy moved Freddy Krueger around to the right place on his neck. "Estelle," he told Toby, "sees everything."

"Now, Roy. How fast will it go?"

"In the desert once I got it up to a hundred and ten."

"The Mojave?"

"Down in the Anza-Borrego."

Estelle smacked her desk. "Boy, I'd like to see the desert," she said. She pointed at Toby. "You better watch out, I may come see you."

Toby laughed. "Well, do. But not in the summer."

"Hey now, you know what?" Estelle was getting ready to set up a date with Toby, out Reed Road on the good, straight asphalt back road where Dub III checked out his muscle cars, but Roy interrupted.

"Did you figure out CHAD?"

Estelle snapped her fingers. "I did. Come look."

She bustled on back behind her desk, where she uncovered and powered up her fabulous new toy, the Toshiba T-2000XE.

She had managed to sneak the purchase by the board, using petty cash outlay and some funds she'd hidden for months waiting for the price to come down. The LCD readout on the laptop was a little hard to get used to, and she had consulted Roy about how to change it. Roy basically favored the Mac, but his friend Huey was plugged into a network of hackers and MS DOS specialists. Huey got as far as CHAD, and Estelle ended up figuring out the rest herself.

"See?" She got into WordPerfect, typed some letters. The background of the screen turned a soft pleasing gray, the letters fat and blue.

"Estelle, you're amazing. Hey, Tobias?"

Toby was looking around the waiting room of Eva Turner, taking in the drippy furniture, the velvet curtains and plush rugs. It looked like the lobby of some decadent old-world hotel. He turned, squinting. "It's so dark in here."

Estelle cleared her throat and brushed the back of her skirt. "Oh, we try to economize, you know. Electricity bills and such."

"Sure, Estelle." Roy waved Toby closer. "You into computers?"

"Full tilt."

"Mac or—"

"IBM. Clones of."

"Good man." Estelle Etheridge was beaming. "I like your hair."

"Oh," he said, smoothing the back part behind his ears. "Thanks."

"His too." She pointed at Roy. "Not that he has any."

After going through a punk phase when he styled his hair in a Mohawk and dyed the brush on top bright blue, Roy had asked his father to shave his head. He couldn't wear a homburg with a Mohawk, and was bored with punk anyway. Baker hadn't wanted to, but when Roy said "It's my head" he gave in, as he had about Freddy Krueger and the pierced ears. Baker told him he was drawing the line at a nose ring, however. Roy could protest and say it was his nose until the end of time, but Baker wasn't about to have him going around town looking like Roxie Sidwell. Besides, who knew what he'd do next— his nipple? Roy claimed he'd never pierce his nipple, and Baker said, "Oh really?"

Roy fingered the soft tufts of hair along the cords of his neck, where Freddy Krueger was perched. "I'll probably let it grow out when school's out," he said. "I just did it to—" he frowned—"amuse people." He turned to Toby. "So," he said. "You ready?"

Estelle put her hand on Toby's arm. "Don't run off. You look exactly like your mother. I guess you're tired of hearing that."

Leland and Dub Jr. had been in school together. Dub was a year older, but everybody knew about Leland, the same way they did Dolly. Dolly Standard didn't go to church. She didn't wear a slip. She started a poetry writing group. Poetry? people said. After some high school boys signed up, there was a scandal.

Tobias rolled his eyes. "All the time," he said, looking extremely pleased.

"Must get old."

"I don't mind."

"So, Roy . . ."

"Yes, Estelle?"

"Y'all are doing supper tonight, I guess."

Roy shook his finger at her. "Estelle. You know we are."

She blushed, then the phone rang. She went for it, and Roy looked out the front doors. Lady M. was licking the glass. "We better go," he said.

Estelle told Sissy Westerfield to hold on a minute, she had something to tell her. "Y'all come back tomorrow, you hear?" she called. "We'll talk some more."

Roy said they would try, and Tobias told Estelle how nice it was to meet her; then the trio headed out.

"Good girl," Roy told Lady Macbeth. From his pocket, he got out a reward biscuit the way the trainer had said to. "Estelle's nice, isn't she?" He looked up at the sky as if to check the weather, then returned his gaze to Toby. "You want to walk a little more?"

"I love to walk. Sure. In New York I walked all over the place, but in L.A. nobody does. They *jog*. Or walk like, you know . . ." He mimicked a race walker. "But they don't just *walk*."

"Like stroll."

"Exactly."

"I'd like to see New York. And L.A."

"Oh, well. You have to."

"My mom tell you about the film script we did?"

"Not yet."

At Manilla Street, they turned toward Main, away from Strange Park and the black part of town. Main was wide, with a grassy esplanade down the middle and huge oaks on either side. Above their heads, the oaks joined, making a kind of protective tunnel. The light dimmed, the air cooled.

Roy adjusted his glasses. "It's a splatter movie." He pointed to the right. "This way." They turned toward downtown. "Which I don't go in for much anymore, but I think this one has a shot."

"How come?"

"Why I don't go for them? I've seen them all a zillion times. Plus the Freddy Kruegers—no, not you, Freddy—got totally corny. I still like Michael Myers."

"Who's he?"

"In the *Halloween* movies? The other ones, Jason Voorhees and—" he pointed to the rat on his shoulder—"could do pretty much anything they wanted. Kill anybody, go anywhere. Plus the people in Crystal Lake—I mean, *gah*. They were so stupid they deserved what Jason did to them. But Michael Myers had to struggle to kill people. I felt sorry for him. Anyway, you seen *Texas Chainsaw Massacre*?"

"No, but I noticed the poster."

"It's basically a fun brutal movie to watch."

Toby took that in. "Okay . . ." he said.

Private adoptions were easy to arrange in a small town, especially if you and the baby were both white and you knew
people. While Mell was in Zurich, Baker had heard from a
lawyer friend that a thirteen-year-old girl was about to have a
baby she wanted to give up. The friend got all the paperwork
in order. Baker had not met the girl, but the lawyer told him
she was white, with a Slovenian background. Her parents had
come south from Chicago to work on the river. River rats, he
called them. And the father? The girl said he was a brain. After
Roy's birth, the girl had disappeared and hadn't been seen or
heard from since. Roy didn't have the slightest interest in
meeting her.

"In our movie, the splatterer's a girl. You like horror?"

"Not particularly," Toby said.

"I like the special effects. Movies don't scare me. My mom
and dad go nuts, but I figure, it's a movie. Anyway, her name's
Lorelei, and she's dead. When she was alive, her father abused
her. I mean, you know . . ."

"Sexually?"

"She never got over it. Eventually shot him, then went out
in her CRX and smashed it into a tree."

"Now she roams the world—"

"Looking for revenge."

"Sounds good."

"She's southern—you know, a cheerleader and stuff. In her
suicide note she leaves the shotgun and the wrecked car to
her mother. The note starts out—get this—'Dear Codepen-
dent . . .'"

"I like it."

Roy giggled. "That was my idea."

They were at the railroad tracks.

"Like I say, I'm not much on the splatters anymore, but I

think this one has a shot—a splatterer for the nineties. A friend of my dad's took it to the film commission, and—"

"If it happens?"

"My mom and dad will get rich. I won't spend the rest of my life in Eunola."

"You won't anyway."

When Mell got home from Switzerland, presented with the hard physical fact of a baby in a crib, she threw a fit. Baker had set up a nursery in the tiny closet of a room Roy had never moved out of. He had gotten temporary custody pending Mell's okay. What was she supposed to do, kick a four-month-old baby out the front door?

Roy held out his arm. "Anybody told you about downtown?"

"What about it?"

"Good." Roy seemed content. "You like cappuccino?"

Tobias nodded, and they set off down Main Street past the courthouse.

18

Baker banged a soup pot against a burner.

Mell put her hands over her ears. "Would you stop? It'll thaw by itself."

"I know, but I meant to take it out last night."

"Well, you didn't."

"Thank you for reminding me."

"There's plenty of time. Use the microwave."

"You know I don't like the microwave."

"So don't use it."

Baker had made a batch of his famous rosemary, chicken and garlic soup, which he then froze in two-quart ricotta cheese containers.

Mell pinned up her hair. "I'll do the dishes."

Baker set three of the containers in a tub of warm water. "Doo?"

She didn't answer.

"What did you mean when you said 'bat wings'?"

"'Bat wings'? What bat wings?"

"At the front door. When you first saw Toby."

Mell had a gift for catching thoughts as they flew by. When she saw the boy on the curb gathering his mother to him, holding her close, she saw trouble. Swirls and red flashes, darkness. Leland the sleeping bat, Toby the wings wrapped tightly around her.

"I don't remember," Mell lied. She dipped a hand-painted Italian plate in hot soapy water. "This afternoon seems a thousand years ago."

19

"It's a kilt," Roy Farrish said. When he frowned, his eyebrows made a ruffled fringe along the top rim of his glasses.

"A what?"

"Kilt. You know, like—"

"Bagpipes?"

"I was going to say 'Scotland.'" Beneath the kilt, Roy wore his kung fu pants, which he had rolled above the tops of his Doc Martens.

Dog and Totty had arrived exactly on time. Mell hated on-the-dot, punctual guests; she was upstairs still getting dressed, while his father was in the kitchen trying to remarry the curdled Béarnaise. Roy had been sent to entertain them, and with practiced grace he balanced a freshly polished silver tray on the flat of his hand.

Dog nodded.

Roy lifted the napkin-swathed glass from the tray. The small silver dagger hanging from his ear jiggled. There was another earring in the same ear, a coiled silver snake with a green stone for an eye.

Dog Boyette accepted his drink and, shifting in his chair, scanned the room. Leland's boy was another strange one, sitting there like a statue. Dog had rejected the dress shirt Totty ironed for him, preferring a royal blue polo shirt. It emphasized the color of his eyes, plus the snugness of the cotton knit showed off his pecs and biceps. His pants were beltless and without pleats. Dog had a paunch, but it was muscled and firm, like a well-filled tire. He sucked it in. "Looks like a skirt to me." He lifted his gin and tonic. "Thanks, pal."

"You're welcome. But it's a kilt." Roy moved across the room to bring Totty her drink.

"The guys at school let you get away with it?"

"They think it's cool."

"Cool?" Dog all but choked on his drink.

"Yes sir."

Dog snorted.

Roy was wearing a huge black T-shirt that had the standard yellow smile face on the front, but with a bullet hole in its forehead. A trickle of blood ran from the hole to where a nose should be. When Totty Boyette looked up and saw the blasted face, all she could say was, "Ooooh, look at that! Ooooooh."

Roy reached for her drink, bourbon and Diet Dr Pepper with a lemon slice. Before he got hold of it, Totty had lifted her glass from the tray, mouthed an exaggerated "Thank you" and smiled. She took a dainty sip, licked her lips and patted his hand.

"And the . . ." Dog backhanded the air, hoping to have his thought filled in. Not especially with words. Put the right people in the room, pause at the right time and who needed words?

Roy unstacked a set of ashtrays and began setting them around.

"Ah, the . . . *you* know." Dog rubbed a cranky place in his neck. He didn't want to kick things off too fast. They had only just got there. Totty was staring a hole. Anyway, Dog had his mind more on the evening ahead—Jane Scott and Totty in the same room together—than on the subject at hand. But still . . .

Roy swiveled on the heels of his boots. "The who?"

Dog didn't like to say "blacks." "Blacks" was their word. And he wasn't about to get his mouth around "African-Americans." Under the circumstances, however, he couldn't use the term he was accustomed to. Totty said he was going to have to get over saying that word at all, and she meant ever, if he wanted to get along these days, not to mention hold a job. Again, he waved the air.

"Blacks?" Roy let Dog off the hook.

Totty cleared her throat at Dog.

Dog lifted his heels and jiggled his feet. "Whatever."

"Like I said. They think it's cool."

"Tobias . . ." Totty cleared her throat again, then either her drink went down wrong or she made believe it did. Sputtering, she patted her chest. "I'll get it out in a minute . . ."

Dog stood up. The look in Totty's eyes sent him straight back down again.

When she spoke, her voice was normal. "Have you had a chance to tour Eunola? I guess it must seem pretty dinky after New York City. Oh, but you—"

"Live in L.A. now, yes."

"Live in L.A. now. Oooh. L.A." Totty got a wide look in her eyes. "Would I be scared to live there? Lordy Lord."

Toby knew what was coming next.

"Were you there for the, well, riots?"

He answered quickly. "The Indian restaurant half a block

from our apartment was burned to the ground. We helped put out the fire. It was awful, all of it."

Totty clucked, ran her hand up the back of her neck, patted her hair and retwisted a spit curl.

"You know, I just don't think I could live in a place like that where there are so many, oh, I don't know, different kinds of people. Especially now, what with . . . Oh, well."

Like Dog, Totty waited for somebody to finish her thought.

Toby shifted back to her original question. "To answer your question: no, I don't think Eunola is dinky. Roy took me around. We went downtown. Eunola is . . ."

She waited.

". . . surprising. Very."

"I mean, I saw it on 'Inside Edition' and Maury Povich."

"Saw what?"

"About the crime."

"In L.A."

"Well, yes. And the smog. All those, what do you call them, *Asians*?"

"We have Asians, yes." Toby felt his cheeks go warm. So far, they'd done blacks, criminals and Asians, and he was pretty sure where she was headed next.

"Well, I know, but—"

"There aren't that many. I mean there are, but you get used to them. To everybody. To difference. It's part of life." He bided his time, hoping for an interruption.

"And the . . ." Totty humped her shoulders. "Well, the . . . you know."

Roy tucked the serving tray under his arm. Totty twirled her hands in circles.

"The . . . ?" Toby offered.

"You know—the what-do-they-call-it." She made a face. "Gays. I mean, now? AIDS and all like that? I'd be scared silly."

Dog lifted his glass, rattled the ice.

Roy moved toward him.

"Totty LaGrande, I don't believe it!" Leland flew down the stairs. Roy turned on his heel.

In one motion, Totty stood and smoothed the back of her skirt. She'd done the same thing ever since junior high, when they all started getting their periods and had to check, smoothing the fabric against their behinds and asking one another if there was anything back there.

"Boyette," Totty said emphatically, and then, "Leland. Isn't this neat?"

"So, I'm curious." Dog and Toby were standing, starting their own conversation. "How do you mean, 'surprising'?"

Toby calmed his breath. "I mean people are more sophisticated than I thought. I didn't expect to have a great cup of cappuccino at the Marriott. Roy's great and so are his parents." He shrugged. "That's snobbish, but what can you do?"

Dog said, "Beats me."

Main Street, it turned out, had been transformed from a standard straight street going through downtown into a series of orchestrated curves, an idea city planners had in the seventies, hoping to save small towns from the blight of suburban drift. There were planter boxes at the apex of each curve, the vegetation carefully tended. The curvy street was supposed to make drivers slow down, notice what was for sale, park, shop and buy. Parking meters, installed in another time, were covered with black plastic hoods saying Free.

As Roy led the way, he pointed out closed shops with Drastic Reductions or Going Out of Business painted in huge white letters on the show windows. A Rexall drugstore was still open, a shoe repair shop, Jack-Mart, a dime store. Next to an ugly monument to the World War II dead at the end of Main was a new Marriott, the cafe of which served espresso, cappuccino and Italian sodas with cream on top.

Leland wore a tiny skin-tight skirt, thin socks with sparkles in the weave, black lace-up ankle boots and a voluminous silk top. She had washed her hair and freshly spiked it. From her earlobes dangled huge aluminum leaves.

"Leland," Totty gushed. "I don't believe it! How long has it been? Just *years.*"

Bent at the waist so they'd touch minimally, the two women hugged. Both of them suddenly remembered that they hadn't particularly liked each other back when they were girls, and couldn't imagine why they should expect to now.

On the upstairs landing, in a black high-necked dress with white lace at the collar and cuffs, Mell wished to hell she hadn't let Baker convince her to invite Dog and Totty. What did it matter that she'd been in their gang? Totty was pure plastic wrap and Dog about as interesting as concrete.

Mell wore her hair down, caught up in small tortoiseshell barrettes at her temples, college-girl fashion. In her severe black dress—preciously tucked and pleated with small jet buttons climbing up the placket between her breasts, and at her throat an enamel cameo—and pale makeup she looked like a mad but beautiful Puritan, just over on the *Mayflower.* She had bought the cameo at a drugstore in Rosedale. The pharmacist was selling his grandmother's jewelry piece by piece, so whenever she went there, Mell had to listen to him rant and rave about the evils of Wal-Mart and Sam Walton. But in the end she felt it was a fair trade-off.

From the shadows, Mell watched Totty smile, jiggle and smooth the back of her skirt. Baker adored inviting people over he knew would clash. Somebody was always stalking off, vowing never to speak to any of them again. By now, Mell should have been used to it—all those people out there not speaking. She was not. Her gray eyes burned with rage, delight and dread.

The doorbell rang, and Lady Macbeth made as if to lunge. But when Roy gave a command, the dog went down as if struck.

Totty and Leland kept on counting up how long it had been.

Meanwhile, Dog Boyette and Tobias Standard considered each other momentarily. Dog smiled faintly, so did Toby; then they both looked away.

Dog went to freshen his drink at the bar in the hall. "What say, Duke?" he hollered at Baker in the kitchen. There was a bucket of huge red flowers by the bar. When Dog moved the flowers out of the way, the bucket tipped. He stuffed the flowers back in every which way, some of them flower-end down.

"This is never going to work," Baker muttered to a saucepan.

"What?" Dog said, pouring his glass full of gin.

"Dog, I'm sorry." Baker appeared in the door, a spoon in one hand, a dishtowel in the other. He shook Dog's hand with the dishtowel. "It's the goddamn Béarnaise," he said, pushing his glasses back up on the bridge of his nose.

"The what?" Dog squeezed lime juice in his glass and stirred his drink with his finger. He had always thought Baker Farrish had a shot at being queer. He tossed the lime toward the bar, and it landed in a glass.

"The sauce. Excuse me, Dog, I have to . . ." Baker set the spoon and towel down, plucked the lime slice from the glass and, cupping it in his hand, slipped past.

For one thing, what kind of man made a living making cheesecake? Those red glasses and the way he flailed his arms—Dog didn't know precisely what it was, Baker just had a girl thing about him. That boy in the living room, Leland's son, same thing.

As Mell began her descent, Baker came in from the kitchen and announced that he was going to the Korean's since the Béarnaise had curdled and all they had was one lousy egg.

"Oh, for God's sake, Baker!" Mell shouted, and everybody looked up. "Serve it curdled."

"Mell, the—"

"The only thing that matters is the taste—just throw a lot of *parsley* on top."

"Don't be silly, Doo." Baker sped past her. In their bedroom he got his wallet, checked the VCR and the sleeping rat.

Downstairs, Roy opened the front door to find Carroll, Jane Scott and Sissy on the front porch. Carroll had swung by Beall Park to pick up Jane Scott. Sissy had pulled her Mustang convertible to the curb the same moment Carroll parked his Lincoln Town Car. Except for Jacky Nelms they all were here.

Toby watched Mell make her way in her own sweet time down the stairs. Earlier, he had walked in on her in the bathtub. He knocked; but if Mell heard, she didn't say. He poked his head in and there she was, lying in the tub with her head against the enamel. Her pinned-up hair made a damp wreath around her face. The water was brackish brown, and soapy rings made islands around her knees. Mell floated a washcloth over her breasts and smiled as if from a great distance. Toby murmured apologies, closed the door as nearly shut as it would go and stood in the hall with his hand on the doorknob, feeling quite faint.

Sometimes a woman got to him. He was mostly drawn to men—when, in these dangerous days, he allowed himself to be drawn to anyone—but from time to time it happened. There was a woman on the Playboy Channel he liked to watch doing herself. He liked the idea of a woman's silky muscularity. He never did anything about it. Women were from another planet; men were himself.

"Toby?" Leland held out her arm to gather him close. Her other hand clasped Totty's. Toby looked the other way, pretending not to hear. The Program had taught him: define the enemy. Tonight, Totty would play the part, without question.

He was heading in the direction of the front door and Carroll Cunningham when he noticed Mell's slippered foot moving from the bottom step to the floor. There were hydrangea petals all over. Mell's slippers had leather soles and were new, so when the toe of her foot touched the scattered white petals, she went down, her black dress puffing up in a pumpkin at her waist. Toby rushed over as Mell grabbed hold of the railing, pulling herself up. Pale cheeks scarlet with rage, she flicked her head in the other direction.

He moved away while she gathered herself together. Melanie never took a bath without thinking of Lucy. Immersing herself in the jelled soup of memory, she let it all happen once again. Blood, ambulance, hospital. She stayed until the water turned tepid, then watched the water run out, her skin dry. When Leland's son interrupted her, she tried to cover herself; but in the bathtub, moving through gravy-thick time, her reactions were slow.

"Sissy," she said. "Hey." Sissy looked gorgeous, her face aglow with careful makeup, her perfectly tinted blond hair in soft curls. She was wearing one of her caftans. She was fat again.

Sissy pulled Mell warmly to her. "Hey, Mell."

Friends were used to Sissy's ups and downs. Thirty pounds off quickly became forty back on. Mell pulled away. "It's too bad," she said, "Hank couldn't come."

"Well, you know . . ." Sissy waved her husband away, in the direction of Cotton Plant and the catfish ponds. "*Dog!*" Sissy cried. She was crazy about Dog Boyette. He was just so lively. "You old mutt."

The two did a sidestep boogie into each other's arms.

From Sissy's soft shoulder, Dog saw his wife giving his girlfriend a polite embrace. Jane Scott's hair was frizzed in wiry plumes, and she had bracelets stacked from her wrist to her elbow, the hippie kind of claptrap Dog hated except on her. She was wearing a wild see-through something, mud brown and thin enough to seine minnows through. Her eyes were heavily mascaraed, with a thick line beneath the bottom lashes, and she'd put a lot of iridescent green on her eyelids.

The two women came apart. Totty leaned around Jane Scott's shoulder and, through the golden frizz of her rival's long hair, aimed a withering glance in the direction of her husband.

Dog's eyes widened, and his wife's tiny face disappeared. He rolled his neck, lifted his chin, pawed Sissy's soft breast. "Lookin' good, darlin'," he growled. "Keep it in. I like it."

Sissy moved his hands to her rib cage. "Dog," she said. "Fix me a bourbon, you dog."

Leland and Jane Scott hugged. Totty stood there adjusting her spit curl and smiling. Toby stuck out his hand to shake Carroll Cunningham's, but Carroll drew him close. Carroll's skin was cool and damp.

The doorbell rang again, and Roy went. When Dog Boyette saw it was the plumber and noted how Sissy, Leland and Jane Scott lit up at the sight of him, he ground his teeth and turned away.

The front door flew open again, banging Jacky in the back. Kicking a small yellow cat back out on the porch with the heel of his sneaker, Baker held up the cardboard egg carton. "Got 'em," he said. "Soon as I redo the Béarnaise . . ."

Dog checked his watch. Eight-ten, and whatever kind of sauce Baker was making was still raw eggs. It was going to be a long night.

20

By the time the Béarnaise was ready and Baker had thawed and warmed the soup and started heating the bread, it was nine-thirty. He put the rice on.

Mell and Baker never served hors d'oeuvres. People just drank. For the first hour Leland took only Perrier, knowing that if she tried to keep up with the locals she'd be on her face before the soup course. At nine-fifteen she had a glass of wine.

Jacky drank Perrier, having given up alcohol some ten years ago.

Baker stirred the soup, checked his meat thermometers. He wanted to have everything ready before people sat down. That way, once they finished their soup they could go straight into the main course. The lamb was perfect—two degrees below medium rare.

To avoid having Mell improvise and sit somebody next to exactly the wrong person, Baker had Roy and Toby do place cards. Baker's place was at the mama end of the table, closest to the kitchen, so he could go in and out. Mell sat at the other end, in front of the windows. On the long side of the table, starting at Baker's left, they put Jacky, then Totty, Roy, Jane Scott, Toby. Mell at the end, then Dog, Sissy, Carroll, Leland. That put Leland between Baker and Carroll and across from Jacky, Roy between Totty and Jane Scott. Toby between Jane Scott and Mell. Mell would have to sit next to Dog, but with Sissy on his other side, that shouldn't be a problem.

When they'd all finally stopped hugging and sat down in the living room, Mell was her usual fogged self. As the evening progressed she began to bloom. Her cheeks turned rosy, her manner lively, and she told stories on everybody in Eunola who wasn't at the party. She was a study in contrasts, lively and bubbling in somber clothes, a pale girl dressed too soon in mourning attire.

Until they got bored with waiting and hunger started to kick in and make them cranky, Sissy and Dog stayed by the bar, telling jokes and engaging in general cutup. Totty was quiet, more or less. Every time she tried to talk, people ran over her with louder voices and smarter—they thought—conversation, as if they all wanted her to just shut up and sit there, so she did.

Leland told about her interview with Roxie, and everybody laughed about how the newspaper had changed and how Roxie Sidwell acted like she owned it. During her story, every time

Leland looked over at Jacky, his eyes were on her. Made nervous by the plumber's obvious attention to his mother, Toby twice leaned forward to ask Jacky a question. The second time, Carroll laid a hand to Toby's arm.

Roy skirted the fringes of the party, serving drinks and emptying ashtrays. When things seemed to be pretty much going on on their own, he stole away. Upstairs, lying on his mother and father's bed, he zapped on the television set, flicking from channel to channel with the remote. He left the sound off. The light from the TV screen flickered and then steadied, bouncing off his glasses, emphasizing his round cheeks and strong chin, his close-together eyes. His head was big and knobby; shaving it made it look bigger. He lay there with his Docs hanging off the edge so as not to soil the satin comforter.

In principle, Dog Boyette was right—it was a skirt. Roy had bought it at a garage sale. The skirt was great and had served its purpose, but Roy was starting to get bored with it. He was keeping an eye on MTV for new ideas. Guns N' Roses was disgusting, but their costumes were good. He studied magazines.

Showtime was running the original *Terminator*. The special effects were great, but there was a long time to go before Arnold took out his eye. With his thumb Roy punched a red button on the remote and the television screen went dark. He checked on Freddy Krueger, who was curled in a quiet ball. Roy reached in and stroked the soft fur between his ears. Freddy shifted in his sleep, then delved deeper down.

The VCR clicked. Roy looked over. Baker was recording a show, either "L.A. Law" in syndication or some "Mary Tyler Moore" he'd missed. Baker was determined to record every "L.A. Law" ever made, and he was nuts over Mary Tyler Moore. He had a whole library of homemade videos: the complete "Family Ties" and "Miami Vice," all the "Designing Women" until they fired Delta Burke and most of the old "Hill Street Blues."

Roy closed the Plexiglas box and, straightening his skirt, went into the hall. To his right was the locked room nobody went in, where they kept all the stuff Baker refused to junk, sell, give away or even organize. They never even thought about it anymore. The door was just there, the room, the stuff. Roy turned on the hall light, in case anybody wanted to use the upstairs bathroom. Lady Macbeth waited for him on the stair landing, looking up and wagging her snubbed tail.

In the living room, a haze of cigarette smoke hung over the guests' heads like a low thunderhead. In her usual chair, Roy's mother was telling Leland, Carroll, Tobias and Totty a story. "So we went to this Japanese-looking, I don't know, *hoshunga* or some such, and sat on the floor eating macaroni and *bean* sprouts . . ."

Mell told stories on herself all the time, mocking her own experience, making fun of what she took seriously.

Roy tiptoed into the kitchen. In the pantry, looking for Lady M.'s doggy treats, he discovered Dog Boyette and Jane Scott Laws. Dog was wiping Jane Scott's eye with his handkerchief.

"Oh," said Roy. "Hi." He gave Lady Macbeth her biscuit.

His father was stirring the soup. "Okay," he said into the pot. And then he saw Roy. "Hey, child," he said.

"Hi, Dad."

Baker cradled his son's head and planted a wet kiss in the center of his forehead.

Roy smiled. Being adored wasn't half-bad.

"We're ready," Baker announced.

The soup bowls were on the chopping table, waiting to be filled. Jane Scott emerged from the pantry. Then Dog.

Jane Scott ladled soup. Roy took two bowls to the table. Baker went to the living-room door to tell everybody to come eat. Mell patted the air to make them stay one more minute, until she finished a story about the time she went to a yoga workshop in a town south of New Orleans and everybody got stoned and one woman, whom they all knew, had a naked massage in the hot tub and, well, Mell was not at liberty to say what happened with the guru afterward, *but* . . . She rolled her eyes.

Totty harrumphed in disapproval at everything Mell said, then got up and went into the dining room.

Dog picked up a place card and held it at arm's length. They had put him between Sissy and Mell. Jane Scott was across from him and one over. Considering everything, he thought that wasn't too bad.

Roy came in bearing soup. "Don't switch them."

"I wasn't." Dog replaced the place card. "Little fruitcake," he muttered as his wife moved to his side.

Roy pushed open the swinging door to the kitchen and held it for Jane Scott, who came in carrying two steaming bowls.

Seeing that Totty was there, claiming her husband like a checked coat, Jane Scott set the bowls down so fast she sloshed broth in a plate. Head down, she made her quiet way back into the kitchen. Her visit to Eva Turner had been a nightmare. She had walked in to find Samme in a puddle of urine, her night-gown and sheets wet to her armpits, Samme lost and gone. Jane Scott was about to fetch a nurse's aide when Samme lifted her craggy head from the pillow. "Sister," she said. Clear as a bell.

"Darling Mommy." Jane Scott moved to her mother's side.

"You," Samme said, pointing her finger, "lock me up in this hotel. I can't pay the bill. You don't care." With one wild foot Samme kicked back the sheet. Her gown was above her waist. Her nearly hairless genitals and pale thighs lay against the wet white sheets, thigh meat lankly folded in pleats. Jane Scott took a step back. Samme had always had great legs. Even through middle age, she'd kept them creamed and shaved to the groin. Golfing, she used to wear short shorts, scandalizing the country club. When Jane Scott tried to cover her up, Samme screamed and drew back against the bedstead.

A nurse came in, Marge Loflin, head nurse and Methodist

drug dealer. Holding her arms out, the nurse gathered Jane Scott close, pressing her head into the valley between her huge breasts. "She don't know," the nurse crooned. "Don't take it hard. She don't know."

Jane Scott felt like a two-year-old having a fit because her mother didn't love her anymore. Mrs. Loflin gave Samme a shot and soon she was quiet again, down in the deep pools of her wrecked and bottomless mind. On her way out, Jane Scott went into Marge Loflin's office and held up four fingers. Mrs. Loflin passed a small white envelope across her desk. Jane Scott slid a twenty beneath her desk blotter.

When she got home there was a message on her machine from Lucien and Tony. "Hey there, you Mississippi Jane," Tony said. "Get your ass back out here with the cappuccino and the faggots." His voice softened. "Stay with us—we miss you." Lucien said simply, "Jane. I wish you'd call sometime soon. We worry about you. Love you." From the background, Tony chimed in. "Love you."

She set down the last soup bowl and took her place between Roy and Toby, who stood behind their chairs. She felt calm. Calm and smart. The pill had worked. And, glory be, she had three more. Toby pulled her chair back.

Baker had lit the candles too soon. Liking the feel of a room with candles lit, he had them going early, so that people felt the pull toward dinner and communion. They had burned halfway down already. "I'll get new ones in a minute," he promised, and asked Roy to start the bread.

There were salt and pepper cellars at each place setting, tiny crystal bowls Mell had picked up in Rosedale, each with its own minuscule silver spoon. Individual butter pats lay curled like small seashells in doll-sized dishes beside each place card.

Roy lifted the silver bread basket, but a quick tap on his shoulder stopped him from passing it.

"Since this is such a special occasion, would y'all mind if

I said the blessing?" Totty folded her hands in a here's-the-church pose.

"Of course not, Totty," Baker said. "How sweet."

"Sweet?"

Dog jabbed Sissy in the ribs. Roy set the bread down and giggled.

Mell groaned, and Jane Scott couldn't tell if the flush in her cheeks was from hormones or rage.

They all held hands while Totty blessed the food of which they were about to partake. Leland kept her eyes open, head slightly raised. Baker's hand was damp and hot, Carroll's cool and papery. When she lifted her eyes, Jacky Nelms was looking at her.

Totty thanked the Lord for healthy children.

Leland held his gaze, and Baker tickled her palm.

Totty acknowledged health, friendship and the blessing of living in a free country.

Leland could see Toby watching from the other end of the table.

By the time Totty ran out of bountiful gifts for which they should all be grateful, it was ten o'clock.

"Amen." She dropped her hands, leaned over her plate and swiveled her head toward Toby.

21

Hank Westerfield ate ice cream from a cardboard container. He had bought the ice cream at the all-night convenience store on the highway, where he knew he would pay almost double the asking price at Food King, but 7-Eleven was quick and secret: you paid, nobody asked, you left.

Hank had never gotten all the way hooked on "L.A. Law," like some. It was a silly show, but he liked anything that made fun of lawyers.

He dipped his spoon in. Chocolate Revel was his favorite, especially if the pint he happened to buy had a lot of chocolate in it. He liked his ice cream soft. By the time he got to the bottom, it would have melted down to exactly the way he liked.

A judge was trying to decide what to do about a couple whose grown daughter had been in a coma for seven years. The parents wanted to pull the plug; doctors were saying no. The judge had hooded blue eyes and slack cheeks and was mostly bald. Hank had started losing his hair in his late twenties. He was not a vain man, but he despised not having hair. The judge had more than Hank, a pad above his ears, and in the back a pelt. The judge looked the way a judge should, wise as Solomon, but of course he was an actor. Hank wondered what he was like in real life. Probably a nincompoop, maybe queer. Life was either a joke or incomprehensible. Hank could not in the wildest stretches of his imagination picture himself wanting to be an actor or queer.

The chocolate ran down his throat. Hank wore jeans, a white V-neck T-shirt, leather slippers. He'd taken a bath after coming in from defoliating the fields. Sissy preferred showers, but Hank never did get to where he felt clean if he didn't lower himself all the way down into a tub. With the help of one of his hands—that was an accomplishment, learning to say "hand" after all those years, not knowing or thinking, just saying the word "nigger" like a definition, like "chair" or "radio," not having any idea anybody might object—he'd had to get completely down into a combine engine when it stalled, so he'd been filthy. After Sissy left, he fixed his own dinner, two baloney sandwiches with presliced American cheese, lettuce and mayonnaise. Potato chips, pickles.

His feet were up, the way he liked them, on a hassock. A

long time ago, he'd suggested buying a La-Z-Boy, so that he could push back and be comfortable when he watched TV. Sissy said recliners were redneck, tacky and out of the question.

He could not imagine how the rest of his life would go. Up until the past few years, it had laid out there ahead of him like those confounded catfish ponds, waiting. The only surprises he'd thought were in store for him were from weather and natural disasters—catfish decline and who knew what else—and those were the kind of surprises a farmer got used to, fast, or got out of farming. But things had changed. He didn't mind learning to say "help" or "hand" instead of the other, not one bit. He never meant to hurt anybody and was happy to oblige; on the other hand, he didn't appreciate being told what to say and how to say it. Especially not by the U.S. damn federal government. It was the government that threw things off and kept farmers going beyond their time, the government that both saved and doomed him.

On TV, the hoods of the judge's eyes came down like window shades and he allowed as how he had given this case and the ethics involved considerable thought.

The newest wrinkle was, to train catfish away from their natural habits, farmers were using puffed feed that floated on the surface of the ponds. The feed lured fish away from the muddy bottom they preferred, so that their flesh was whiter. The wrinkle on top of that one was birds. When the catfish came up to eat, the birds attacked. So now farmers were setting off butane cannons all day long to scare away the birds. If that didn't fit "incomprehensible" or "a joke," he didn't know what did.

Hank set the ice cream on the arm of his chair and wondered what it must be like to have a daughter dead and at the same time not. Naturally, he'd assumed he and Sissy would have a family. Not too big, because of Sissy's ambitions. He knew from the beginning that Sissy wasn't cut out to have a lot of children—her nerves wouldn't take it—but maybe a boy and a girl. They never found out whose fault it was. Back then, before all these tests and fertility drugs, babies weren't conceived in a saucer. People got pregnant or they didn't. Hank and Sissy didn't find out what the problem was, they just stopped trying. A live daughter meant the possibility of a dead one. Like Mell and Baker. Hank shivered.

The judge called a recess, saying he would hand down his decision tomorrow. Everybody stood up, the lawyers looked at one another, the parents stared at the floor and the judge, in his flowing black robe, turned to go out. The judge's back was replaced by a bottle of green mouthwash. With his remote, Hank turned the volume down. As soon as "L.A. Law" was over, he was going to bed.

Down at Baker and Mell's, they were probably just now getting rolling. At lunch, the minute Sissy started tap-dancing around the subject, Hank knew she was going to end up believing that she made him think he was the one who decided he wouldn't go tonight. Hank didn't give a possum turd for dinner parties. He only went to watch after Sissy.

He dipped up a tablespoon of ice cream. Sissy didn't know his heart, how much he adored her. She couldn't afford to. She had to keep her own heart calloused against him or she might go soft and love him all the way, and she didn't want to do that. It didn't suit her sparkling ideas and dreams about herself.

After mouthwash came tires. Hank was tempted to switch channels to see if maybe Atlanta was playing, but resisted. He didn't want to get caught up in a baseball game and miss out on the judge's decision.

Sissy knew they were in debt—farmers were always in debt—but she had no idea how close they were, this minute, to going all the way under. The word "bankrupt" used to give him a hard chill, like "abortion" or "fuck." But no more. People had lowered their standards. Too many good men had gone down.

Used to be, Hank knew every single teller at every last bank in Eunola, Cotton Plant, Eustace, Lula and pretty much anywhere in the Delta. Not anymore. Kids left the state as soon as they could; new people came in. Yankees, blacks, Orientals—and not just Chinese. Thai, Korean, Vietnamese. They didn't give a rat's ass how honest he was or how Hank Westerfield's word had always been his bond. To the new ones, he was just another broke white man about to lose his land.

Sometimes he wished the government hadn't bailed him out way back, so he would've had to face doing something else when he was young enough to bounce back quicker. Now? Who wanted a washed-up fifty-eight-year-old farmer? And what would he do? He used to think if all else failed he could always pump gas, and now that everybody knew how to fill it up and check the oil for themselves, he couldn't even do that. He was good with machines, so maybe he could hire on somewhere as a mechanic. The world had gone crazy. The homeless. Queers getting married. He couldn't imagine Sissy with a grease-monkey husband.

The "L.A. Law" logo came on, then the judge. Hank turned the sound back up. The judge said that after long deliberations he had made his decision, and would the parents please approach the bench? The two people—actors, Hank had to remind himself, actors—came close. The mother's eyes filled, and the father looked like somebody had beat him to a pulp, then left him to die, but he hadn't.

"We are only human," the judge began, and Hank knew how it was going to go. "We reach for the divine." Then he leveled his blue eyes on the parents and proceeded to explain how it wasn't given to us to decide when a person died. The parents ducked their chins, like children being scolded. Hank scraped up the last of his ice cream and tossed the spoon in the carton. There was a tag-on scene, of course, where the lawyer who represented the parents was being consoled. The drama was the lawyers, not the parents.

When the credits started to roll, Hank switched the set off and sat in the dark. From time to time, Sissy got restless. Hank knew when it happened. He didn't think she did anything about what she called her "fidgets." Sissy wasn't as sex-minded as she gave herself out to be. She was a lot more interested in shoes, clothes, makeup and her singing career. Hank had had his two little hiccups. M.L. Brown called that time in the middle of the night when she knew Sissy was in Memphis doing jingles. "I'm coming over," she announced. In minutes she was at his front door. That was a long time ago, and by now he could look at M.L. without a blink, as if she were a stranger. He had left the light off that night and remembered only the thinness of her rib cage, vulnerable as a girl's. And the other time, drinking with a friend who'd been elected constable, they all got loaded and . . . that was nothing. Less than nothing.

Was he a fool? Men were drawn to Sissy. When they went to parties. When she walked across a room full of strangers and nobody knew they were connected, he saw. Heads turned. Eyes measured. Passions stirred.

He didn't know if he could hold on to the world he'd promised her, and helped her create. She didn't like being in the country, took no pride in his profession or in him. But he gave her a lot: her house, her dressing table and private bathroom, the built-ins he'd made in the walk-in closet with the special shelves for her shoes.

Hank pushed himself up from his chair. If he got into it tonight, he wouldn't sleep until it was time to get up. He would lie there and see the lines of figures totted up, see the face of the Oriental who was now his official loan officer at the Cotton Plant Bank and Trust, giving him that flat, calm look. The Oriental's words were kind enough, but his look was cold, cold. As it was, he'd be awake until Sissy got home. Which was late enough.

Hank leaned forward, with his elbows on his knees, and let his head hang. He either had waited too long to get out or should never have gotten into farming in the first place. On the other hand, who could tell a young man what not to do? When his father died, his brothers wanted to parcel up the land and sell it to developers. Hank and his mother said no. They lucked out, had a few good years; things rolled. In the beginning he liked even the bad times, the challenge, the sense of continuum year to year, the kinship they all felt. Farmers were at the top of the heap back then—no real money, but cotton was king. People admired the farmer, looked up to him. Back then was the time of the white man and the farmer, and Hank had been proud to be both. Now they were no better than welfare recipients, on the government tit. They *were* welfare recipients if you didn't get touchy about words.

He should go to bed. The thing about the daughter in the coma, he knew it was cheap, a TV show written to stir people up. But he couldn't help it, it got to him.

Sissy's dog sashayed into the room, nails clicking on the cypress floor. Hank never thought he'd see the day when he cared about a pissy little woman's dog, but Lil was special. She had a contemplative nature. She tipped two steps closer.

Hank chuckled. "You trying to tell me something, Miss Lil?" He held out the carton. In the dark, the white dog stuck her head in to her ears and lapped up the last drops of ice cream. When she was finished, Hank heaved himself up.

"All right," he said to the dog. At the kitchen door, he tossed the empty carton in the sink and turned out the light. He and Lil went out on the porch. Stanley roused and came to Hank's side. Hank rubbed the bird dog's silky ears, and the two of them stood on the dark porch, looking at the moon while Lillian had her pee.

Six days beyond new, the moon was a thin sliver, three-quarters risen. Almanacs said plant by it, and maybe he should

have tried. Stanley yawned. In the distance Hank heard the
burble of an owl.

Around him the fields. The endless flat fields.

22

"Tobias . . ." From two people down, the voice of Totty Boyette
rang out.

The soup course was over. Platters, bowls and baskets had
been passed for the main course: garlic-and-rosemary-stuffed
leg of lamb, artichoke hearts with Béarnaise, rice, bread,
chilled fresh asparagus with roasted peppers and cherry toma-
toes. Wine had been poured, a nice soft Médoc that Jacky—
knowing Baker's chintziness when it came to wine—had
brought. The candles were on the verge of guttering. Glasses
clinked, forks scraped, dinner moved into second gear.

Fork aloft, Toby turned to his right. He had cut and speared
a piece of meat topped with artichoke heart and a slice of
roasted pepper. He was looking forward to the bite a lot.

Totty craned her head around Roy and Jane Scott. Making
a gesture of helplessness, she smiled broadly, Coke-brown
eyes asparkle, all apologies for the inconvenience, having to
lean around people to talk, like in church when the pews are
full.

Toby set down his fork, allowing it to clank against his
plate. "Yes?"

When he leaned forward, Jane Scott moved back so he
could see around her. To talk over Roy, Totty lifted her chin.
Roy kept his head down.

"I notice Roy here"—Totty aimed a fluttery gesture in his
direction—"calls you Tobias. Do you prefer that?"

Jane Scott moved forward, cut an asparagus spear, leaned back.

"Actually," Toby responded, "I do. But . . ." To his left, Mell ate her food in small bites, taking a sip of wine after each swallow. Across from him, Dog and Sissy had resumed their intense and often raucous exchange. If he turned his face entirely in Totty's direction, Toby would ostracize Mell, showing her the back of his head. Not that Mell cared—by the look of her, she was on the moon—but it was still rude. So he turned halfway to his left, offering her that part of his face.

"But," he continued, "I don't mind Toby."

"Anyway, To-*bi*-us." Totty giggled. "I was wondering, what do you *do*?"

Head down, his face close to the plate, Roy caught his mother's grimace and rolled his eyes. One elbow on the table, Mell held up her wineglass.

"Excuse me?" Toby said, stalling for time. If figuring out what Totty was asking was tricky, understanding why she asked it was a lost cause.

"I mean, my boys . . . Well, there's no need to get off on *my* boys, is there? They're older, and . . . But I mean, like, you know, job? School? Like ambition?" She jiggled her head to let him know that while ambition was far too lofty a concept for her even to think about, much less dare to apply to herself, when it came to boys it was crucial.

Toby was quiet. He had thought about this moment a lot, before he agreed to come with his mother, after she had committed to the trip herself. Knowing these kinds of questions would be asked, and that his mother preferred that he not answer them straightforwardly, he had let her know that he would be discreet, but he would not lie. Now, in the face of Totty Boyette's hard dark stare coupled with her soft sweet smile, he could not come up with a flip answer.

Shifting forward, Jane Scott spoke to Mell, praising the

meal, declaring the lamb perfect, the wine superb, the combination of taste and textures inspired. Mell said she should tell Baker.

Jane Scott turned toward Baker's end of the table but said nothing. The bravado she'd felt before the meal was ebbing away. It was depressing, Dog across the table and Totty one person down. They were married, for God's sake; a couple. She was too old to be in love with the wrong person—and what did love matter anyway? She was a fool. She scanned the dinner party. When you'd been to bed with every grown man at the table at least once, maybe it was time to think about leaving.

Patient as stone, Totty waited for Toby's answer.

"Oh . . . ." Toby's voice faltered. "Not that much, really."

The table was divided into splintered chips, separate conversations. At the other end, Leland, Jacky and Carroll laughed at a story Baker was telling about the time when, hired to stage a debutante party, he used "The Death of the Southern Virgin" as his theme and wrapped the country club in black. Carroll confirmed his story. Mourning ribbons, he remembered, were draped from the chandeliers. With his graceful long hands, Carroll conjured these swags in the air. Meanwhile, to Mell's left, Dog and Sissy discussed catfish and hard times. Mell, Jane Scott and Roy were quiet.

"I mean, but everybody does something. Me, I take care of Dog." Totty batted her eyes.

"That's nice," Toby said. Helplessness was a cover. He knew men who milked that one. Totty wasn't just phony. She asked direct questions and then, once they were answered, slithered away, as if somebody else had done the asking. She was out to get somebody, though Toby wasn't sure who. Not him, probably, but he'd do in a pinch.

What he had *done*, in the way Totty was asking, was get mired down. He had not finished high school and only last year had gotten his equivalency diploma. Drugs were not the only thing; drugs didn't necessarily take people over the way do-gooders would have you think. What he'd gone through was a period of feeling so lost, so inconsequential. He was better now, but only just.

Could he tell Totty Boyette he was a nineteen-year-old child and skip the rest when, given her conversation in the living room, the rest was likely her real interest? Could he say to her that his job was taking care of his mother? Surely Totty Boyette never asked a question she didn't know the answer to. Somewhere in her thwarted shrunken soul, Totty Boyette sensed, suspected, *knew.* Toby lowered his eyes. He wanted to proceed slowly, carefully, to take this woman very, very seriously.

"Or, I don't know, am I asking the wrong question?"

"Of course not." He looked longingly at his bite of food.

Hard by Totty, shoulder pressed against that ruffle of her pinafore, Roy Farrish held up a chunk of lamb. Bits of browned garlic and rosemary decorated the meat, Roy having chosen a piece from the outside edge.

He spoke in a clear, loud voice. "Does anybody know . . ." He raised his voice and tried again. "Excuse me, I said does anybody know . . ." The eyes of his bullet-ridden yellow smile face peeked up over the edge of the table. Roy's child's voice rose above the others with a youthful conviction they had lost long ago.

The splintered chips went silent. Leland laid a hand on Baker's arm, raising one finger to let him know that his son was requesting the floor. Dog was happy to get Sissy off the horrors of catfish decline, which she was describing in detail. Dog had a funny stomach.

They all looked at Roy. It was one of those moments in a dinner party when the party either jells and becomes one event or stays splintered, usually for the remainder of the evening. With this many people you could never predict, especially after the bourbon and the gin, the wine and the waiting. It was only because Roy was a child that the others felt in any way obliged to listen.

Totty withdrew her head. Jacky Nelms, on her right, didn't know what was going on, but he could feel Totty's fury, her upper arms and shoulders stiff as a wired puppet's.

Totty did not believe in allowing children at table. When her kids were little and she and Dog had people over, she made Jody and Art stay in their rooms.

Momentarily off the hook, Toby sat back. He slid his fork between his lips—his first bite of food. The lamb was juicy and nicely rare, the Béarnaise creamy and pointed, alive with tarragon and vinegar.

Roy pushed his glasses back up on his nose. "Does anybody know which animals, of all the species in the animal kingdom, are omnivores?" Then he shoveled in the lamb.

"Omnivores?" Sissy pondered out loud. "Now that—"

"Means everything," Mell blurted.

"Hey, Mell. I was going to say—"

"Sorry. I thought you didn't—"

"You didn't give me a chance to finish." Sissy pouted.

"One is obvious." Jane Scott turned her hand palm-up, aiming fingertips at her plate.

"Exactly," Carroll agreed.

"What?" Totty played dumb.

Jacky Nelms bent his head in her direction. "Well, so there's us." The thing to do with a woman like Totty was respond to the question she asked, not the implications, inferences, tone or, most importantly, her own feigned stupidity. "People," he continued. "Human beings. We eat anything."

Totty cocked her head and lifted her chin.

Roy nodded. "Right. And?"

Baker's bald head gleamed. He did adore his daring, eccentric young son and, to encourage him, was happy to play the straight man. "How many are there altogether?"

Catching Baker's eye, Jane Scott narrowed hers. The minute

he saw the place card arrangement, Baker knew it was a mistake to put Jane Scott and Totty on the same side of the table with only Roy in between. But the situation was complicated, and there were only so many ways to divide people up boy-girl-boy-girl. Mischief moved him to leave the women where they were. If push came to shove, Jane Scott would have Totty Boyette for breakfast. To acknowledge her silent message, Baker ducked his head. Jane Scott didn't look so good.

The table was quiet, waiting. Roy held up his hand, indicating food in his mouth. He chewed.

Mell gestured Toby closer, and he leaned his head in her direction. "Don't let her get to you. She's a cunt," she whispered. "Cunt" came out louder than she intended.

Toby straightened, blushing. Dog looked around.

Roy swallowed. "Four," he said, holding up four fingers.

"Four!" Dog remarked. "Isn't that fascinating."

It was Sissy's turn to jab Dog in the ribs. Dog winced and put his hand there. His stomach was acting really funny now. He was always getting sick feelings.

Carroll flashed Roy an admiring glance. The boy would never get it. Dinner conversation was supposed to be polite chatter, small talk and gossip, not games, open questions, real discussions. It wasn't just his age; Roy was a new kind of citizen in this worn-out relic of a town, a person of curiosity and sheer plainspokenness. In his presence, Carroll felt hopeful and even thought things might actually change here, someday. If there was some way to persuade people like Roy to stay.

"Okay," Baker said. "So humans. Lions?"

Roy rolled his eyes. "Sure, Dad. You ever see Mama Cat eat a banana?"

"She likes cherry pie."

"I mean in the wild, not in a Jim Beam box on the front porch. Lions are carnivores."

"Hogs." When everybody looked over, Sissy was almost sorry she had spoken. She shrugged. "Hogs eat anything. Chickens, chinaberries, dog doo." She held up a finger: "Your this." She shrugged again. "You name it." She shivered. "Hogs," she said. "I hate them."

"Hogs are right." Roy sipped a bit of wine. He liked wine with his food, had been allowed to drink it at table since he was eight. "That's two."

"Hey, darlin', that's *good*." Dog jostled Sissy's shoulder with his own. "You some kind of brain or what?"

Dog rubbed his taut paunch, fingering his belly button. He didn't know if it was catfish decline or what, but his stomach was starting to feel seriously strange.

"No, I just grew up with a *hog* around back by the chicken house. Are you going to eat that piece of bread?"

"Me? No." Dog handed Sissy a hunk of bread from his plate.

"Sissy, there's plenty of bread." Baker turned to his son. "Roy?"

"I don't want a whole piece. I want Dog's." Sissy held up her hand to keep the bread basket from being passed.

Dog lifted his wineglass. Sissy clinked hers against it and they turned them up.

"You know what?" Mell said to her husband. "We forgot Carroll's champagne."

Baker slapped his forehead.

"Mell, never mind, it's okay. I brought that champagne for you to have whenever you wanted."

"*God*, Carroll," Baker declared, bolting up out of his chair. "Of course it's not okay. What an idiot." The chair tipped backward, and his napkin fell to the floor.

Jacky steadied the chair, bent forward to get the napkin. When he raised his head, he found that Leland had set her foot on the empty seat. Jacky ran his hand up her muscled calf to her knee. Her skin was very white, her bare legs smooth and hairless. Like all dancers, Leland was a maniac about hair. She spent hours removing all trace of it from her legs, groin and armpits. From the kitchen they heard the pop of a champagne cork. Jacky thumbed the soft, cordlike muscle behind Leland's knee. Another champagne cork popped. Leland withdrew her leg.

Jacky placed Baker's napkin on his chair, sat back, turned to the others and said, "Bears." Jacky knew all four omnivores, but he held off, in the interest of general conversation and to save Toby Standard from whatever wickedness Totty Boyette was brewing.

Leaning around Totty, Roy held up three fingers. "Bears," he said, "are three."

"I thought bears ate berries."

"They do."

"*Choke*cherries. That's in a children's book. I never knew what chokecherries were."

"Me either. What book was that?"

"*Blueberries for Sal?*"

"That was blueberries, Leland."

"Oh, right."

"You always see bears in magazines with a fish in their paw."

"Like *Sports Afield.*"

"They do eat fish," Roy confirmed. "And berries. That's the point."

"Some kinds will eat out your liver."

They looked at Sissy. "Liver?"

"Not mine," Dog said.

"I didn't mean yours, Dog. I meant, you know, the in-general 'you.'"

"Are you sure bears is right?" Dog shifted his feet.

"We could look it up."

"Never mind." Dog took all games seriously and didn't like to see Jacky Nelms scoring a point.

The door to the kitchen swung open and Baker made a circle around the table, setting a champagne glass at each plate. "It's French," he said over his shoulder. "The real goddamn thing." He disappeared through the kitchen door.

"Otherwise it wouldn't be champagne," Jacky said, smiling. There was a line in his life, marking off the time before, when he drank. Since he quit he'd come into his own, had begun to learn things, to look around, to have the self-respect to be quiet within himself. He still went to meetings, not wanting ever to chance thinking he was cured, or that he'd made the change on his own. It took him two years to apply the term "alcoholic" to himself. After accepting that, he settled in for the long run. And there was a stillness about him now that, he knew, was worrisome to other people. Sometimes, in conversations, he just listened. "Where are you?" friends wanted to know. "Here" was the answer, right here—where, when he was drinking, he never had been. Like all alcoholics, he had to let go of certain dreams. The dream of being different, of being special. Some people liked him better back then, when he was wild and made trouble for himself every day of his life.

"Everybody give up?" Roy was grinning.

When people asked Jacky if he missed drinking, he had to laugh—quietly, because he didn't mean to ridicule the genuine concern and curiosity beneath the question. And in fact, there were people who discovered, once they got out of hell, that they missed the horrors and the remorse, the morning-after phone calls. *This is Jacky Nelms, I'm sorry about last night. . . .*

"Okay," Mell said, "I give up. What's the fourth one?"

"Did anybody guess bears?" Leland looked into a flickering candle flame. "Somebody ought to . . ."

Everybody seemed to be staring at her.

"Mom?" Toby hated it when his mother got drifty and made mistakes like that.

Baker swooped back into the room with the champagne bottles.

"Where's yo' head, girl?" he teased. "I heard that."

"Somebody did guess bears," Jacky offered. "And he was right."

"Oh . . ." Leland looked toward Jane Scott. "I guess I was . . ."

Jane Scott twirled her hair, winked. "Okay, Roy, what? We give up."

"Rats." Roy cut into his meat.

"Rats?" Totty frowned. When she turned to look at Roy, it put a crick in her neck. "Are you saying *rats*?"

Mell rolled her eyes. "Oh my God," she said. "Back to Freddy Krueger."

"The movie?" Sissy sopped up gravy with a piece of bread.

"I mean rats." Roy took a bite of artichoke, chewed, fixed his glasses on his nose. "*Rattus norvegicus.*"

Totty fluffed up her ruffle. "Oh well, of course. Rats."

They looked at her, and she jiggled her head. "Well, I mean . . ." She lowered her voice. "Those stories, you know. Those poor little black babies with milk on their mouths? The rats come in and . . ." She twirled her hand.

Dog dropped his fork.

Totty corrected herself. "White babies too," she said, directing her remark to Leland.

"Totty!" It was Dog's turn to shush her.

"What?"

"That's a misconception," Roy explained. "If you keep a rat in a clean environment, it's meticulous, cleaner than a hamster by three thousand centuries."

"Roy has a rat," Baker told the table.

"What do you feed it?"

"Nuts and grains."

"Cheese?"

"I don't. Raisins, almonds—he likes lettuce."

Leland chuckled. "A vegetarian?"

"Well, yes. If you feed them meat—"

"Roy." Filling Leland's champagne glass, Baker tried to shift Roy's line of thinking.

"—they turn feral," Roy concluded.

"*Roy.*" He filled Carroll's, Sissy's, Dog's.

Roy was on a roll. "I heard about this case. A kid fed his rat raw hamburger."

"What happened?" Sissy was game.

Baker half-filled Mell's glass, set the first bottle on the windowsill, picked up the second, finished pouring Mell's glass. Toby, who had dumped Diet Coke into his champagne glass, held his hand over it. Baker filled Jane Scott's.

"The rat went crazy, bit the kid's finger."

From behind Roy, his father filled his glass.

"And?" Sissy's eyes shimmered like bright water.

"He got blood poisoning." They waited. He shrugged. "Died."

"The boy?" Totty was seated so close to Roy he had to go cross-eyed to look at her.

"Not the boy, Totty." Jacky kept his voice low.

"The rat," Sissy was quick to add.

"A toast." At the foot of the table, Baker raised his glass. "To our good friend Leland and her son, Tobias. Welcome. May there be many more such occasions."

Jacky clinked his empty champagne glass against the others', dipped the tip of his index finger in Leland's champagne and tasted it. "To you," he whispered.

Leland proposed another toast, to friendship. Again, Jacky clinked his empty glass. When Leland held hers out once again, he refused.

Roy sipped his champagne. He wanted to talk more about rats, but Mell was giving him a look.

"So, Tobias . . ." Sensing that bears, rats, hogs and little black children had run their course, Totty once again leaned around Roy and Jane Scott.

The table was silent. Now that the fractured conversations had come together, nobody wanted them to fly back apart again. Not that people felt particularly united, or even that interested in one another. The mood of the table had shifted, that was all, the shape of the evening altered. To deny that was to defy convention and manners and the natural flow of things. Nobody wanted to be rude. After all, it was a party.

Toby could feel the others' eyes on him.

Totty pressed on. "Are you in school out there? Or what?"

Jane Scott didn't rile easily, but sense flew right out the window when she did. She could surprise even herself with a wild outburst, the occasional hurled object. The champagne was having an immediate effect on them all, after all the other drinking, not to mention, in Jane Scott's case, Mrs. Loflin's pills. "Totty," she said without turning in her direction. "For God's sake."

"For God's sake what?"

"Give it a rest."

"Give what a rest, Jane Scott?" Totty cast her eyes toward the ceiling, as if seeking help from above. "What?"

Dog's heart thumped like a hammer.

When Jane Scott lifted her glass to her mouth, her bracelets jangled. Her left eye twitched. "The subject, for God's sake. Can't you figure *anything* out?"

Totty gave a sarcastic little laugh. "Oh, well, some things. Yes I do. Yes indeedy. I certainly do."

Dog waded in, not knowing what else to do. "Anybody heard the one about—" The two women's eyes—*his* two women's eyes—burned a hole in Dog's joke. He shut up.

Next to Jacky, Totty's body was like a stretched wire.

Toby pressed hard against Jane Scott, who suddenly felt light next to him, as if she might be going.

Anybody at the table who had not, prior to this second, heard the news about Jane Scott Laws and Dog Boyette now knew, including Toby.

Totty shifted her rib cage to the left; pressing against the sheer white fabric of her pinafore bib, her nipples were small pebbles, like pea gravel. Dog's mouth flew open. At home, he'd brooded so much about the prospect of being in the same room with his wife and his girlfriend that he'd hardly noticed, until now, what Totty was wearing. He wanted to throw his napkin across her chest. The way everything was sticking out, every man in the room could look to his heart's content.

Totty ran her hand up the soft burr at the nape of her neck. "I may not know stuff like biology and, well—" she made a big show of searching for the word—"'omnivores,' but to set the record straight, Jane Scott Laws, I am not stupid. Some things I figure out quick and good."

"Good for you." Jane Scott tossed back her hair. Her spine was going liquid on her. "Then pick on somebody grown-up. Leave the kids alone."

"Nineteen is hardly—"

"Carroll, this champagne is divine." Baker lifted his glass.

At the other end of the table, Melanie's gray eyes circled the table and came to focus on Baker.

Carroll concurred. "It is good, isn't it?"

"Where'd you get it?"

"Oh, Shamoon's. Duke keeps it in the back. You have to ask."

Assessing the possibilities of risk for her son in advance of the guests' arrival, like a travel agent advising which roads to take and where the speed traps were, Leland had underestimated Totty Boyette's dogged need for a general evening-up of whatever scores of whichever old and lost games were being kept and played. Even now, she didn't quite get it, still thinking Totty only a silly, empty-headed and very pretty girl-woman who thought the sun rose and set in Eunola, Mississippi. Under the table, Leland thrust her foot out and placed it against Jacky's. He pressed back and they sat there, like children at secret games.

"Shamoon's," Mell declared, "is my bank."

"Your bank is a liquor store?"

Mell leveled her eyes on Toby, the first time she had fully

looked at him since the incident in the bath. He returned her calm, flat gaze for a second, then backed off.

"Duke cashes my checks. Holds them when I need him to. Things like that."

Observing the warm exchange of looks between his wife and Toby Standard, Baker's heart lifted.

"That's cool." Toby turned to his mother, who wasn't listening.

"Not like L.A., I take it?" Carroll's eyes were lively. He was trying to help Toby out and, at the same time, to let him know he might as well forget about steering his mother out of trouble. She was too far gone to turn back now.

"No."

"Speaking of bears . . ."

"What about them?" Roy was pleased to get back to animals and surprised to find that of all people it was Sissy Westerfield giving it another shot. Roy liked Sissy. She was just so sad.

"Did anybody read that book *The Night of the Grizzlies*?"

When nobody said anything, Baker rotated his hand in small circles to encourage her to keep going.

"Where the bears in Montana ate those girls?"

"God, Sissy." Dog covered his mouth with his napkin. "Get crude, why don't you."

"Well? It happened." Sissy didn't understand it when people got upset about horrible things that had really happened. She found crime and horror and grisliness entertaining, enlivening. At night, she pored over the paper looking for nightmare murders, horror-story suicides. Awfulness gave life a wider scope. And in the end, you could fight it all you wanted, but things happened. Things just did.

"Grizzlies don't usually attack people." Roy looked skeptical but interested.

"I know. But they did this time. You get a lot of information reading true-crime books, and this one went into grizzlies and how they live and all that, so I know." She folded her hands together in a basket. "It was about twenty-five years ago. Nineteen sixty-seven, actually. I don't know why I remember that kind of thing, but I'm sure that was the year. Nobody ever figured out why it happened."

"Did you say 'girls,' plural?"

"People came up with theories, but—"

"Plural?"

When Sissy nodded, the blond curl at her left eye dipped and brushed her eyelid. With one finger she flicked the curl back into its proper place and wondered how her Very Peach blush was holding out.

"Two different bears." Her voice was as matter-of-fact as the subject demanded. "Two different girls. On the same night."

"Imagine the odds against—"

"Hard to believe."

"They dragged them off." Sissy looked up. "The bears."

"Yes."

"Dragged the girls off."

"Yes."

Somebody clicked silverware against a plate. A champagne glass brushed the bread basket and made a soft ringing sound.

"There was one theory. Both girls had their . . ." Sissy made the same gesture as Baker, making circles with her hand. "Had their, you know . . ."

"Monthly?" Roy suggested.

"Thank you."

Dog doubled up his fists and pressed them against the table. If there was one thing he could not stand to think about it was blood. He was known for fainting in the locker room if somebody came in cut and bleeding, and he'd never fucked a woman when she was having her period.

Disapproving, Totty tapped a nail against her plate rim.

"Do you know how to tell the difference between a grizzly and another kind of bear?" Sissy said. When engaged, she looked about Roy's age, her face a map of unabashed vulnerability.

"Is this a joke?"

"No."

"The hump?"

Sissy nodded. "The hump on their back, behind their heads." When she reached back and touched her shoulder blades, the neck of her caftan came up to her ear.

"The grizzlies *ate* the girls?"

"Well . . ."

"All of them?"

"Roy!"

"Well, if you mean all—"

"Sissy!"

"Not all their whole bodies, Roy. Just . . ." Emerging from the enchanted heart of her tale, Sissy cast her eyes around the table. Toby frowned, Totty was appalled, Dog looked ready to puke. Mell and Roy were the only interested parties, and for them she finished her sentence. "Certain parts." For the others, she lowered her voice.

"Sissy, my God."

"Well, heck, y'all," she said. "It happened."

"Do you still have the book?" Mell asked.

"I gave it to the dialysis center." Sissy nodded in the direction of Cotton Plant.

Dog harrumphed. "They must have been grateful." He was starting to feel really sick now, a blackness developing behind his eyes, pulsing like a toothache.

Sissy turned to Dog. "They were."

"I'd like to read it."

Baker spoke to Leland. "Knowing her inclinations," he said, nodding toward Mell, "I'm surprised she missed it."

"I'll see if it's still there. It's not the bears so much that got to me as the . . . as the . . ."

"The mystery?" Jacky suggested.

"Exactly."

"The menace," Mell added.

Sissy sighed.

As guest of honor, Leland felt obliged to fill in the silence that followed. Even though she'd waited until past nine o'clock to have her first glass of wine, she was tired from the drive and quickly had grown fuzzed and loopy. When she spoke, it was as if she fell into words instead of thinking them through. "That," she murmured, "is very interesting."

Champagne glasses came up, went down. Baker went for dessert and coffee while Roy and Sissy gathered plates.

"So. Tobias." Even before Totty said the boy's name, no one had the slightest doubt where she was going.

Across the table, holding two plates, Sissy stood behind Dog's chair in disbelief. "Do something," she hissed in his ear. "Stop her."

Dog kept his head down. If Sissy thought he could do any-thing to slow Totty down when she had the bit between her teeth, she was nuts. Anyway, he felt too sick to stop a gnat.

Sissy bolted toward the kitchen. Sleeping around was so complicated, so scary. So many things to be afraid of. She didn't know how people managed. In the kitchen, she whis-pered to Baker that Totty was back on the rampage. Then, us-ing a crust of somebody's bread, she wiped up a clot of Béarnaise and concentrated on that.

Roy went out to gather up more plates.

Meanwhile, Toby's heart felt like one of those frozen blue things you put in an ice chest to keep food cold. In the past few years he'd discovered courage within himself he had thought was simply not in his nature. Two friends died, then a teacher he particularly admired. He did not like to think where he'd be without the Program. He'd worked hard. But the missing time in his life, the years he had in one way or another blanked out, left him unformed. In a lot of ways—books, social clues, methods of behavior beyond the walls of his and his mother's apartment—he felt clumsy and adolescent.

He looked across the table at Carroll Cunningham. With a slight tilt of his elegant head, Carroll gave him a high sign. Toby laid his hand on the back of Jane Scott's chair and said simply, "Yes?"

What he had now was his honesty, the need to speak. Sometimes he went too far and told too much. Maybe someday he wouldn't have to, but for now it was a necessity. He had his drill. He went by it. He let his index finger drop to Jane Scott's neck, to let her know he was grateful for her help but didn't need it anymore. "What was it you wanted to know exactly?"

Totty sniffed. "Well . . ." She didn't particularly want to defend herself and her family and friends and Mississippi and the entire South against the onslaught of slippery ideas and immoral actions, abortion, drugs, homosexuality and crime and the rest. But if she had to, she would. "You still haven't told me what it is you *do* out there in, umm . . . Yankeeland."

That was brilliant. Toby had to laugh.

"What?" She rescrewed a spit curl.

"Nothing."

"Must be something. You laughed."

"In Yankeeland? I mean, what I do is . . ." He took his hand from Jane Scott's chair. "Mrs. Boyette, what exactly is your problem?"

"I beg your pardon? *My* problem?"

"Forgive me for being blunt, but I keep thinking you're asking some other question."

"Why would I—"

"I don't know. You tell me."

"You brought it up, so you should—"

"Tell her." Leland felt calm and certain, no longer fuzzed at all. If Toby needed her approval, he had it.

In the kitchen, Baker scraped Béarnaise from Sissy's chest.

He wasn't entirely sure, he explained, that she'd ever get the grease spot out of the silk. Roy poured up the coffee.

Toby looked at his mother. He knew it was hard for her, all of this. She wanted to think she was fine about who he was and how his inclinations went, but she wasn't. He addressed Totty. "Is it by any stretch of the imagination my sex life that you're curious about?"

"Your . . ." Totty's hand dropped into the vegetable bowl. She wiped her fingers. "Sex? Whatever gave you the idea that . . ."

"That what?"

"That I wanted to know about your . . ." She wiped her knife with her napkin.

"So what is it you're asking, exactly?"

"Now that's too . . ." She fluttered, looked to Dog.

Jane Scott slid her chair back.

"Oh, I don't know, it's just that when you—"

"No." Totty made a basket of her hands as if preparing to pray. "Absolutely not. I am not interested in *anybody's*. No."

The kitchen door swung open. Roy held it for Baker, who was bearing fluted crystal goblets on a tray. Roy lifted the goblets off and placed them around the table.

Her hand over the spot on her dress, Sissy came back in and took her place beside Dog. She tucked her napkin into the neck of her caftan. "Y'all are in for a treat," Sissy said. "Baker let me taste it and y'all are not going to believe this dessert."

"What is it?"

Roy announced, "Marrons glacés."

"Marone what?"

"Chestnuts."

"Do bears eat chestnuts?"

"That's not funny."

"Mmmm," said Totty, spooning up the rich dessert. "Mell."

"Don't look at me." Mell pointed her spoon at Baker.

"Then mmmm, *Baker.*"

Spoons clicked. Jacky leaned over to Baker and told him, in a whisper, what had been said. Roy, Jacky and Leland had coffee.

Toby waited. The tables had turned, and he was into it. "I meant to ask," he said, "what is it you like to be called, Totty or Mrs. Boyette?"

She turned her spoon upside down in her mouth. "My name is Wilhemina." She batted her eyes in Dog's direction. "But everybody calls me Totty. Don't they, Dog?"

"Huh?"

"Call me Totty."

"Call you Totty."

"Dog, I think you—"

"Let Tobias finish his thought, Totty." Mell felt she was finally in touch with the strongest sense of herself. It took a while, many checks and balances; a milligram in the wrong direction and she could go goofball or flat. "The dessert, Baker, is superb." Through the guttering flames she looked down the long table at her husband. Her eyes simmered like a thick hot roux.

"Thank you, Doo. I thought you'd like it."

"You were right." She studied him through her lashes.

Jane Scott tossed her napkin down next to her spoon. "Does anybody care if I smoke?"

"While we eat?" Sissy said.

"Don't worry. I'll be careful."

Baker shoved his open palm in Jane Scott's direction and whimpered. Jane Scott took two cigarettes out of her purse. Roy offered to light Jane Scott's, but she was too wrought up to notice. Jane Scott and Baker lit up. Then Mell, who hardly ever smoked, requested one, as did Carroll, who hadn't smoked a whole cigarette in four and a half years. Jane Scott passed around the pack. Leland had stopped only six weeks ago. So far, her longing had not let up one iota. She still smoked from time to time, though never in front of Toby.

He didn't have to make announcements, Leland had told

Toby before they left. People in the South didn't like announcements. She hated herself for saying it, even as she spoke the words. The meetings, his group, what Toby called the Program, demanded that he not shy from the truth but speak it whenever possible. Come out, declare yourself. At home, she was used to it. The past few years she'd changed her expectations with such regularity that she thought she was up to anything. But L.A. was one thing. Here it was different.

Jacky blew out the candles, which by now were down to their holders, then leaned forward to pour himself another cup of coffee.

Carroll Cunningham covered Leland's thin wrist with his hand.

"Because," Toby went on, "if you have a problem with who I am or what I do, I'll be happy to—"

"I think it's time for us to go, Dog."

"If what you're thinking is I'm one of those fruitcakes you were talking about earlier, running around L.A. giving everybody a disease, you're right. What did you call them in your day—'queer'?"

"I can't believe y'all aren't eating this dessert." Sissy spooned up the last bits in her goblet, her spoon scraping against the crystal. "It's the very best thing I ever put in my mouth."

Jane Scott passed her untouched dessert across the table. "I made jelly all afternoon. I'm up to my eyeballs in sugar."

"Are you sure?"

"Positive."

"If you're sure you don't want it . . ."

Baker drew on his cigarette. Leland touched his hand, took a drag. Her hand was cold.

Baker tapped ashes in a small crystal bowl. He didn't want to think about AIDS and HIV just because Toby was a homosexual. He'd read up on things for Roy's sake. He knew how the disease was transmitted and how it was not, but still . . .

"I wouldn't want it to go to waste." Sissy pulled Jane Scott's goblet closer.

Totty pushed back her chair. "Dog?"

"Dog's gone. He's a dog gone."

"I said, Dog!"

"Do what?" He came to. "Totty, for God's sake." He handed her his crumpled napkin. She didn't know what it was for, but she took it.

In Dog's stomach, food and all the talk roiled together like trash in a flooded ditch. It took every thread of his strength not to let go and throw up in his marrons glacés.

"Let's go, Dog. You're plowed."

"My God, cover your tits, Totty. I can see everything you've got."

His wife's eyes were livid, but she spoke in a measured voice that was new. "I said we should go, Dog." She tossed his napkin across the table.

It was the meat getting to him. Dog liked his meat cooked until it was gray, especially lamb. This lamb had been soft in the middle and the blood ran. There had been too much talk about meat and teeth and blood and queers. Dog had gone wild boar hunting once; he had seen what kind of tusks a hog had. He could imagine what kind of damage those long sharp teeth could inflict. Especially on a girl. As for bears . . . Montana was a long way away—where was it, next to Idaho?

Around him, the world moved slowly and on its own. His wife's eyes burned holes in him; then there was that fruitcake boy of Baker's, who looked like a little old man. And Leland's fruitcake son, the queer.

Jane Scott blew cigarette smoke in his direction. Nobody would believe this, but Dog Boyette loved Jane Scott Laws. There she was in her wild frizzy hairdo and that drapey top and she looked like she might melt at any minute, the way she did when he went down on her and it happened and happened. He had never gone in for going down on a woman, just wasn't in his repertoire. If a woman didn't go for fucking, then fuck 'em, was how he felt. But Jane Scott . . . Now Dog's stomach felt like somebody was stirring it up inside with a rusty spoon.

"We had a wonderful time, Baker." Totty had gone back to her familiar singsongy flutter.

In the thirty-what? years they'd been married, Totty had stayed the same as she was in high school, hanging on Dog like a pet monkey. She listened to the same music, wore her hair the same, did that swoopy thing with her eyelashes, raised that one eyebrow when she got mad, the way movie stars used to. When Dog went off to State to be a football star and Totty was not smart enough to go, she wrote him every day, came to every game, even the dumb ones with Mansfield State and Northwest Louisiana and hung all over him afterward like a hero's crown. Made him feel nine feet tall. Sucked his cock until he felt his soul empty out and pour down her throat. Offered herself butt up, cheeks pulled wide, calling him Dog, Dog. . . .

She was a clever girl, his Totty. Knew what she wanted and went for it. She'd given him everything she had, except the one place she declared sacred and off-limits. She would not, she announced, get pregnant. She'd be a virgin in white when they got married. She let him put his cock everywhere except there. Held off until they had a big wedding at the Baptist church. And when Dog took her to the Gulf Shores in Biloxi, there was blood, blood. It wasn't her period, she swore, it was because she was—well, he knew. But there was so much. And then she held off a day or two, taking him in the usual other places; but Dog had never been sure. The meat came up. Dog closed his eyes. It went back down. Seeing Totty now, you wouldn't know. In that way she had changed, once she had her sons. Their life was like a secret bird he kept in a closet, where no one could see. He nursed the bird when it was sick, fed it small bits of grain from his fingers. Covered its cage, would not leave it, not ever.

Totty stood up. "Dog."

Baker stood. "Do y'all have to go so early?"

Totty waited. Dog didn't budge. Neither did Totty. If Dog thought she was leaving without him, he could think again. If Dog and everyone else thought she was going to sit there and be insulted by a California homosexual, they had another thought coming.

When Jane Scott shot another big puff of smoke in his direction, Dog heaved.

"I feel like . . ." he began.

"Dog—don't!" Totty bounced over toward him.

Sissy moved away. "Are you okay, Dog?"

Dog stood. "I feel like I'm going to throw up or faint."

Roy covered his mouth to keep from laughing.

Hoping for "faint," Baker went to Dog's side. "Let's get some air." He took Dog's arm and led him out.

On the porch, Dog heaved a couple more times and then let go. Vomit spewed out in the berry bushes. The food came and came. All he could taste was raw meat. When he thought he was finished, his stomach roiled again and more food came out. He felt a soft sliding in his gut. Dog squeezed his muscles back there hard, but he knew it wouldn't do any good. It all came down on him. His bowels let go and his pants filled. He heaved again.

Totty got her purse and rushed outside, in time to see Dog crumple to the sidewalk in a dead faint. His face was in the berry bushes, his cheek resting in puke. His eyes were closed, and he looked altogether peaceful and beatific.

"Pee-yew, Dog," his wife said, wrinkling her little nose. "Pee-*yew*."

23

Dog thought he'd died and gone to heaven. Lying on a soft white cot, afloat in a sea of shatteringly bright light, he felt weightless and free, as if his troubles and responsibilities and all the problems in his life had been a heavy coat somebody had lifted from his shoulders.

At his feet, a white shape. He studied it. The shape moved. It wore white. An angel?

She ran a washcloth up and down his legs, pressing the hair first against the grain, then with it. He felt the warm soapy water trickle down his shinbone to his ankle and thought about Jesus. Who was it washed Jesus' feet?

His leg was raised up, then scrubbed on the underside, from the back of his calf up to the knee. The woman pressed his ankles together and lifted him so that his buttocks came up off the cot. Like a mother diapering a baby, she wiped him clean, running the cloth up and down the crack of his ass.

Dog moaned. He didn't know if he had died or what, but this had to be heaven.

"Dog?"

He didn't answer. Like a child he burrowed down and pretended to be sleeping. From somewhere, a breeze ruffled the hairs of his legs. The bather toweled his shins, knees, thighs, moved the basin of soapy water to the other side of the cot.

"Dog."

She placed her hand between his thighs, soaped his groin, went up and down the length of his cock. Dog had not been circumcised; she pulled back his foreskin, and with the deftest motion and the smallest amount of water cleansed him there.

Dog moaned again.

"*Dog.*" The angel's voice bore down.

Dog stirred, peered through his lashes. The world was a blur, the woman's head surrounded by a pulsing halo of white. Angel or whatever, the woman had the biggest tits he'd seen in a long time. She moved and they bounced.

"Tits." He reached for one, made a sucking sound.

The angel thumped the head of his dick.

"Hey," he protested.

"Wake up, Dog."

He shook his head and tried to get up.

"Don't even think about it." The woman pushed him back down. "You'll jar the IV."

He lifted himself to his elbows and saw that a needle protruded from the crook of his left arm. Above, a bottle of clear yellowish liquid swung from a gleaming steel bar.

"Shoot!" Tears filled his eyes, and like light through a cracked door, the evening came back to him: the vomit, shitting his pants, the collapse. "Just, I don't know . . ." He slid from his elbows back down flat on his back. "Shoot." Then he started to bawl.

"Hey, Dog. Come on." The woman pulled Dog to her chest, held him hard. He buried his face, letting the tears pour out into the crevice between the soft pillows of her breasts. She patted his back, pressing his head deeper.

He snuffled. Nobody knew what it was like being a star, grinding out the yards inch by inch until you speared your way past the goal line. Nobody knew how it felt hearing the crowd roar "DOG! DOG! DOG!" Then came the bark—they *all* barked, not just some of the crowd. When he walked into a room, people knew who he was. He had thought life would always be like that. People made him such promises. Jobs, money, special treatment. His father, who was nothing but an ignorant sharecropper with a head as thick as a concrete block, told him not to dream too high. People get too high, his father used to say, they jump out of windows. He would rather just about anything than for his father to be right.

Dog cried until the tears went dry and there was nothing left except the slightest heaving of leftover spit and dribbles.

The woman held him hard.

Dog's father died at forty-seven. His mother now lived alone in a shacky pigsty, on a diet consisting mostly of mustard greens and bread pudding. Who was Dog supposed to be like? To look up to and admire?

The woman loosened her grip and he pulled away. There was nobody. "Where am I?"

"You'll be out as soon as I get you stabilized."

Dog looked down. He was wearing his blue knit polo shirt and nothing else. From the waist down he was damp, scrubbed and slightly shriveled. He covered himself with a sheet.

"Don't worry about the hard-on," the woman told him, and for the first time he noticed she was quite old. "I'm flattered."

As she turned away he thought he heard her giggle.

It was Mrs. Loflin, the head nurse and Methodist drug dealer.

"Am I in—"

"Never mind. In five freckles short of a flash we are going to forget where you are and who cleaned you up and stopped you from vomiting up the lining of your gut. We are never going to mention this little episode again—we are not even going to remember it. Do you understand?"

Mrs. Loflin had come to Eunola from Minnesota. She had never learned to flutter, flirt or play verbal dodge ball. Some people found her rude and uppity when she was really only plainspoken. She lowered her face down close to Dog's neck. "Do you understand?"

He nodded.

"Excuse me?"

"What?"

"I need the words."

"What words?"

"Do you understand what I just told you?"

"I said I understand. I do."

"Good."

"But . . ."

She stiffened. "What."

"Tell me I'm not in the white ladies' rest home."

"You are not in the white ladies' rest home, Dog. No."

He sighed.

"Your wife is bringing you some clothes. Now, can you sit up?" She came behind him and with one stout arm hefted him up.

"Good God, you're strong."

"I have to be."

"Well, but still . . ."

She rubbed his back. "How do you feel?"

He shook his head. "Woozy."

"You should be. Squirting at both ends."

"How'd I get here?"

"Your friends. That plumber's a strong one."

Dog's heart sank. "You should have let me vomit my gut up and die."

She whacked his ear.

"Ow!" He cupped it.

"What a thing to say."

"I mean it."

"You'll get over it."

There was a vile smell in the room. Dog looked down at the needle in his arm, the bubble of skin where it went in. "What's this for?"

"Electrolytes, potassium—getting your system back to normal."

"What happened?"

"I'm not sure. Something you ate."

"Food poisoning."

"Not food poisoning or everybody else would have it."

"Then what?"

"Stress, maybe."

"I hate that."

"What?"

"Stress. It's all anybody talks about. When you were growing up, you ever even *hear* of stress?"

Mrs. Loflin shrugged. "It's the all-purpose garbage can of causes. What about allergies?"

"I think so."

"What do you mean, 'think'?"

"Ask Totty."

Mrs. Loflin checked her watch. "Your wife."

"Totty keeps up with all that."

"You're a lucky man, Dog Boyette. Now swing around this way, let your feet hang off the table and I'll take the IV out."

He did as he was told. The room was small and shiny and white, all tile surfaces, marble and bright lights. There were shower heads in the walls, and in places the tile floor sloped down into silver drains. "What the hell is this place?"

Mrs. Loflin looked around. "Used to be a steam room, back when this was a fancy place and white ladies came here for comfort and rest and time off from their husbands."

"I thought you said I wasn't in the white ladies' rest home."

"You're not."

"Then what?"

"You're in Eva Turner all right, but there are a whole lot more folks than white ones here."

"God."

"And I don't have any right to be treating you, Dog Boyette, and I could lose my state certification if anybody found out. You are going to go home and flat-out forget you ever saw me tonight, you hear?"

He nodded.

"We brought you back here because nobody comes down here. The hall crooks, gets dark and nobody uses it. It stays locked, so nobody knows. I happened to be working late doing paperwork. Your friends carried you in like the sick dog you were."

Dog thought about Totty, and the two late pregnancies she'd said ended in miscarriages. He'd never quite believed her. He would have liked to have had a daughter to pamper and dress up and show off.

"I don't know whose idea it was to bring you here. Somebody said the child."

"Which? The fruitcake in the skirt?"

"Now, I wouldn't know which child, would I?"

Dog did not do drugs of any kind—he liked whiskey—but he knew Mrs. Loflin's reputation and had a good idea what she meant when she said she was there late doing paperwork. He had the feeling he was not the first person Mrs. Loflin had brought to the steam room. "You know, Mrs. Loflin, back there when I first woke up?"

"What about it?"

"I thought I was in heaven."

"Hmmp," she said.

"It was nice."

In one quick motion, Mrs. Loflin pulled the needle from Dog's arm, pressed her thumb down on his artery and slapped a Band-Aid over the hole in his skin. "Well, don't worry about it. It happens."

"I don't mean the hard-on. I mean the whole thing. It was like I had gone on from my body, like I could—"

She pressed her thumb down so hard into the soft meat of his arm it felt like she was touching the other side. "Ouch."

"What?"

"You digging to China?"

"Sorry."

"I mean, I hate that, you know, outer-body woo-woo stuff, but I have to tell you . . . Do you know Jane Scott Laws?"

Mrs. Loflin let up on her thumb. "Well, of course I do."

"She does her horoscope. Has her charts read, talks about that out-of-the-body California crap." He couldn't believe he was telling the nurse all this, but there was something about her. She listened, that was the main thing, and did not react until he had finished his thought. Meantime his life was running out like water down a drain. "Not that I know Jane Scott that well."

"No."

"But I like her."

"Your wife will be back soon."

"I always tell her, 'Jane Scott, you stayed in California too long.' You know? What do you want to get into this past-life shit for? People are alive or dead, and when you're dead that's it. Am I right?"

Mrs. Loflin cocked her ear and laid her hand on his shoulder. "Dog . . ."

"But tonight, when I was lying here between conked out and alive, I knew what she meant. I didn't have a worry in the world, I was light as a feather, and I floated above the weight of my life and it was sweet. So sweet. I—"

"They're here."

There were three sharp little raps at the door and then Totty's perky little face poked in. "You decent?" Her eyes were bright and she was smiling. Why the fuck didn't Totty ever stop smiling?

"Hey, darlin'." Dog pulled the sheet up tighter. "Your man wasn't much of a man tonight."

"Now, Dog." Totty came over and handed him a pair of wide-assed khaki pants.

Mrs. Loflin turned her back and went over to a white metal chest of drawers and put something in one of the drawers. It was then that Totty did something Dog had never seen her do in his life. She ignored the other woman, did not make small talk or fill the air with chitchat, but fixed her concentration distinctly and unwaveringly on Dog.

"I can't wear those."

"I guess you're going home stark raving bare-assed naked?" She giggled behind her hand.

At the chest of drawers, Mrs. Loflin acted busy.

"Aw, Totty."

Totty placed her hand at the corner of her mouth as if confiding a secret. "You sure can't wear your other pants home."

"Oh . . ." He rolled his eyes. "All right."

The two women kept their backs to each other and were quiet. It was odd.

Dog pushed his clean soaped feet and legs one at a time into the legs of the khaki pants. When he stood up, his knees buckled slightly, and Mrs. Loflin came back to his side. The two women held him by the elbows, one on either side. While they braced him up, he pulled the pants to his waist. The women were amazingly strong. "These Baker's?" he asked Totty.

"Yes," she said.

Dog pulled at the back seam. "Looks like a family of Bohemians moved out of here."

"Well, you know Baker's not as firm and trim as you, Dog." Totty smoothed his hair with her hand.

Mrs. Loflin brought him his shoes. "Your socks," she said, "are . . ." She waved her hand in front of her nose.

"Never mind," he said.

"So. Are we ready?"

"Yes ma'am," Totty said.

Mrs. Loflin held the door open and they went down a long hall, their steps echoing. From the floor above, a woman whimpered, a high, persistent yipping cry, like a weaned puppy trying to get through her first night alone. Ahead, Dog saw a small porchlike room with no furniture.

Hearing Baker's voice, he shook off Totty's arm. "Hey," he said. "Duke."

Baker leaned against the door, talking to Jacky Nelms.

"Say hey, guys." Dog's words were jauntier than his tone. "Shall we make like a tree?"

"And leave?" Totty finished up for him.

When the men asked Dog how he was, Dog said he'd been better but he'd live, and he thanked them for taking care of him, but did not look Jacky Nelms in the eye. At the door he turned to shake Mrs. Loflin's hand and thank her, but she'd retreated to the dark part of the porch, away from the street-lights on Manilla, where she couldn't be seen.

As Dog and Totty took their first steps down the concrete back steps, they heard Mrs. Loflin telling them to remember their agreement, and they saw her white hand waving them on. Her voice came from the darkness, as if Eva Turner herself were speaking.

The last one to leave, Jacky Nelms handed Mrs. Loflin an envelope. They had pooled together what cash they had, which came to just shy of two hundred and fifty. Mrs. Loflin did not open the envelope, but gauged the number of bills inside with her thumb and forefinger.

"Can you walk all right, Dog?" Baker asked.

The night air was warm and still and thick with the sweet scent of flowering ligustrum.

"I'll be fine once we get past these goddamn flowers."

Jacky Nelms lingered behind the others, careful not to crowd Dog and force a show of gratitude.

"Did she say what happened?" Baker worried about the freshness of the lamb, the chicken in his soup.

"She said stress."

"Oh God, *that*."

"Or garlic."

The three men stopped. Totty walked on a step or two until, realizing she was alone, she turned back, pumped her shoulders and ran a hand across the back of her skirt. "Dog's allergic to garlic."

"I am?"

"Dog, you know you are."

"I forget." He turned to Baker. "Was there garlic in something we ate?"

Baker laughed. Then Jacky, then Dog and Totty. And the four of them began moving again, taking slow, careful invalid's steps down the sidewalk toward Strange Avenue. As they went, Baker explained about the soup and what was in it and how nobody ever guessed the secret ingredient and once they found out it was garlic, they could not believe how many whole heads been boiled in the broth, then pureed into it.

"Really?" Dog was saying. "You hear that, Totty?"

As Baker told how he made the soup, he was very much aware that he was repeating himself. He had spoken the exact same words earlier in the evening, when the soup was served and they began to eat. At their end of the table, he and Jacky put Leland, Carroll and Totty to the test. What, they asked, was the main ingredient? Carroll said rosemary; Totty said chicken broth. Leland said she was no cook and had no idea; she only knew the taste was wicked, slightly erotic. Jacky turned to Totty and, wanting to include her in the conversation, asked if she agreed with Leland. Totty hemmed and hawed and finally said she wouldn't say *erotic* exactly, but it was certainly an interesting taste.

"Well, no wonder." Dog felt relieved. "I'm sure glad it wasn't stress. I hate stress."

Totty was quiet as they crossed Strange Avenue.

In the short walk to Baker and Mell's house, Baker and Jacky remembered that earlier exchange and paused to consider the complexities of the human heart and wonder why Totty had remained silent on the subject of Dog's allergy until he'd nearly puked up his stomach and soiled himself like a child in the berry bushes.

Five cars were parked in front of Baker and Melanie's house: Totty's five-year-old mint-condition white Eldorado; Jacky's beat-up Cimarron; the two Toyota wagons; and, between them, Toby's Zee. Carroll, Jane Scott and Sissy had gone home.

Dog wondered if Jane Scott had seen him in his shameful state. Tomorrow, he thought, he would call her up, do his song and dance. She'd come around. Jane Scott loved him, he was sure of that. If anybody ever loved him it was Jane Scott.

"Baker." Jacky spoke for the first time since they left Eva Turner. "You ever think about turning off any lights?" The house was lit up like a chicken coop.

"No," he said.

"I didn't think so."

Through the large clear windows of the living room they could see Mell and Leland sitting very close to each other. Leland gestured, Mell nodded. Leland brought her hand to her face, dropped it. A slow stream of cigarette smoke came from her mouth and rose to join the low ceiling of haze which hung in the air above the women's heads.

"How long was I . . . ? What time is it?"

"Midnight or so. Do you want to come in?"

"In these?"

"No thank you, Baker. I need to get Dog to bed." Totty unlocked the passenger door to the Cadillac and held it open. Like a child, like a *woman*, Dog meekly got in. He couldn't even roll down the window to spar with the guys or tell them good night until Totty turned on the key to release the automatic windows. When she did get in and started the car, they all said good night and then she pulled away from the curb and roared off.

Baker and Jacky watched the Cadillac's taillights. "Poor dumb son of a bitch," Baker muttered. "I never thought I'd come to feel sorry for Dog Boyette."

Jacky touched his shoulder. "Don't go soft on him. Tomorrow he'll be appalling and hateful all over again."

"People die from allergic reactions."

"I know."

"She knew about the garlic."

Jacky put his arm around his friend's shoulder. "Hey," he said. "They're married, remember?" The two men turned toward the house.

At the broken-up sidewalk, Baker pulled back. "You watch yourself, bud. With her." He nodded toward the house.

"Me?" Jacky pointed at his own chest. "You're worried about me?"

"Damn right. She's—"

"Hey, pal. Life will unfold. It will unfold."

"Can you slow down? A little?"

"No."

"I didn't think so." The yellow kitten hurled itself between Baker's feet. He stumbled, caught himself. "God damn you." He kicked the kitten behind him with the heel of his sneaker.

Through the windshield of the Eldorado, Dog and Totty saw Toby Standard and Roy Farrish heading down the middle of Strange Avenue where the streetlights were brightest. Even though the night was sticky and warm, Roy was wearing his cape and homburg, Toby his satin jacket. Lady Macbeth rumbled along between them. Toby had the boxer's leash wrapped around his arm.

Totty pressed down on her horn to let them know she was coming by. She loved the sound of a Cadillac horn, like a church-organ chord.

As the car washed past, the boys looked over and, seeing who it was, waved.

Dog and Totty kept their faces straight ahead.

In the headlights, over Roy's shoulder, Totty had seen two tiny red spots, red and menacing. "He's got that rat. If we'd had time . . ."

"What?"

"I'd have gone up and fed him some meat, just to see."

Dog chuckled. "Totty. You're wicked." He rubbed the soft meat in the crook of his elbow. "I hope that needle was clean."

"Dog," Totty said, then wheeled the car to the left, went two blocks, turned left again and, now on the wide clear street, floored the accelerator. "I am not going to say another word about this after tonight, but I am going to ask you to do something for me, and I think I deserve your cooperation. I think I do."

"All right, Totty. What?" Dog liked feeling like a child. He wanted this small, thrilling, hot cotton gin of a woman to take care of him, forever. *Dog and Totty*—when they were in high school, she'd carved that into trees, benches, bathroom stalls, the dark cherry wood of her bedside table—*Forever.* And she drew a heart around their names. And everywhere Dog went he saw those public testaments to her love. And he had thought then, they would be high school sweethearts forever. And still did. He didn't know what she was getting ready to ask for, but whatever it was—except give up Jane Scott, and he couldn't imagine her giving even the slightest indication that she knew—the answer was yes.

"I want you to get a blood test. For . . . well, you know. I'll get one too. After tonight . . . I mean, it makes me sick to think about that boy, just sick. I don't know if he helped cook or what."

Panic was a small bird in Totty's chest, flapping its tiny wings, pecking at her soft silky insides. To calm herself, she took a deep breath. "Anyway. That's all I ask. And I think you owe me."

Dog said he would. Dog loved his wife. His wife saved him from total, head-first failure.

Noting the taillights of a car ahead, where the street narrowed and curved and went by the old cemeteries, Dog's wife reached across the seat and tugged at her husband's shoulder. "Are you okay?"

"Aw, yeah. I guess I'm just so . . ." Dog's lower lip quivered. "So disappointed."

"Dog." She tugged again. "You're my man."

Dog gave in and lay down on the seat with his head in her lap. Totty kept clean. The scent of Safeguard soap clung to her long after she had bathed, and he had to press deep to catch the slightest whiff of her womanly smells. His face buried in his wife's tiny white pinafored lap, Dog had a flash of memory—the moment when Totty entered the white ladies' steam room and Mrs. Loflin turned her back and the two women very carefully and very purposefully did not speak.

Totty pushed Dog's head down deeper in her lap.

Dog let the memory go. Jane Scott was a dirty girl. She had a funky smell. Dirt had its appeal, but not in a wife.

Passing the car, Totty floored the Eldorado and, thrusting her free hand deep into Dog's baggy trousers, sped home.

24

Carroll noted the Cadillac whizzing past. "There they go."

"Who?" Jane Scott was looking the other way, out her window.

"Nobody."

"Did you ever used to go there?"

"The cemetery? No."

"Clyde and I used to roam through the Jewish one. We'd study the Hebrew letters and run our fingers in and out of the grooves and . . . it was a wonder, you know?"

She looked up in time to see Totty's Cadillac disappearing ahead into the dark night. Totty was driving. There was no sign of a passenger. "Maybe Dog puked up his heart and died," she said.

"You should be so lucky." Carroll had been advising her to dump the Dog for months.

"Don't be mean." They passed the Catholic cemetery.

Sometimes she and her brother went to that one too, and then to what they thought of as the regular people's, not knowing what any of that meant, "Jewish," "Catholic" or "regular." It was just how things were.

"One time we were in the regular people's graveyard and—and—wasn't it awful we called it that?"

"A different time, Jane Scott. And what?"

"We uncovered an honest-to-God adultery."

"In the graveyard?" Carroll rounded a curve, swerved to miss a dog.

"The woman was—do you remember Pete Ross?"

"No."

"She was the golf pro's wife. Pete wasn't her real name, but it was her all right. I didn't know the man. But when we came home and told Daddy about Pete, he told us to stay out of the graveyard and never talk about what we saw again."

"What did they do?"

"Drove up in two cars. He went and sat in hers, they smoked cigarettes, sat there and when it was over they hugged. The man came over and told us we shouldn't play in the cemetery. We ran home. It was exciting, back then."

"Are you okay?"

Jane Scott was too far gone to lie. "No. I am definitely not okay." She felt like she might be melting, her bones disintegrating into granules of white which if heated, stirred and tended would turn to syrup.

"When we get to your house I'll make some coffee."

The car filled up with Jane Scott's thoughts. "Carroll?"

"Whatever it is, be sure you want to ask."

"What's to lose?"

"I don't know. I'm just saying."

"Are you that boy's father?"

Carroll took the last curve before Beall Park, then slowed down. As a philosophy, he did not believe in telling people more than they wanted to hear, the way Toby did. Confession was good for the soul only of the confessor. In New York and then Los Angeles, he and the boy had had long discussions on privacy, social responsibility and the movement in the homosexual world called "outing." They had not reached any point of real agreement, but only argued points pro and con, Carroll standing firm on an individual's right to have—and keep—secrets.

"Leland thinks I am."

"Do you?"

He didn't answer right away. She waited.

"It'll do."

"You don't really, do you?"

"Not much."

"He looks so much like her."

"It's funny. Because of all of this, I've taken a special interest in what people look like and who resembles whom, and of course there are genetic family traits that seem stamped on. Yours, for instance. Nobody would ever take you for anything but a Laws. Other people . . . it's hard to tell. In Toby's case, I stopped looking a long time ago. What's the use? I've claimed him." He clicked on his left-turn blinker and wheeled the Lincoln into Beall Park.

"How do you mean 'claim'?"

"He doesn't know this, okay?" She nodded.

"I want him for my son. I'll act as his father in whatever way he wants me to—if he does—and however it seems appropriate. I couldn't care less who else he tells, or what he tells them, or doesn't. He has enough on his plate already. As you know, unlike Toby I'm not one for making announcements. But if something happened to Leland, then—"

"What do you mean, 'something happened'?"

"Nothing specific. Just if."

"Really? Because I keep wondering why she came home right *now*."

"Really. A general just *if*."

Without fully believing him, Jane Scott let it go. "You've been seeing him all these years?"

"For a long time I didn't want to; then I did. Then I didn't. Now I do."

"And *if*, you were saying?"

"Leland . . . well, died? He's old enough not to need a guardian."

"He seems such a child. Roy seems more grown-up in some ways."

"Well, there are reasons." Carroll turned into the long pea-gravel drive leading to the House of Laws.

"That's why you always used to go to New York and now L.A."

"You know it's not the only reason."

"No."

"But it is one. Yes." In the center of the circular drive, Carroll parked at the front steps. When he cut his headlights, black night wrapped around the car. "Don't you have a porch light, Jane Scott?"

"Out."

Carroll opened his door. "Don't you have any bulbs?"

"I don't know."

In Beall Creek, bullfrogs crooned a courting tune, lusty and low.

"You should get a dog."

"We had one."

"Adele was a hundred and three."

"I know. But."

"You don't want to get another one. You keep thinking you'll leave."

"And if I do—"

"You won't want to have to part with a dog."

"No." Jane Scott got out of the car, trudged through the gravel. At the front door, she reached inside and switched on the hall light. "Are you coming in?"

"God."

"What?"

Carroll stood beside his car. "Those frogs."

"What about them?"

"They go on and on."

"You've heard the frogs before. Now, are you coming in or what?"

"I promised you coffee."

"Well, then?"

He came up the steps and walked past her into the house.

"I warn you, the place is a wreck. I made jelly."

"I'm sure I've seen worse."

Behind him, she closed the front door. "Maybe."

"On the other hand . . ."

"Maybe not. You do the coffee—I'm switching to near nothing. Would you like to share a joint?"

"Do you think that's a good idea?"

"Meaning?"

"Added to whatever else you've had today."

"I think it's an excellent idea." She wheeled and went out.

Carroll looked around the kitchen. On every surface, ashtrays overflowed with cigarette butts and ashes. A bowl in the sink was crusted up with morning cereal and fruit. A pot of jelly was sitting on the stove, burned around the edges. "Jesus, Jane Scott," Carroll muttered. He discovered a coffee pot in the sink, a glass Chemex, the wooden collar of which had long since been burned up and discarded. Carroll lifted a teakettle from the stove.

He and Leland had not been in love. They had slept together exactly twice, when Leland came home for Annie's funeral and afterward had stayed a week or two, to see to her mother. By then Dolly Standard's brain was floating in a lifetime of bourbon, like a pickle preserved in brine. Leland was running out of money and had stayed with Carroll, who was still in the big house then. There was plenty of room, and they didn't have to cross paths. But a couple of bourbony, sleepless nights they had found consolation in each other. Then Leland went back to New York, and Carroll withdrew from the world again, trying to harden his heart against more hurt and disappointment.

Leland hadn't told Carroll about the baby until after he was born. She would never, she vowed, ask him for anything, or put any strings on him, but she thought he should know.

Carroll filled the kettle with water and put it on to boil. He was never sure the baby was his. Those years, cynicism and doubt suited his new resolve. Sealed off, he did not call or write, and neither did Leland. When Dolly died, she came home alone. No mention of the baby. No pictures. In time he grew curious. On a trip to New York he called and asked if he could come by, climbed the five flights to Leland's floor-through and presented the baby with a stuffed gorilla too big for him to hold on to. Looking hard, all he saw was a miniature, enchanting Leland.

"Penny." Jane Scott had on knit shorts and a tank top. The shorts were not good on her, her thighs soft, her behind going saggy. Tossing her long hair over one shoulder, she cupped her hand around a tightly rolled joint, lit it and took a deep drag, sucking the smoke into her lungs and holding it.

Carroll felt bad for her. Her looks were starting to go and she knew it. When the teakettle sang, he turned off the fire. There were no coffee filters. Jane Scott expertly folded a length of paper towel, pressed it down into the point of the Chemex, told him to pour slowly, then picked up her boombox and took it to the sunroom to wait for him.

There had been another phone message from Lucien and Tony, saying they hadn't heard in too long and thought something was wrong and would keep calling until they got her. She flipped open the cassette slot, took out the Percy Sledge she had been listening to earlier, replaced it with *Chet Baker Sings*. "Carroll?"

"One minute. I'm—"

"Do you think I should go back to San Francisco?"

He was quiet.

"Did you hear me?"

"Don't you ever wash any cups?"

"Not until I have to."

"Jesus, you have a dishwasher."

She hadn't rewound the tape, so it came on in the middle of "My Funny Valentine." Jane Scott sank into a pillowed wrought-iron chair. She did love to hear Chet Baker sing. She took another hit of grass and closed her eyes. "I don't like the sound of a dishwasher." She said it low, to herself, starting to relax now, to feel herself coming back together again.

Tonight had scared her. People who had not seen the trails and colors, been on the moon or traveled with stars could not understand how fast it happened. How you could be in the world one instant, gone the next.

"It's murky."

She opened her eyes. She thought he meant the music.

He handed her a cup. "The paper towel collapsed."

"I don't mind." Jane Scott put out the joint and tasted the coffee. "Thanks. It's fine, but I don't want to wake up."

Chet Baker's voice melted into the horn, which became the voice again, wobbly and muted, a ghost voice.

Carroll lowered the volume and sat in the chair beside her. "So what is this about San Francisco?"

"I was thinking about going back."

"To stay?"

"I don't know. Start my third life."

"Third?"

"I read somewhere . . . we all get three."

Carroll sipped his coffee and grimaced. "God, that's awful." He had turned down the music so low they could barely hear the end of the song, but Jane Scott knew it perfectly, note for note. "I guess it's not too late to start another one."

"We're young and strong."

Mostly Jane Scott forgot about age. She was too busy to think about things she couldn't do anything about, anyway most days she felt pretty young. Tonight, for a moment, she pulled back from the table and the conversation and saw how silly they all looked, still squabbling over who had whose boyfriend and who was never going to speak to somebody else ever again. And just like that, she felt old and silly. She had stopped bleeding last year, read the books, went on H-10 to balance her hormones. Now she thought maybe it was all a mistake, trying to hold on. Why not just get old and ugly?

"What I think is, you're losing it. You need to get out of here. I don't know about moving, but at least for a while. This house is grim, Eva Turner is grim. Nothing is going to change with Samme. Whether you move or not, you ought to sell the house."

"To whom, would you suggest? Nobody's buying anything in this town, which you know."

"You haven't tried."

"No."

"Give it a go. If you get stuck, I'll buy it."

"No, thanks, Carroll. Really."

"Why not?"

"I wouldn't dream of—"

"Do you think I'd do it as some great sacrifice?"

"Yes." She paused. "No."

He laughed. "Well, then."

The tabletop in front of them had so much stuff on it you couldn't see the wood. Stacks of material for dolls and pot holders next to stacks of bills and papers and government forms, next to magazines Jane Scott combed for ideas. On the other side of the table sat two sewing machines. On one wall, she had hung costumes from San Francisco: tie-dyed silks, a feather boa, a southern-belle straw hat, its ribbons trailing leaves and flowers and red plastic hearts. On the other wall she had nailed up her white satin debutante dress, onto which she and Baker had pinned colored pictures of naked people.

"Close up the house and go. You could probably find somebody to rent it. Or stay in it."

"Like Jet and Roxie."

"Who?"

"Jet Taliaferro. You know, Paula. Did you know she was gay?" The Taliaferros were an old Eunola family.

"Since when?"

"Since Roxie Sidwell got to be her girlfriend."

"Roxie's black."

"Yes."

"It could be a fling."

"Jet says it's the turning point in her life. At forty-seven she's figured out she's been a lesbian her whole life and never knew it. Now she's happy."

"Good for her."

"You sound dubious."

"You know Paula. I think it's a great way to hear new gossip, get in on different parties. Have a group."

"She says it's like born-agains. She's seen the light."

"Good for her. Although—"

"You wouldn't recommend it."

Carroll said nothing.

Jane Scott sipped her coffee. "I do like Roxie."

Carroll gestured, waving at the sun porch. "This . . . *mess* is why you should leave. You're too angry, and now you're getting grim. Like this house. Dog Boyette is your revenge against your best self. . . ." He thought about that. "Or some such—I don't know."

"Hey. Sigmund."

"So there's my answer. Yes. You should go to San Francisco."

He took one last swallow of coffee. "And as the cat said after making love to the skunk—"

"You've enjoyed about all of this you can stand."

"It's mud." He stood, took her hands, pulled her to him. Against his chest he felt her body go soft and vulnerable.

She spoke into his neck. "You want to stay over?"

He pulled away.

"I don't mean . . . I mean, just stay over? Sleep in Gus's lair?"

"No thanks."

"You have somebody coming."

"Later." He checked his watch. "A lot later."

"So go."

At the front door she kissed her fingers and put them to his cheek. The hum of the frogs' song filled the night. Then he cranked up the Lincoln, waved and drove off.

Jane Scott stood at the door, looking out into the darkness. They were all too old for all of this. By now they were supposed to be beyond some of this; when her parents were this age, they . . .

They what? What did she know about what went on with Samme and Jake when they were in their fifties?

In the sunroom, she turned the music back up. Chet Baker was doing "I Get Along Without You Very Well."

Jane Scott flopped into a chair. She couldn't get Pete Ross off her mind. So pathetic—the graveyard, cars, a little small talk, a couple of cigarettes, one hug and it's back home to the golf pro.

"Tooky," Jane Scott said aloud, remembering the golf pro's name. She fooled with her hair. "Or was it Pooky?"

She was losing it again, going woozy and soft, and wondered if she had the energy to dial 415.

25

Singing along with *La Bohème,* Sissy took the idiotic zigzag of Main Street fast, letting her hair fly.

After saying her goodbyes and driving to a dark corner where she could not be seen, Sissy had stopped to put the top down. Instead of taking Strange Avenue out to the highway, she turned toward downtown.

Leontyne Price was singing Mimi's "Addio." *Addio, senza rancor.* Sissy had learned the aria phonetically, sitting with a CD and the Italian lyrics. The next song was Musetta's Waltz, which she used to know as "One Night of Love," maybe from an MGM musical, she wasn't sure which one. As a girl she loved musicals and the stars with the pinched waists: Kathryn Grayson, Jane Powell, June Allyson. Now she listened to Leontyne Price.

Downtown was dead enough during the day; after midnight on Friday it had gone cold and stiff. Sissy took the curves fast, hogging the street, Puccini bouncing against the dark, painted-over show windows, coming back to her like crickets screaming in the trees. At Robertshaw, a block before the war memorial, she ignored the blinking red light and wheeled hard to the right. She had to go through some scary black areas of town before she came to the gravel road that ran up along the levee. She knew it was dicey at this time of night, to be alone and blond and very white with the top down, but she'd done it before. Nobody bothered her, not ever.

At one corner a man, obviously drunk, called out, "Hey, sweetie! Now *that's* music." Sissy waved and went on. Her digital clock said 1:15. Her computerized fuel gauge told her she could go forty-four miles before she ran out of gas. She should have filled up before going to Baker and Mell's; the last question Hank asked before she left was, did she have gas? When she said yes in her what-do-you-take-me-for? tone, he ignored it. Sissy couldn't exactly say why she didn't want Hank to do things for her, she just didn't. Still, he never let up. His last words were "Now you're *sure* you have gas?"

At a stop sign, Sissy slowed down. The turn toward the levee was pretty much right-angle. When she hit the gravel road, a ball of dust rolled above her head, then settled back down inside the car. Sissy pinched the end of her nose and turned left toward the levee. There were three songs from *La Bohème,* then some other Puccini. When Leontyne finished up Musetta's Waltz, Sissy pushed Rewind. There was no way to get too much of *La Bohème.*

The dinner party had ended badly. After Dog rushed out with Baker and Totty hard on his heels, the rest of them had sat there eating the fabulous dessert and saying precisely nothing until Baker roared back in. Dog, he announced, had fainted in the berry bushes and needed help. Jacky Nelms went out to see what he could do. The others sat there eating.

Jane Scott looked on the verge of falling apart. Leland's son had brightened considerably. Cheered by Totty's departure, he started in on his marrons glacés. Leland and Carroll chummed it up at the end of the table. Nobody thought anything serious was wrong with Dog at first. Except maybe Mell. Who just sat there, Miss Gloompot. Of course she had reason, but still . . . Finally, Sissy said she thought she'd better go on home, and for a minute or two there wished she hadn't made Hank stay back. It might have been better to have had somebody with her at the end of the evening. She'd grown tired of Dog even before he got sick. Dog could be amusing, but he didn't know when to lay off.

The tape clicked back to the beginning—*Sì mi chiamano Mimì,* Mimì telling how it is to be always alone, making lilies and roses. Lonely, alone.

At the base of the levee Sissy pressed the gas pedal to the floor, and the Mustang shifted to a lower gear. With the top down, climbing the road to the top of the levee, Sissy had the glorious feeling of being on the kind of carnival ride that made you think you were on the verge of tilting over and falling out, but you never did. Hank didn't approve of her little car. He didn't like cars so small he had to put them on instead of get in. This was one of his standard lines; when he said it in front of his farmer friends they snorted and slapped their legs. Sissy didn't care. She loved her red Mustang. It was like an Italian leather shoe, the fit of it getting better as time went on.

At the crest of the levee, she turned north. She would drive along it as far as the Indian Mounds, then turn back east to the highway that ran past her house. Going this way took longer, but Sissy loved it, the dark night air whipping her hair in peaks like meringue. Down the levee on her left was the lake—far away but out there—and on her right, more flat endless cotton fields. The river had been rerouted and straightened out a long time ago, after the 1927 flood, when downtown Eunola was all but destroyed. Except for barges and towboats, the river did not have much effect on Eunola anymore. People lived on the lake, fished in it, sailed, played. Barges came and went. The towboat business was belly-up, just like cotton and soybeans.

The "Addio" came back on. Pressing the accelerator, Sissy began to sing again.

What a silly group they all could be, still trying to figure out how to live in the world and what they wanted to be when they grew up. Not a nine-to-five job in the bunch; not one pension plan, and all of them over fifty. They should be where they were going by now, not still poking along, starry-eyed and with their fingers up their whatever. The sense of things she got from her own parents was, there was a time when your life became calm and leveled out and you knew. Knew what? Nobody ever asked, or wondered that far. And come to think of it, who wanted to be like her parents?

Sissy settled her haunches on the gray leather interior, lifting one buttock, letting it spread, lifting the other. She pressed her left knee against the car door. She was so proud of herself! She had gotten one of the omnivores right. She had won the game. Who never won Smartest or Most Likely To. She couldn't wait to tell Hank.

After the final notes of the "Addio," this time Sissy let the tape run. Without slowing down, she slipped off her left green shoe and then her driving one.

Maybe they thought she was kidding when she said that about a hog eating anything, including your finger. She wasn't. One almost took off the tip of her pinkie once. She had been reaching inside the pen for a doll she'd dropped; her mother was running toward her, yelling for her to stop, get away, but she wanted that doll. She knew the hog would gobble it up, and even though it was a silly little rubber thing, it was hers and she liked it.

The hog had eyes only for the doll until he saw Sissy's white little hand. She wouldn't have thought a big hunkering thing like that could move so fast. She felt the drip of his snout, the heat of his ugly breath. Sissy's mother got to her just in time, picked her up, held her close. The hog had only nipped the tip of her finger—it hadn't even hurt—but Sissy screamed so hard her daddy said he heard her out in the fields and came to see what was wrong. It wasn't the pain; it was the threat, the unknown. Like the grizzlies in that book: they weren't supposed to attack, but they did. Sissy had looked into the hog's tiny eyes, had seen the potential menace. She shivered.

Tosca was up. Sad, wounded Tosca. Sissy didn't know which role was her favorite, Mimì or Tosca. She lifted her voice, humming along.

The gravel road was narrow, with barely room for two cars to pass. People had been saying for years they ought to widen the road; then road engineers said it would take hundreds of thousands of dollars, so people dropped the idea. If a car came, she'd pull over to the shoulder and stop, hope it was somebody friendly, then go on. This time of night, she almost never had to. People didn't come up here anymore, not even teenagers. She didn't know what teenagers did for fun or where they went.

The elastic at the waist of her pantyhose felt tight. She should not have eaten the second dessert, but she hadn't exaggerated when she said it was the best thing she had ever put in her mouth, and didn't it make sense to go for what was there when you knew it might never show up again? With her left hand, she pushed the elastic band down until it was beneath her belly. Rounding her hand, she cupped her fat. Fat could be a comfort. With three fingers she punched the soft flesh in, let it go, punched it in, grabbed a wad of it in her fist.

It was Roy who suggested they take Dog to Eva Turner. What an idea! Sissy thought they should put his feet up, keep him warm and wait him out; but Baker said they had to get help, Dog was out cold and still puking—probably doing the other as well. Roy went first to make the contact; then Baker and Jacky got Dog over there, Sissy didn't know how. The rest of them stayed at the table until Dog was good and gone; then Sissy, Jane Scott and Carroll said their politest goodbyes and left. She let her belly go. She had done this before, once at sixty-five mph on the interstate to Vicksburg. It was exciting. You had to concentrate on two things at once. Lifting her pelvis, she let one finger slide inside.

She didn't care if she ever had sex with a man again, didn't want to share herself anymore or give away her secrets. Secrets were about the best thing she had, and she wasn't about to toss them out like so much confetti at New Year's. She also did not want to be in love, whatever that was. What she wanted was to be recognized. To be heard. If she could become

Manon, pretending to remember a lost time of love and peace, what need would she have of the real thing?

She went through a sudden patch of fog. Moved her finger, fast, then slow, then pulled it out and did other things.

One fog scrap ended as the love duet from *Madama Butterfly* began, and then there was another.

26

"We are too *old* for this." Baker waved his arms. "God!" He clamped both hands on his bald head, like a prisoner, then dropped them and reached for a cigarette.

"Doing what, Baker?" Mell let cigarette smoke drift through her nostrils.

"These intrigues and this . . ."

"What?"

"I don't know—*mishmash.*"

"Are we going to clean up the dishes tonight?"

"Good God, Leland—what an idea! We never clean up until the next morning."

"It'll be worse in the morning."

"I don't care." Baker waved the thought away. "Where are the boys?"

"Walking Lady M. and the rat."

"The rat was a star tonight."

"Not our rat exactly." Baker corrected Leland. "Rats."

"Well, let's be sure and be picky, Baker."

"Roy's a sweetheart. Who'd have thought it? Omnivores!"

"God." Mell felt depleted and wonderfully calm. The crisis with Dog had seemed an appropriate end to the party, better than somebody storming off and vowing never to speak to any of them again. Watching Baker handle the situation, Mell had felt astonishingly proud, and very content. She turned to Leland. "Do you think Toby's okay?"

Leland frowned. "I know he's okay. I worry for him all the time, of course. But he's fine. I just hope you don't think he . . ."

"What?" Sitting slightly behind Leland in a straight-back occasional chair, Jacky leaned forward and took her hand. "Spoiled the party? Got too serious? Told people more than they wanted to know?"

"It's not done down here, is it?"

Baker wanted to approve of Toby's little speech more than he actually did. "It should be."

"Totty's a grown-up. She asked for more than she got." When Jacky took his hand away, Leland's moved reflexively after it.

"I suppose." She let her hand fall into her lap.

"Why didn't you tell me about Jane Scott and Dog?" Mell sat tall in her chair.

Baker shrugged. "She asked me not to."

"And so you didn't."

"She's a friend."

"I'm your wife."

Baker wagged a finger at Leland and Jacky. "You two."

"Yes?" They answered together, looking up at Baker, who stood nervously in front of the fireplace, shifting his weight, one foot to the other.

"If you're going to go, then do it while the boys are out. I'll tell them you went for a drive."

Jacky reached for Leland's hand again, and for the first time since he and Baker got back from Eva Turner, she looked at him full in the eyes. She turned her hand over, offering him the open softness of her palm.

"Shall we?" He smiled at her, letting her know that if she

wanted to hold off because of Toby or for any other reason, he understood.

She answered by slipping her feet into her shoes and standing.

"Do you need a purse?"

"What for?"

"I don't know. Most women don't go anywhere without their purse."

"Are we going to make a purchase?"

"I don't think so."

"Do business?"

Jacky shook his head in mock exasperation. "Baker, would you get this upstart some house keys?"

"'Upstart'?"

Baker came up with a set and walked them out to the porch. Jacky put his hand at Leland's waist, and she felt her spine warm to the tips of her hair. When she turned to say something to Mell and Baker about what time she would be back, Baker waved her on.

As soon as the door closed behind them, Leland moved into Jacky Nelms, found his mouth.

When they pulled apart, he touched her lip. "Let's go. I warn you, my car's a junk heap."

"I don't care. Where are we going?"

"My place?"

"Yes."

"It's—"

"I don't care."

"—tiny."

"I don't care."

His car was a black, beat-up diesel Cimarron. "Isn't this a Cadillac?"

"Their attempt at an economy car. It's a piece of nothing."

"But a Cadillac."

He opened the door for her; she got in. The car smelled of oil and damp, old books. At his door, Jacky knocked at the window, gesturing at her. She opened the door.

"The handle's broken." He slid beneath the wheel and pumped the gas pedal a number of times before turning the key. The car didn't start and then it did. Black smoke belched out the exhaust pipe. "Junk heap. Like I said."

"You're right." She placed her small, daring hand on his thigh.

He held it there. His hand was barely bigger than hers, and one finger was crooked at the knuckle, as if it had been broken more than once. Backing up, he turned his head to look through the rear window. "What?" Leland was staring.

"I don't know. Just you."

"What about me?"

"Nothing. Just . . . nothing."

He closed her hand inside his fist. "Go with it, Leland, go with it."

"There's stuff I need to—"

"In time."

"Like . . . ?"

"When we get to my house."

"All right. But then."

"Yes. All right. All the delicately dangerous and throbbingly unspeakable subjects."

Leland's fingers uncurled. "They are."

"Fine," he said, releasing her hand and shifting the car into drive.

27

When Mell came to bed, Baker had the TV on, his eyes glued to the set.

"What's on Showtime?"

With the remote he flipped channels. "Nothing. I'm scanning." He didn't look up. "What a night."

"Can we talk about tonight tomorrow?" She closed the bedroom door. "I'm too tired to think, much less speak."

She was wearing her silk kimono, beneath which Baker could see the cup of one breast. With his thumb he pushed a button. The television picture narrowed to a speck, then went dark.

"Leave it on." She turned off the bedside lamp.

Baker pushed the red button again and the picture came on. He dampened the sound until it disappeared.

Mell slid into bed beside him, lay on her back, arms by her side. "Did Roy get the rat box?"

"He did."

"Good."

When he reached for her, she drew away.

"I've taken a sleeping pill." She crossed her hands at her middle, spoke with her eyes closed.

He did not touch her. Her dark hair lay like a mannequin's wig beside her face. She had brushed it, readied herself, left on her makeup. In repose Mell looked amazingly like Lucy.

"Wait until I drift off?"

He told her he would, and in the light of the flickering television screen, he watched his wife lie submissive and still. Sexpot Mell. Love of his life. He thought of her softness, belly and thighs and white white flesh.

He pulled back her kimono. Her breasts were large, with pale pink nipples. A rippling swirl of black hair ran from her navel to her pubic bone. She stirred. Not yet.

Of course he had seen the exchange between Mell and Toby and, knowing his wife, understood that the boy's age and declared inaccessibility made him that much more appealing to her. Not that Mell wanted Tobias Standard; not really. What she wanted was this.

She lightly grazed his hipbone with the back of her hand.

Baker had no complaints. Desire played by its own rules. He would take what he could get.

Her breath deepened.

Mell felt herself going thread by thread into a delicious drugged blackness, where imagination would break down the walls of her carefully defined daytime self and allow her truest feelings to unfold their wings and, under the cover of night, fly and fly.

28

"We shouldn't go too far."

"Is it dangerous?"

Roy's eyebrows came down. "Most of the kids in my school are black, you know."

Beneath the shivering leaves of a cottonwood tree, Lady Macbeth squatted. From inside Roy's shirt collar, Freddy Krueger poked his head out and sniffed the night air.

"They live around here?"

"I just meant, I know how some of them think. And they're mad." He shrugged. "I don't blame them, but what can you do?"

"Any of them friendly to you?"

"At school?"

"Whatever."

"They're not *un*friendly."

"But they're not pals."

"No."

"Any friendships at all between black kids and whites?"

"No."

"None?"

Roy shook his head.

"That's depressing."

"What can you do?"

"The riots? She asked earlier? I was on Pico in my car. This group of guys in ripped T-shirts stopped me. I sat there, they came over, and the thing is, it didn't matter what I'd done or who I was. I wasn't them, that was all that mattered, and so I was the enemy. For some reason they let me pass, I don't know why. When I got home I thought, That's the way they feel all the time. But at the time? When they were stopping me, and had baseball bats and probably guns? I had no sympathy— none. I was mad. And scared. Really scared."

Lady M. finished up her squat and rejoined them, and they walked the railroad tracks awhile. Clouds covered the moon. The night was black, the air still and close.

"We should head back," Roy said when they got to Main. Then he stopped. "My best friend is gay."

Toby started. "Is he your age?"

"Fourteen. Most of my friends are older, but he's fourteen."

"And he knows he's gay?"

Roy shrugged. "He says he is. I believe him."

"The world does change. At fourteen, I was a baby."

"People think I am, because of this." He flipped his skirt hem. "But I'm not. People are stupid, thinking if a guy wears a kilt, it means—"

"He's queer."

"I wear it because I wear it. But I wouldn't care if I *was* gay."

"No?"

"I'm just not."

"It's easier not to be."

"I know."

They turned down a dark block. Something moved in the trees—a scrambling sound, some night creature taking cover. Looking up, Lady Macbeth growled and the hair along the ridge of her spine lifted in a stiff bristle. Freddy Krueger hunkered down.

Toby felt his heart go cold. "Should we worry?"

"Keep going. Just keep going."

They took steady, unhurrying steps. At the corner, there was a streetlight. Lady Macbeth's bristle flattened.

"Probably a bat. Or a cat."

Toby blew out his breath. "Life is dangerous," he said.

"Everywhere, I guess."

At home, they noted which cars were gone. The house was still lit up like a Halloween pumpkin. Inside, Roy went around turning off lights. "I have a Watchman," he said. "If you want, I could bring it down, we can watch a Letterman rerun."

"Sure," Toby said. "That's a good idea. But where will you sleep?"

"Upstairs at the end of the hall, in a double sleeping bag." When Toby started to protest, Roy held up his hand. "I like it. Lady Macbeth gets in with me. It's fun."

Toby did not go up to check on his mother. He hoped she was asleep, and not off somewhere with Jacky Nelms.

Roy went out to the back porch and came back with Freddy Krueger's box. "All right, little guy. In you go." Safe in his Plexiglas nest once again, the rat jumped on his dancing machine and went to town.

Roy glanced up. "You want anything to drink—juice or anything?"

"No thanks," Toby said, then waited while Roy went and got the Watchman and brought it into the living room. "My mother may be sick," he said. "She has this . . . thing." He put his hand on his chest.

Roy plugged the set in, frowning. "Is she going to die?"

Toby's head snapped back. "Why did you ask that?"

"My friend's mother died when he was six. They still give him drugs. Prozac. They say he's depressed."

"Is he?"

"I don't think so. He just—"

"Needs his mother."

"I didn't mean to say that."

"It's okay. You didn't."

"Dying's all that matters." Roy pulled up the antennae. "I had a sister."

"I know about her."

"My parents never got over it when my sister died."

Toby was quiet.

"I hate it when they give kids drugs. Five of my friends are on Prozac."

"She may not even be sick, actually. But she's having a biopsy next week."

"Is that why she came here?"

"One reason. I don't"—Toby hesitated—"know them all."

Roy switched on the set. "This is probably stupid."

"What?"

"If you need a place—you know, anytime?—we have the extra bedroom."

"Thanks."

Gallagher came on, Letterman's special guest.

"You like this guy?"

"I used to."

"Me too."

The rat went around, dinging his bell.

"He used to be funny, but I don't know."

"Me either."

29

Hank Westerfield sat in the living room in the dark. Sissy hated it when she got home and he was on the front porch looking for her. She said it made her feel like a dog, the same as when Stanley went off and Hank stood outside whistling and whooping and calling him up. She didn't want to think he didn't have anything else to do except wait for her. Sometimes he hid behind a curtain in the dark. He tried not to rile Sissy if he could help it.

One forty-five. They probably didn't eat until after ten. Take two hours to eat; then the women would get into it, back to high school days and all. Take another hour. It wasn't late yet. At two he would start to worry.

He went to the bedroom, where he would lie in the silent black dark and wait for the sound of her Mustang, the ribbon of double lights across the ceiling of their bedroom when she turned in.

30

"I need a drink."

"Dog, I don't think you—"

"Shut up, Totty. I said I need a drink." He stuck his glass in the icemaker cubbyhole in the refrigerator door and chipped ice sprayed out. "I actually feel hungry too, believe it or not. But . . ." He turned up the bourbon bottle, poured a glassful.

He looked around. Totty wasn't there. Dog lifted the kitchen receiver, punched a set of numbers, let the phone ring once, twice, then thought better of the idea and replaced the receiver.

"Dog?"

"Now what?"

Totty stood in the kitchen door, flatfooted as a country girl. "Why don't you take off those silly-assed pants and come in here with me?"

She wasn't wearing a thing except that see-through pinafore, and no body stocking underneath. Dog set down his glass.

In the living room, Totty fluffed up her skirts and went straight down on her knees. Sitting on her heels, she beckoned Dog over. When he got to her, she unbuttoned his pants and unzipped them and pulled them down. Dog slipped out of his shoes, lifted his feet out of the pants. Totty cupped his buttocks with her hands and took him between her lips until he was stiff—as close to stiff as he got these days. Not the boner he used to have but, well, it worked.

Once he was hard, Totty lay down on her back. Dog knelt over her, one knee on either side of her head. He rubbed his cock against her neck and then her cheek and then the soft burr of her hair.

Totty put her finger in her mouth. He pulled it out. And then he fucked her mouth, as far down her throat as he could go, feeling the soft flaps of skin back there, taking him in. She curled her tongue, opened her throat.

Totty was slightly beginning to know who she was again, but not all the way. When he jammed himself so far down that she gagged, he pulled out. Totty reached for the container of clear jelly on the table, squeezed some out in her palm and applied it to his cock, rubbing it up and down.

Dog sat back on his heels. She kept going. He reached for her, pulled her lips apart, caressed her soft silky opening, groaned. "Totty, I . . ." He wanted her there, in the heart of her womanness, where the real Totty was. Totty said no. She flipped over, pulled her white ruffled pinafore to her waist, used her hands to open up for him. Dog lay facedown with his chest against her spine, and held her hard, pinning her down so she couldn't move or do anything except be there for him.

"Where do you want it?"

She spread her cheeks with her hands. When he tried to go into the other place, she banged against him with her behind.

"All right." He moved the head of his cock against her rectum, to spread some of the jelly there, and then pushed in. No woman had ever made Dog feel like a man the way Totty did. Her flanks were small and poignant, slight as a child's. He hammered at her.

"More," Totty whispered. "More." She had never in her life had that feeling magazines wrote about, which women described as just short of heaven on earth; but she did sometimes get to a place of recognition and light which felt like home— her destination. She was on her way now. Soon she would know who she was, her curled self, down there where nobody, not even she herself, could find it.

She opened up instead of tightening. He pressed so far into her she thought something might tear, and when he did that, she knew what it was again to be her self, to be Totty, the real Totty. It both hurt and did not. If his blood test showed anything, she would have it too, the big disease. They would be Dog and Totty Forever.

His pubic bone pressing hard against his wife's behind, Dog cried out. For a moment the events of the night and his life disappeared and he felt like a king again. A man in charge. A man on the football field, spying daylight, going for it, making the score, hearing the cheers. He jabbed at her one last time.

Totty whimpered. She was the girl she knew she had to be.

31

Coming through the second patch of fog off the lake, Sissy was touching herself and didn't see the rabbit until it was too late. And when she did, the eyes held her, gleaming in the black night like toy headlights. Blinded, the animal stood as if paralyzed in the middle of the road, facing the oncoming car as if a silver bumper was what it had come out to find.

Sissy swerved—I should not have, she thought as soon as she did it, tried to miss it—and her front tires went to the left, hit the soft gravel of the shoulder, then the shoulder itself. She was going too fast, and the wheel jerked in her hand when she stomped on the brakes. The Mustang hit the rabbit and fishtailed to the field side of the levee, then the lake side, and flew over the edge of the narrow gravel road.

She had not buckled her seat belt, thinking that buckling a seat belt didn't make much sense in a convertible; it kept you inside so the car could come down on top of you. Better to fly through the windshield, and fly she did. The car flipped and Sissy went, out into the dark night, and the Mustang kept going past her. In the corner of her eye she saw it as she went through the air, was amazed how much *time* there was before she hit, time enough to see her small red car turn over twice and come to rest upside down at the bottom of the levee.

As she flew, a wild thought ran through Sissy's mind. Eleven for dinner. *Odd one out. Somebody had to die.* And she heard Hank's wry sarcastic voice, one of his favorite, self-deprecating lines: "A dirty job, but somebody has to do it." And then she saw the eyes once again, not the silly rabbit but the hog, his dull victorious stare. She did not feel herself touch the ground, hit, snap, come to rest. There was only the flight, the vision of her car, the wild thought, the hog and nothing.

Sissy lay curled in a ball in her bright caftan, hands crossed at the wrists. The grass beneath her was the same emerald green as her dress. During the night, dew would form and her body would dampen. The engine would run until the forty-four miles of gas had been used up, Sissy having hit the gearshift with her knee, knocking it into neutral.

The battery was new and strong—Hank Westerfield took good care of his wife's car—so the tape ran on. When Leontyne Price finished Lauretta's aria, the one from *Turandot* came on. Then nothing. The end of side two. The tape ran to the end, clicked into automatic reverse after a time, switched back to side one again, Mimì in the dark with Rodolfo, telling of her lonely life with her flowers and embroidery.

Sissy and the rabbit were still.

32

"Would you like some wine?"

"You don't drink."

"No, but you do."

He switched on the light. He lived in a garage made into a dark two-room apartment with a tiny kitchen, a small bathroom. Except for windows over the kitchen sink, the walls had been shelved over. "My hideaway," he said with a little smile.

Books ran from floor to ceiling. There was very little furniture, just a double bed covered with a light spread, a large oak library table with two chairs, a leather chair with an ottoman and a reading light. The room had been divided in two with a section of bookshelves, which flanked one side of the bed.

"Spare." Leland felt slightly sick with desire. "I like it."

"Can I get you a glass of wine?"

"I thought I'd had enough."

"Then Dog sobered you up."

"Fast."

"I'll get a glass."

She took off her shoes and went to his bed and, propping up two pillows, leaned against them and waited. She heard the soft pop of a wine cork from the kitchen, a glass being set down. On the shelves running alongside the length of the bed were reference books, the four-volume edition of the OED, an *American Heritage Dictionary*, a set of encyclopedias, books on plant life, animal life, a thesaurus. There were stacks of books and magazines on the bedside tables, a small clock radio, an address and appointment book.

"I only have red, but it should be good."

"Red is fine. From Shamoon's?"

He came back in with a wineglass. "Where else?"

"Do you remember Twyla Rose? Little Twyla Rose?"

He frowned. "I don't think so."

"It's odd, having been gone so long, hearing names I thought I'd forgotten. I might never have thought of Twyla Rose again." He handed her the glass. "Thank you."

He sat in the leather chair beside the bed.

"Was she a Shamoon?"

"Mmm. Twyla Rose Shamoon. She was the first kid I knew who died. We were in the fifth grade. She got leukemia, went down to nothing, then no more Twyla Rose—she was gone. The next year Buddy Neighbors got it."

"Leukemia?"

She took a drink of wine. "This is wonderful. He was my first boyfriend, handsome and athletic. Pretty much of a bully, as I recall. The boys were all afraid of him. It was such a shock. Back then we didn't think it would happen to the strong ones. His mother was a nurse. I don't know if his father was alive or dead; I only remember the mother—thin and drawn in a white uniform. Buddy was her only child. He was gone for a while, for treatment. We knew he was dying. Then he came back. There was a party. He was white and thin with a big, bloaty stomach. We played spin the bottle. I got Buddy and had to kiss him. It was scary and I hated it, but didn't say anything." She looked up. The wine was woody and fine, with many layers. "This is really good." She swirled it against her tongue.

"Good."

"What made me think of Twyla Rose Shamoon?"

"Shamoon's is where I got the wine."

She nodded. "Anyway . . ."

"Yes?"

"Have you always lived like this?"

He looked around. "I used to have a house. I have had a couple of houses. Nice ones. Two wives—two daughters by the first, one by the second. I left both times. What my wives didn't get—and they deserved it—I lost."

"How?"

He rubbed his thumb against the tips of his fingers. "Sharp dealing. Gambles. Deals. But mostly—"

"Drink."

"It's good you didn't meet me then."

Leland drew her feet up under her. "I wonder if you'll be glad you met me now."

He folded his hands in his lap. "It's time."

"I know."

"I'm staying over here in this chair until you say whatever it is you've been burning up to tell me since I met you."

She looked down, into her wineglass.

"Not that you have to."

"Yes, well, I do have to."

"All right." He sat apart from her also to slow things down a bit, take stock, check himself, get his breath. He had no fear of what might happen next—he didn't think anything would make him really afraid again—but she did make him nervous. He knew she was special, that this was, that they would not be able simply to take what they could from each other and go on. They would either plunge in more deeply than maybe either of them was ready for or find some way to break apart. If they were going to do that, better to do it quickly. Before things got more complicated. First she had to make her announcement. Announcements. Whatever.

She toyed with her glass. "I'm not exactly clear where to start. I don't want to lose you, but the one vice I never got into was what shrinks call denial, so I have to say it. I don't guess you have a cigarette?"

"The one vice I never got into. Sorry."

"I shouldn't anyway."

"I have enough grass to roll us a nice joint. Would you like that?"

Leland brightened, then reconsidered. "Some other time," she promised. "Tonight—"

"Tonight we'll be clearheaded."

"Yes. Anyway . . ."

"Anyway?" He waited. "Look, is there somebody else?"

She didn't answer.

"Because if there is, that will change things. I like to think I'm not possessive, Leland, but I won't share. I'll get out of your way."

"That means you are possessive."

"I don't know. I just know I can't stand sharing."

"There was somebody, but how did you know?"

"I know. Look at me. I will always know. I've done it too many times myself. Are you finished with him?"

She was quiet.

"Is he finished with you?"

"Yes."

He dropped his head. He didn't particularly like being territorial about women he loved, jealous of the slightest whisper of sexual betrayal. There were only so many changes a person could make. This one was set in stone. "How long has it been?"

"Six months."

"Since you've seen him?"

"Since I talked to him. Since he went back to his wife. I loved him more than he loved me."

"How old is he?"

"Young."

"Go on."

"Thirty-four."

He laughed. She pouted.

"Well," he eventually said. "I can't compete with thirty-four, now can I? So let's get all of this out of the way. What was his name?"

"Simon."

"Simon what?"

She shook her head.

"What?"

"You are a lunatic."

"You should know. So Simon what?"

"Addison."

"Like the disease."

She was quiet. She did not want to talk about Simon; Simon was not the point. "He's not the main thing."

"Are you finished with him?"

"Yes."

It was wishful thinking; he knew it, let it pass.

She held out her hand. "Would you come over here?"

He sat on the bed beside her. She took his hand and brought it to her left breast.

"There's a problem," she said. "Here."

A muscle in his forearm flinched. "Does it hurt? I don't want to hurt you."

"No, there's nothing to cause pain, at least not yet. Nothing hurts. That's the problem. I feel the same. But I may not be."

He withdrew his hand from her breast and laid it alongside her face.

"Then again, maybe I am." She set her glass on the bedside table. "I don't like or trust doctors, and I've tried all kinds of alternative methods, but they keep scaring me with facts and figures and medical reports. Toby's on their side. And so . . ." She turned her face into his hand. "So, I'm scheduled for surgery next week, only they don't call it surgery."

"A biopsy."

The gold flecks in her eyes flashed. "Yes."

"Leland . . ."

"We can stop now. We probably should. We could be smart for once, have a swell time together tonight, then go on from one another, me to L.A., you to your . . ." She fixed her eyes on the dictionary shelf. He waited until she brought her gaze back down to him. "Don't you think?"

"This is going to sound crazy."

"But?"

"If there's somebody else, that changes everything for me. But this—" he placed a careful finger on the tip of her nipple—"will not. Does not."

"There is no one else."

"As of when?"

"As of this very moment."

"Good." He drew her to him. "Everything else is part of life. Part of you."

They lay down side by side and held one another. Letting her head rest on his shoulder, she told him everything. About Dolly and the Cuban, the injuries. Living with Toby in New York in the floor-through with one bathroom and him in the bedroom so she had to go through it, and how they moved to

L.A., and all the important things she left out of the interview with Roxie Sidwell.

By the time she finished, she was lying with her head at his feet, her feet in his armpits. He told her about his daughters. Two were grown, one was married. The youngest was a mess, but he was hopeful. "Her mother used to tell her, 'Don't you pull a Jacky Nelms on me.'"

"That was cruel."

"She was scared."

They moved around again. He lay with his head on her shoulder. She pulled him close. They curled in a ball together. Leland dozed.

Making lists in his mind, Jacky set aside the what-ifs. One day at a time. At something after four, he woke her up. "You should go back. Your son will be worried."

"I don't want to wake up."

"This is important. We need to go slow."

She knew he was right. He took her back to Baker and Mell's house.

Leland crawled into Lucy's freezing bed—the air conditioner blasting full force and she couldn't figure out the knobs—and pulled the covers up.

33

There were blips on the line.

"That's your call waiting."

"I'm not answering. It's Dog."

"Who's Dog?"

"Don't ask."

After two more blips, the call waiting stopped.

Lucien and Tony had two phone lines. Tony was on the other one, checking plane schedules. She could hear him asking for flight numbers.

"Do you need me to come down there and get you? Because you know I will."

"No. I mean, yes, I know you will, and no, I don't need you to. I have a good friend who can help out."

"The one you call Dog?"

"Not Dog. Carroll. I can call him anytime."

"Carol? What's her last name?"

"It's a he. Carroll."

"Carroll who?"

"Cunningham."

Jane Scott thought maybe she didn't need help. Lucien's voice was doing the trick, pulling her loose nerves together, bunching them like flower stems in his great fist. If he kept talking, maybe she could settle herself enough to pack, make it to the airport, follow a plan. But if he stopped . . . After Carroll left, she had gone down again. There was a place inside, way deep. Once she got there, she could not stop the downward slide.

"We passed the cemetery tonight," she finally said.

"Who was buried there?"

"Everybody. Well, not in one place. First came the Jews, then the Catholics, then the regulars. The dead version of us."

"All right."

"And I remembered how my brother Clyde and I used to play there. We discovered a couple one time—they were meeting in secret and . . ." She began to cry.

"Jane . . ."

"It doesn't mean anything, Loosh. She wasn't anybody I really knew. I don't know why it makes me so sad."

"Jane . . ."

She blew her nose. "Okay, I'm listening."

"Promise me you won't take anything else tonight."

"Yes, all right." She felt like a four-year-old. "I promise."

"And give me your friend's phone number."

"Dog?"

"Not Dog. The one you said would help."

Lucien cupped the telephone and told Tony to put the travel agent on hold and find out Carroll Cunningham's number and have him go help Jane get packed and to the airport, then said to wait, Jane was calling him.

"I'm clearing, Loosh," she said. "Talk to me."

Clarity came in fits and starts, between which shadows again descended. A lucid moment and then a wild breakout of flecks and motes and dust balls. But the moments of clarity were more frequent now and lasting longer.

Lucien told stories. He and Tony had gone to a gay pride party that day and had no fun at all, as everybody wanted a piece of Lucien and they all seemed stuck at a stage he and Tony thought they'd been through and gone on from a long time ago. Jane Scott said she had been to the same party, only not gay, or not exclusively, and then she told him about Toby and Totty.

"What a time to be this age, Loosh. Our parents getting it on one end, which at our age you have to expect, but now the young ones are getting it on the other end too. Sick all over, dying right and left. We're in this, like, *vise*."

Lucien said that tomorrow morning they were going to the Zuni Cafe for buckwheat pancakes and would probably see that redheaded waitress with the wild blue eyes, did Jane remember her?

"Keep going, Loosh. A little more and maybe I've got it."

He kept talking and she kept pulling herself together and asked that Tony not call Carroll, she thought she could make it on her own, and they ended up staying on the telephone for more than two hours, until Jane Scott's head was clear enough to hear the plane schedule and tell them that yes, she could pack and would drive to Jackson early in the morning instead of taking the commuter flight, which was completely undependable. She would have to leave before seven to make the flight, but she could sleep on the plane and at their apartment when she got there. When the phone blipped again, Jane Scott said ignore it, she wasn't answering.

It was almost four in the morning when she hung up the phone. Jane Scott pulled the cord from the wall. She did not want to be tempted to answer, since there was no one she wanted to talk to now.

At three Hank made his first call, to Baker and Mell. When Mell picked up, Hank said, "Mell, I hope I haven't—" then Mell's disembodied voice droned on—"You have reached . . ."—and her voice gave the number. Hank hung up. He hated talking to machines.

He turned on lights all over the house, went to the kitchen for a can of soda, took Lillian outside for a pee and stood on the porch. The moon was high. Clouds made the stars impossible to see. The owl whoo-whooed.

He waited half an hour, got Mell's machine again, hung up. Fear turned his stomach to a rock. In fifteen minutes he would start calling the others. And then the police.

Baker heard the four rings, the silence as Mell's voice came on, the click of a receiver being replaced. He had heard the boys come in. He had given Leland a key, so it wasn't Leland. Wrong number, more than likely. Beside him, Mell slept. Her kimono was open all the way. He had waited to touch her until she was all but comatose. When he sucked her breast, she took his cock in her hand—a reflex, he suspected.

When he placed a finger between her thighs, she opened them. When he entered her, she responded with passion and need, but didn't open her eyes or emerge from her dreamy state.

At the end of the hall in his sleeping bag, Roy had on earphones and was listening to a Dead Boys tape. At his feet, Lady Macbeth snored like an old man. In Roy's bedroom, Toby stared up at the horror masks on the wall, which he could not see but knew were there.

He had knocked on the door to his mother's room and eased the door open when she didn't answer. She was with that man, the plumber. His mother was not careful. He was the one everybody warned about safe sex, but he was the safe one, who said no and took precautions. His mother threw herself in, tossed herself off the edge of cliffs. It made him furious that she would take such chances with her life.

Toby could not stand to think what would happen next. He was going to visit Carroll tomorrow. He could talk freely to Carroll, who knew them both and understood. In a couple of days they would head home. And then, who knew how it would all go.

He heard the phone, wondered if it was his mother, if she had a key; then nothing.

Carroll was halfway through the new Sue Grafton, just out in paper. Mysteries had gotten him through many hard nights. Robin would arrive shortly, after the Yacht Club had closed, the cash register been cleared, the glasses washed, the bar wiped clean. Nobody knew about Robin and Carroll, and so the stories flew fast and furious across the bar where Robin worked. A lot of people would be mortified to discover into whose ear their gripes and confessions and declarations of love and lust had been poured.

They slept close, Robin and Carroll, on their sides, fit together like spoons. They didn't always have sex, didn't always feel the need; they craved the holding more, the closeness, the contact.

Robin arrived. They were in bed when the phone rang, Robin telling stories in the dark. Carroll heard the telephone, the click of the machine, then silence. If it had been Jane Scott she'd have left a message. Jane Scott loved talking to an answering machine and would gab on forever, even at this hour of the morning. Jane Scott was the only one Carroll cared about talking to.

Dog washed his cock. When he got to bed, Totty was in her nightgown, turned away from him on her side. He touched her hip. "Are you—"

"Forget it, Dog."

"I just wanted to make sure you—"

"Forget it."

On his side of the bed, he turned in the other direction and was asleep in no time. He did not dream of his wife or of his girlfriend. He dreamed of the Methodist drug dealer. In his dream Dog Boyette was weightless again, flying through the long black night, Mrs. Loflin above him, giving instructions. "Up, Dog," she was saying. "Come higher up."

Stark dead awake and still in her pinafore, Totty restaged conversations from the dinner party in her mind and thought about people who'd be sorry when she died. She and Marge Loflin had handled themselves well, she thought, acting like they'd never seen each other before when Marge Loflin had been the one to scrape out Totty's womb, way back all those years ago. She didn't think anybody suspected anything—least of all Dog, who was about as smart as a sidewalk.

She shifted her body. When Dog's breath deepened and slowed and she was certain he was sleeping, she reached back and touched herself. The soft puckers of her rectum were sore and raw but not damaged.

When the phone rang, Totty jerked back her hand as if she'd been caught. Let it ring, she thought, clenching her fists at her chest. Ring and ring.

34

In a small house by the levee, the boy stirred in his bed. He had been dreaming about his grandmother. When he heard the singing he thought it was her, crooning her church songs. It was his grandmother who had told him, Always keep your window open a crack, so the light of Jesus can reach you. Never shut yourself away.

The boy, Matthew, opened his eyes. The singing stopped. He held his breath. It started again. He went to his window, put his ear out the open place. He had never heard such a high voice, even in church. Barefoot and on tiptoes, he walked to his door and, holding on to the frame, looked around it.

The house was dark, quiet. He could hear his mother's breathing, the rough breath of the man who slept with her. The man was not his father or her husband, but he was there. The boy feared him, and so did his mother.

He was afraid of his mother, too. His grandmother was dead. He did not tell them he cracked his window, because the air conditioner in the living room window was supposed to cool the whole house and they wouldn't like it. He could hear the sound of the floor fan in their room going from side to side. The air conditioner changed gears.

He was wearing white cotton underpants and nothing else. He tiptoed to the front door and, turning the lock and the knob at the same time, slipped out onto the front porch. From under the steps Mokey emerged, come to greet him. Mokey kept her eyes shut tight so she wouldn't wake up completely in case he went right back to bed. The boy patted her between the ears and she wagged her great tail.

The night was warm and close. The mosquitoes hadn't got too bad yet, but they would. From his front porch the boy could see the levee, rising up in front of him, keeping watch over their house like a giant soldier. He listened.

The voice was high and sweet and there was music behind it, coming from the other side of the levee, the lake side.

He bent down to Mokey's hairy ear. "Hear that, Mokey?"

"Matthew!"

"Hear that?"

The dog licked his face.

"Matthew!"

"Mama?"

"Get back in this house and go to sleep."

He went to her door. The man snorted but did not rouse.

"It's a lady," he was whispering, "singing." The fan whizzed and squeaked as it rotated.

"I said get back to bed."

He obeyed.

The voice stopped. He held his breath. And then it returned, slipping through the window he kept cracked as sure as his grandmother's love.

35

Toby stirred. Someone was knocking. "Come in," he called. The light was still gray.

Roy stuck his head in. He was wearing his cape and homburg. "Don't wake up if you don't want to."

"No, it's fine. Did my mother come in?"

"Yes." Roy didn't want to say when. When Lady Macbeth woke up and went downstairs, he'd taken off his earphones and from the end of the hall had heard Leland tiptoe into her room, not more than an hour ago, five a.m. or so.

Lady Macbeth stuck her face in the door.

"Do you want to go to the Marriott for a cappuccino?"

"What time is it?"

"They stay open all night." Roy was whispering. "It's nice downtown this early."

"Why not." Toby threw back the covers and quickly dressed.

When he got downstairs, Roy was at the front door, talking to a uniformed policeman, a black man with a trim moustache. Roy shrugged at Toby.

Having been given her sit command, Lady Macbeth kept her place by the hydrangea-filled umbrella stand. Though trembling with desire, she did not budge. The house smelled of garlic, wine, cigarettes and lamb fat.

"Looking for somebody," Roy muttered, then ran upstairs.

He knocked at his parents' door. When Baker answered, Roy eased the door open a crack. "Police."

"What?" Baker bolted upright.

"Police."

"Where?"

"Here."

"Here?"

"On the porch."

"What for?"

"I don't know. They want you. We're taking Lady M. for a walk."

"*God.*"

"Baker? What is it, Baker?" Mell wore her black satin sleeping mask. Her voice was trembly and uncertain.

He pulled the comforter above her shoulder.

"Roy says police." He patted her. "Don't get up."

Baker reached for his worn blue terry-cloth robe, tied it tight around his middle, slid his toes into his sneakers.

Roy held the bedroom door open. "I'm history. Okay?"

"Where did you say you were going?"

"For a walk." Roy did not look at his father. There was something in the room he did not want to know about.

"My God, Roy, it's the middle of the night."

"I know. Me and Toby are going for a cappo."

"'Toby and I.'"

"Later."

Roy went quickly down the stairs. The black policeman had been joined by his partner, a chunky white woman. The two of them waited politely on the porch.

"My dad's coming," he told them. "Let's go, Toby."

"What do you think this is about?"

"Beats me. Let's go."

"Is that a rat?" The policewoman drew back.

Roy took Freddy Krueger off his shoulder. "Want to pet him?"

The policeman stepped between Roy and his partner.

Roy jogged down the steps. Toby followed, holding Lady Macbeth's leash.

"This way." Roy pointed Toby toward the Eva Turner Home for Ladies.

"I thought downtown was that way."

"We're going to get Estelle."

"This early?"

"She doesn't sleep much. Weekends she has these all-night people she communicates with on her modem."

They crossed the street.

"I'll wait here and let Lady M. do her thing while you get Estelle."

Roy disappeared in the double doors of Eva Turner while, down the street, Baker invited the police inside.

Standing in an awkward circle in the front hall, they asked what time the party broke up and if he knew when Mrs. Mildred Westerfield left and if she was alone and what route she might have taken home.

Baker could not tell the truth, or say that he wasn't there when Sissy left, he was at the Eva Turner Home, where the Methodist drug dealer stabilized Dog Boyette and stopped him from puking up his stomach lining and shitting his pants even more. And so he said what time he thought it was when Sissy left. One of the guests had taken ill shortly before that, he explained, and Baker had taken him for a walk in the night air to clear his head. When he got back, Sissy was gone.

The policewoman looked at him. A walk in the night air?

"Would your wife know?" the man asked.

"Oh, Lord," Baker said.

They waited.

"My wife won't be able to talk until she's had at least one cup of coffee."

The chunky white woman nodded up the stairs.

"Baker?" Mell was standing there, her hair in a wild tangle, clutching her kimono tight around her.

"Who died?" she was saying. "Is somebody dead?"

36

Matthew followed the music to the top of the levee. When they got there, Mokey sniffed at the rabbit carcass, then picked it up and tossed it in the air. The boy yelled, and the dog set the rabbit down. Mokey and Matthew both knew she would come back for the dead animal's soft sweet innards and luscious meat, but they went on, the dog acting like rabbit eating had never entered her mind.

The red car was upside down. The music was starting to wane.

At first Matthew didn't see the woman. The green of her dress matched the wet grass. Mokey went toward her. The boy called her back.

He had seen his grandmother on her deathbed and in her casket. She was the only dead person he had ever seen, and that time his mother held him up over the casket for five seconds and then it was over. This time, he didn't have to hurry. He didn't want to see the dead woman in green but was curious. He wanted to take death face to face until he got it straight, what it looked like, how it would be.

She was on her side with her wrists crossed like a handcuffed criminal's. Her knees were drawn up, one higher than the other. A curl of her yellow hair lay tangled in her lashes, which did not blink but remained wide, wide open. Her eyes were green, matching the soft dress and the grass. Her neck was at a funny angle to her body, otherwise there was nothing except the wide-open staring glassy eyes to indicate anything was wrong.

Her silk dress was hiked up in the back, exposing her soft white behind. The boy wanted to cover her; it wasn't right for her to be out in the air like that. He reached over, lifted the slippery silk for a second; but when the side of his hand brushed her flesh, he quickly let the dress go. His hand felt scalded, like he'd put it in boiling water.

He ran up the levee and over, down the other side to wake up his mother, who would not believe him and would probably smack him for telling lies. He had to risk it. Eventually she would have to go see, or send the man to do it for her. And then she would be full of regret at how she had smacked him when he was telling the truth.

He did not look back to see what Mokey was up to.

37

Leland stirred. She had not slept.

She thought she heard a commotion from downstairs, talk, something going on. She sat up.

Her spiked hair had fallen. With bangs she looked extremely young, and more tenuous and uncertain than she liked. She ran her hand through the top part to shove it up.

Jacky Nelms had told her he didn't quite know what to make of what he called "all of this," but he knew he could not let her go. Once she got home, had settled in a couple of days with Toby, he would come out. "Before the—" He stumbled.

"Yes?"

"Whatever. I have to tell you, I'm not sure I can live in L.A. But I'll come out."

Leland pulled on a long gray T-shirt dress. Jacky Nelms's territorial declarations had at one and the same time infuriated, shocked and thrilled her. This morning she felt pretty energized and dizzy from it all. She couldn't see what else there was to do except ride those feelings out, see what happened. She went down the hall to see what was the matter downstairs.

Mell and Baker were in the living room talking to two police officers.

38

At the war memorial beside the Marriott, Toby asked if they could walk up the levee before having their coffee. Roy and Estelle agreed, although Estelle said there was nothing to see up there this time of the morning except a muddy old lake and some river rats with fishing poles.

The grass was lush, the spring having been wet. Toby went first, taking wide strides, gathering the ground beneath him.

Behind him Estelle Etheridge chattered on. She had talked to a hacker up in Maine this morning, and she bet nobody else in Eunola was at their modem on a Saturday morning making small talk with an eighteen-year-old hacker in Bath, Maine.

Roy said he was sure that was so and they followed their guest up the levee. When Toby got to the top, Lady Macbeth was beside him, sniffing the air and peering down her blunt nose at the lake. On Roy's neck, the rat kept a sharp lookout, eyes fixed hard on the direction they had come from.

Somebody was taking a pleasure boat out for an early morning ride. The boat cut through the warm brown water, sending gently lapping waves against the levee.

A NOTE ON THE TYPE

The text of this book was set in Electra, a Linotype face designed by W. A. Dwiggins (1880–1956). This face cannot be classified as either modern or old style. It is not based on any historical model; nor does it echo any particular period or style. It avoids the extreme contrasts between thick and thin elements that mark most modern faces and attempts to give a feeling of fluidity, power, and speed.

Composed by Graphic Composition,
Athens, Georgia
Printed and bound by Arcata Graphics, Martinsburg,
West Virginia
Designed by Brooke Zimmer